THE YEAR WE HID AWAY

Ivy Years #2

by Sarina Bowen

D1452789

~ Rennie Road Books ~

The Ivy Years, Book #2

Published by Rennie Road Books
Cover image: L e s B y e r l e y / Shutterstock
Cover design by Tina Anderson
Copyediting by Nancy Smay

ISBN 978-0-9910680-2-9

http://www.SarinaBowen.com

The Year We Hid Away is a work of fiction. Names, places, and incidents are either products of the author's imagination, or used fictitiously.

PART ONE

"Ah, but let her cover the mark as she will, the pang of it will be always in her heart."
— *The Scarlet Letter by Nathaniel Hawthorne*

Chapter One: *The Goalie's Job*

— *Scarlet*

The minute I heard the hum of the garage door opener, I was in motion.

I didn't need to look out the window to check that my parents were driving away. When there are three news vans parked on the edge of your lawn, you don't raise that door frivolously. Over the past year, the news networks had taken thousands of shots of the interior of our garage. Just in case it proved newsworthy.

But this was not the moment to dwell.

By the time I heard my parents' car accelerate up the street, I had already yanked my closet open. Out came the duffel bags — already packed — and the box of books. One at a time, I lugged these things down the stairs to the mud room.

Then I went upstairs again to pull my getaway note from the desk drawer and place it in the middle of my bed.

Mom and Dad — I got the time wrong for move-in day. It

starts at 3. So I'm on my way. I'll call you tonight. Sorry for the confusion. Love, S.

There were so many half truths in that short note that it wasn't even funny. But that's how we did things here at casa Ellison. We bent the truth when the need arose. It had been that way my entire life, even though it had taken me seventeen years to figure out how deep the deceptions went.

The last thing I brought downstairs was Jordan — my guitar. I wouldn't want to go anywhere without him.

Then I ran back upstairs, darting one last time into my bedroom. It wasn't for sentimental reasons. Though the room was beautiful — generously sized, and with pretty maple furniture — it had been my prison cell for the past year.

My last task was to haul my hockey gear into the walk-in closet. The skates, the goalie stick, the pads. I hid them all, hoping that my mother wouldn't find them for a while. The choices I'd made these past few weeks had already given my mother fits. The longer I could forestall an argument over quitting hockey, the better.

Closing the closet door, I went over to the window to take a peek between the slats of my blinds. There were three cameramen clustered on the lawn. That was illegal. They were supposed to stay off the property. But the cops in town didn't enforce the rule. Not for my family. If our house was on fire, I'm not sure they would even bother to put it out.

The newsmen on our lawn were probably chatting about sports, or the weather, or whatever it was they talked about when there wasn't any news to shoot. One of them was shuffling a deck of cards in his hands, which probably meant they'd sit down in their lawn chairs to a game of poker soon.

Perfect.

Running back down the stairs for the last time, I threw

open the door which led into the garage. As he always did, my father's bodyguard had closed the garage door as he drove away. At least that creep was good for something. My parents referred to him as "our driver," but that was just another euphemism. Nobody wanted to talk about why he was needed.

But a man who had been indicted for multiple counts of child molestation felt safer having an ex-military sniper at his back when he left the house.

As quickly as possible, I hauled all my gear into my vehicle, closing the doors as softly as I could. Behind the wheel, I took a minute to take stock of my belongings. I had my handbag, with my new driver's license inside. I had all my luggage and Jordan.

But no hockey gear.

Right.

I cranked the engine and hit the garage door opener at the same time. I'd been taught that it was a crime to put a car in gear before you gave it a chance to warm up. But these were desperate times. The fancy German engine would have to forgive me just this once, because I needed the element of surprise on my side.

As soon as my SUV could clear the still-rising garage door, I gunned it backward down the driveway. The news trucks blocked my view of the street, unfortunately. So I had to stop for a moment to make sure that nothing was coming.

The cameramen rose from their card game, looking uncertain. They'd just seen and photographed my father's car as it pulled away — just in case the day would prove newsworthy for him in some way. They'd have it on film.

But I wasn't newsworthy, especially on Labor Day weekend. Especially *alone*.

A hasty glance showed nobody lunging for a camera.

Yesss!

I backed out carefully — because hitting a news van would not make this getaway any smoother — and idled down my street. Even as I passed the other houses in our tidy New Hampshire college town, my heart beat wildly.

My escape was finally in motion. For a *year* I'd been waiting for this moment.

By sneaking out, I'd avoided an our-perfect-daughter-goes-off-to-college scene staged by my tearful mother in front of the TV cameras. I was finished with command performance photo ops.

By sneaking out, I'd also sidestepped a goodbye with my dad. Even before the upheaval, things had never been easy between us. I'd always thought of him as a last century father — strict and too busy for me, unless I was wearing skates. (He wasn't too busy then, but he was still strict.)

Our relationship had been chilly before, but now it was absolutely Antarctic. Formerly a workaholic, my father now spent all his time in a recliner in the den. I never went into that room anymore, where the air was thick with anger and silence.

Though sometimes I snuck looks at him. And I wondered if he'd done all the things he was accused of doing. And why.

And how I could have lived under his roof for so long without guessing.

My heart was full of ugly questions. But even if I'd asked them out loud, nobody in my family could be trusted to answer them truthfully.

Picking up speed, I wound through the back roads toward highway 91. It was Shannon Ellison who was putting Sterling, New Hampshire in the rearview mirror. But ninety minutes from now, it would be Scarlet Crowley who climbed out of the car in Harkness, Connecticut.

"Scarlet Crowley," I whispered to myself. I'd have to learn to answer to my new name. That was going to feel strange. But if I had to guess, it wouldn't be even half as strange as giving up hockey. I'd started playing when I was five. For fourteen years it was my life. At age eleven I'd become a goalie, spending so many hours between the pipes that I even saved goals in my sleep.

The goalie's job isn't just to lunge for the puck. The goalie's job is to see the whole ice at once — to watch the drama unfold well before the puck comes flying toward the net. I'd taught myself to tell who had the puck just from the way she held her shoulders. I studied my opponents, predicting who would shoot and who would pass. I watched it all unfold the way a chess player does — readying herself several moves ahead of time, preparing for all the possible outcomes.

My school won the last three state championships. In a row.

There was a row of trophies in our family room attesting to my strengths as a goalie. And up until a year ago, I assumed that the accolades were well deserved. But it turns out I wasn't nearly as great as I thought I was.

The goalie's job is to foresee the defensive gaps. But in my own life, I'd failed to do that. When the ugly stories about my father began to leak into our lives, I hadn't seen it coming. At all. Like a high-powered slap shot to the chest, all the ugliness hit me hard, knocked me back, and stole my breath.

The life I'd had before was over now. I'd had a year to get used to the idea, so I'd moved beyond shock and denial a long time ago. Now there was only Plan B. It wasn't perfect, but it was all I had.

Two hours later, I stood on a flagstone pathway in a beautiful courtyard. But it wasn't easy to appreciate the Gothic architecture and the perfectly mowed lawns while my heart did speed drills around the inside of my chest.

Probably all the First Years were nervous today. My classmates were likely worried about getting lost, or meeting their roommates. But my biggest fear was something else entirely. Would the registrar's office have the correct name on my paperwork? And what the hell was I going to do if they didn't?

When I reached the front of the line, I waited there, mute and anxious, while a cheerful upperclasswoman flipped through a stapled list of students. She chanted my brand new name under her breath while she looked. *"Scarlet Crowley. Scarlet Crowley. Scarlet Crowley."*

I began to sweat.

Passing by the front of the alphabet, where I should have been found, she flipped to the last page. *Additions and Changes*, it read.

"Ah, here you are," she said, brightening up. She offered me a paper chit which would allow me to have a student ID made. "You were lost, but now you're found."

I hoped she was right.

With my shiny new ID, complete with my newly minted name, I found my way to Vanderberg Hall, entryway A. The lock gave a satisfying click when I passed the ID in front of the scanner. Hefting my duffel, I climbed two flights up the old marble staircase to the third floor. Each floor had two rooms on it, and a door between them marked *bathroom*. I didn't need to try my key, because room 31 was standing open. I leaned into the doorway, spotting two girls bent over the opposite ends of a bright red rug. "Hi there."

Two heads popped up together. The next moment was taken up by their unapologetic examination of me. One of the girls had gorgeous blond hair, while the other sported a perky brunette ponytail. "Hi! I'm Katie!" they said in unison.

Remembering their names would not be difficult. So I had that going for me. "I'm Scarlet," I said, wheeling my giant duffel bag into the room.

But Ponytail Katie tipped her head to the side, questioning me. "Our third was supposed to be someone named Shannon?"

"There was a switch," I said. "Shannon isn't coming." *Because I left her at home.*

"Oh!" Blond Katie said. "Where are you from, Scarlet?"

"Miami Beach," I told her. *Time Check*: I was thirty seconds in, and I'd already told either two or three lies, depending on how you counted them. And each was a whopper.

It took me three trips to the parking lot to move in. The Katies didn't offer to help. Instead, they decorated their desks with photos from home, and tried to decide which of the First Year mixers sounded the most promising.

But I was too happy to be here to let their indifference bother me. And Room 31 was in a gorgeous old U-shaped dowager of a building. The Katies and I had been assigned to a triple, which had a tiny bedroom for Ponytail Katie and a slightly larger one for Blond Katie and I. Our suite also featured its own wood-paneled common room with a window seat looking out on the courtyard.

It was pretty darned cool.

"We need a sofa, like, yesterday," Blond Katie observed. "They're selling used ones outside."

"Okay, I'll chip in," I agreed, sounding for all the world like Miss Eager. But after the lonely, friendless year I'd endured, all I wanted was to be one of the girls. And even then, I didn't need much from them. I didn't come here to be popular or extraordinary. I just wanted to blend.

Even if I had to lie all the time to do it.

"We'll look at them on our way to the dining hall," Blond Katie suggested.

"Great," I agreed.

An hour later, I followed The Katies out of our dorm toward Turner House. At Harkness, the student body was divided into twelve Houses. It was like Hogwarts, but without the sorting hat. Every First Year living in our entryway of Vanderberg had been assigned to Turner House, but we wouldn't live in the Turner building until next year. For now, we were housed with other First Years on Fresh Court.

Swiping my ID at the Turner House gate, I heard another satisfying click. It was hard to conceal my glee when Ponytail Katie swung the unlocked gate open and held it for us. Scarlet Crowley was *in*, people! My escape was working.

The Turner dining hall was old-fashioned in a stately way. There was a vaulted ceiling two stories overhead, leaded glass windows set into marble sills, and a giant fireplace at one end. I followed the Katies into a kitchen area, where we had to make sense of the various lines and self service bars.

"Okay, that wasn't so hard to figure out," Blond Katie said after we'd found three seats together.

"My boarding school dining hall wasn't this nice," Ponytail Katie observed. "It always smelled like bologna."

"Ew," Blond Katie agreed. "Where did you go to school, Scarlet?"

"I was home-schooled," I lied. I had spent the entire

10

summer crafting the story of my new identity. I could have chosen a Miami school to claim for my own, but that posed the risk of eventually running across someone who had actually gone there. And wouldn't *that* be awkward.

"Wow," Ponytail Katie gasped. "But you seem so normal!"

I laughed. If she only knew.

That night, I came to sudden wakefulness on a gasp. For a moment, I didn't know where I was. The room was strange. And my dream still clung to me.

It was the same dream I'd had all year. I was playing hockey, of course. That was no nightmare. But in the dream, I darted out of the crease to get the puck, which skidded away from me. The crowd was yelling, wanting me to send it zipping away from our net. But the puck kept going, pitching into a dark hole. Even as the voices around me grew more urgent, the hole was dark and frightening, and I did not want to fetch the puck from down there. Something in my gut stopped me.

At that point, I always woke up in a sweat.

Lame, right? You'd think my mind could come up with something better, like chainsaws, zombies or vampires. But it was always the same dream.

I rolled over in my narrow dormitory bed, and listened to Blond Katie's snoring. I'd let The Katies drag me to an off-campus kegger that they'd heard about. I'd drunk a warm beer from a plastic cup, and swayed appropriately to overly loud music. The purpose of the party was not at all obvious to me, but on the way home The Katies tallied up the several dozen numbers they'd added to their phones.

"And that lax player with the tattoos? Oh my God — so

hot!" Blond Katie had enthused.

"I heard he's pierced... *down there!*"

They'd shared gale after gale of laughter. The Katies were proving to be the sort of girls who Knew Things. They knew the name of the football quarterback, and which fraternity he'd pledged. They knew the names of the secret society buildings littered around the campus — odd granite, windowless buildings. ("You're supposed to call them 'crypts,'" Blond Katie had emphasized.)

It was also proving apparent that The Katies had much more in common with each other than with me. They both loved Sephora! They'd both played field hockey in high school! They were both into Maroon 5! *LOL* and *OMG* and *WTF!*

I wasn't jealous. Not exactly. (Field hockey? *Please.*) But I was keenly aware that the past year had put a wedge between myself and the rest of the world, which even a complete identity change could not undo. By dropping out of life for a year, I'd become an observer — a watcher and a thinker. Before that, I'd been a doer and a go-getter.

I used to be more of a Katie. Well, technically I'd been a Shannon. But... same thing.

To amuse myself, I tried to imagine how it would go if I told The Katies the truth about me. What would happen to the perky expressions on their faces?

Well, Katies, I'm not from Miami, although we used to go there all the time on vacation. Actually, I'm from New Hampshire, where my father was a famous hockey player and coach. He was a Stanley Cup winner for Toronto before I was born. He coached defense for the Bruins when I was little, and then he took a college coaching job when I entered kindergarten.

Unless they were uber perceptive hockey geeks, the Katies' faces would still be lit with interest at this point in my story, considering all the hot athletes I would (and did) meet over the years.

Also, my father started a charity whereby underprivileged kids all over New England could learn hockey for free. Wasn't that a generous thing to do? Especially since my dad always was — and is — a hyper aggressive asshole. But in hockey they pay you more for that. Anyway, things went swimmingly for him — and me — until about a year ago, when a kid two towns over decided to kill himself.

Were I to say these things out loud, the Katies' faces might start to cloud with concern at this point, whether or not they read any of the major national newspapers.

The boy — his name was Chad — left a suicide note. And in the note he told the world that my father had raped him repeatedly the year he was twelve.

That's the point in the story where any self-respecting Katie would run in the other direction. Their tentative warmth toward me would never survive that kind of darkness. It wouldn't matter to them that I'd learned about my father's alleged crimes in the *New York Times,* just like everyone else.

This past year I'd come to understand something about bad news. It didn't come quickly, like the bad news in movies. It was never just a midnight phone call, or a knock on the door during supper. Real life bad news — the messy stuff — came at you slowly. The midnight call was just a preview of coming attractions. It would be followed by one news truck in front of your house, and then two. And then ten. And even when the trucks went away, it was only a temporary reprieve. Because three other boys would eventually come forward with similar stories. And then the whole cycle began again.

When I'd told the Katies I was home-schooled, I'd almost wished it was true. Last year, I'd kept exactly one friend. One person stood by me while the whole town turned their backs. And worse. It didn't matter that I wasn't the one accused of a crime. No one except for my friend Anni would sit next to me, ever. I didn't go to a single party or event for a year, because I was a pariah. The hockey team voted me off my captainship a mere two weeks after voting me on. Even the coach began to favor the younger goalies. (Unless we were losing. And then he had no trouble playing me.)

Public opinion about my father had congealed into horror almost a year ago now. He'd been arrested and then indicted for just about the worst thing a man could do. And it didn't matter that I hadn't known — *still* didn't really know what had happened. I was the product of a sick man, from a sick home. And anyone in our town who treated me civilly risked getting too close to the stench.

So it's no mystery why I'd gone to the courthouse this summer to file for a legal name change. And then, when the paperwork came through, I called the Registrar's Office at Harkness and gave them my new information.

Shannon was gone, and Scarlet was born. I hoped she could save me.

There was always the possibility that I'd be recognized and outed. There was really nothing I could do about that, short of adopting a cheesy disguise. Luckily, there was only one guy at Harkness who'd gone to my high school. He was two years ahead of me, and I didn't know Andrew Baschnagel well, aside from remembering that he was a pretty big nerd. Since the college's undergraduate student body was 5000 strong, and I'd never had a real conversation with Andrew, it was a risk I could stomach.

Not that I had a choice.

Scarlet Crowley had no Facebook account, and no Twitter handle. If you Googled my new name, you found very little. (This was lucky, because I didn't check ahead of time.) Apparently, there was a Mrs. Scarlet Crowley who taught 8th grade algebra at a middle school in Oklahoma. Her students didn't seem to like her very much, judging by the things they tweeted from her class.

But, *please*. If the choice was to be mistaken for an ornery teacher who gave frequent pop quizzes, or for the daughter of the most infamous alleged pedophile in the nation, which would you pick?

I'd take the algebra teacher every time.

Chapter Two: *Hello, Stalker*

— *Scarlet*

Okay college. Let's do this thing.

It felt good to be striding into the September sunshine on the way to my very first lecture. Thanks to Labor Day, the first day of classes was a Tuesday, so I navigated to the hall where Statistics 105 would be taught. The course was a requirement for the pre-med major, and I was a little afraid of it. Setting my pack on the floor beside a vacant chair, I glanced around at the other students filing into the room, as if inspecting them would reveal whether or not I was smart enough to keep up in the class. Would there be other nervous-looking freshmen? Or would they all be hardened math whizzes?

The results of my search were not encouraging. I saw a lot of skinny boys with rumpled hair. There was not a Katie to be seen for miles.

My sweep of the room ended when my gaze fell on a set of broad shoulders two rows ahead of me. They were attached to an exceptionally handsome guy, with a thick head of dark red hair. As I admired him, he turned his head, catching me in the act. Too late, I dropped my eyes to the notebook open in front of me.

Luckily, the professor began speaking then. All eyes turned to the front of the room, where a thin man in a stiff white shirt introduced himself. "We're going to dive right in with the concepts of estimation and inference! Let's get to it."

With a white-knuckled grip on my pen, I began taking notes. Within a half an hour, it became very clear that statistics was a course requiring coffee as a side dish. As the professor drew yet another graph on the white board, my gaze wandered back to the only interesting person in the room.

His hair was a lovely warm tone — like dark caramel with a hint of cayenne. He looked strong, but not hulking like a no-neck football player. His was a chest you could lay your head upon. I was busy admiring the twitch of muscle in his arm as he took notes when he looked up *again* to meet my eyes.

Ugh. Busted twice! How mortifying.

I stapled my gaze to the professor for the rest of the hour. The moment that class was dismissed, I snatched my things and bolted outside. My next lecture — music theory — was three buildings away, and I had only a few minutes to get there. But the lecture hall didn't seem to be where I'd thought. So I dug the campus map out of my bag feeling just like the idiot First Year that I so obviously was. Reorienting myself, I ran off in the right direction. When I finally reached the door, someone held it open for me. "Thanks," I panted.

"No problem," said a deep voice. The hint of amusement in it made me look up.

It was *him* — the hottie with the auburn hair. He gave me a quick grin. I took a tiny fraction of a second to admire the freckles on his nose before darting past him into the lecture hall.

This time, I sat in the front of the room, where I wouldn't be tempted to stare.

— Bridger

For the first twenty minutes of music theory, I was doing fine. The professor began by explaining how sound waves vibrate the human eardrum. Science had always appealed to me, and the material was easier than the graduate level chemistry courses I'd been taking. Giddyup.

But then the lecture veered in another direction. "When sounds are organized into music, and that music is played slowly, and in a minor chord, the listener will often become sad," the professor said. He hopped over to a sound system and hit "play" on a three-minute segment of Mozart's Requiem Mass.

The music began low and soft. As it began to build, the sound waves vibrating off the wooden desks and the leaded glass, the hair stood up on the back of my neck.

"Close your eyes," the professor commanded from the front of the room.

I complied, letting those violins and the choir's Latin chorus wash over me. The mood of the piece was dire and dramatic. There was no arguing with that. And my heart bought into it. I began to feel overwhelmed, and all because of a recording of a song that was first performed over two hundred years ago.

If I'd taken this class a year ago, maybe it wouldn't have hit me like that. But I was having a rough time. If my life were a movie, the sound track to this year would be written in an ominous key. And there was nothing I could do about it. My role was to suck it up and stay the course.

The song ended, and the professor began to talk about tempo and rhythm. I took notes, trying to tame the unfamiliar jargon on my notebook page. I'd never been interested in classical music. But there weren't any better options for the time slot, and I needed more arts and literature courses to graduate. Harkness was picky like that — they wanted me to be more than just a science nerd. And a hockey player.

A *former* hockey player.

At the end of the week, my teammates would all sharpen their skates and report to the rink. They'd go back to practicing their shooting drills, and arguing about which toppings to order on their pizza.

What would I be doing? Eating ramen noodles and tinkering with the spreadsheet I'd written to keep track of my grueling schedule. This year was going to be a gauntlet of classes and part-time jobs and studying. And childcare.

And keeping secrets.

I couldn't even count all the ways that I could crash and burn. I could lose my part-time job, or I could get sick. My little sister could get sick. My mother could get into legal trouble. The list was a mile long. And even if none of that happened, I was still vulnerable. The college could discover the secret I was keeping — a sixty-five pound, red-haired secret — and show my ass the door.

So even though I was sitting in an opulent old room, in the dusty hush of one of the oldest schools in America, I was on edge.

A couple of rows ahead of me sat the girl who I'd caught checking me out during statistics. Now she tipped her head into one hand, causing her glossy hair to tumble to the side. The creamy skin of her neck was exposed, and if I'd been seated closer I would have been tempted to reach out and test its smoothness with my fingers. On the notepad in front of her, she wrote notes as if her life depended on it.

With that sort of first day diligence, I clocked her as a First Year. No question.

Last year at this time, I'd been looking over the class of freshmen girls the way a guy eyes an all-you-can-eat buffet, wondering which flavor to sample first. By the end of the year, my teammates had a running joke. "What's Bridger's type?" The punch line was, "He likes 'em breathing."

Say what you will, but there was a reason I was such a hedonistic... well, *slut* if you didn't want to mince words. On some level, I'd already known where my life was headed. It's not that I'd predicted my situation exactly. It's just that I could tell that things were going south — that my mother had bought herself a one-way ticket to hell. Last year was my last shot to be a carefree drunk. And I took it. I don't regret it for a second.

So you'll forgive me a few lingering looks at the pretty girl seated two rows ahead. Because a look here or there was all I would get.

After class, I headed over to the newly renovated student center to buy a sandwich and do a little reading. Only First Years and ubernerds started their schoolwork on the first day of classes. But this term was about to become the most difficult of my life, and I was going to have to change my ways to make it work.

I sat down at the last empty table. Before I got a chance to dig in, I saw the hottie from this morning's classes weaving through the crowd, looking for a place to sit. She had that deer-in-the-headlights expression typical of First Years. The campus map was sticking out of the back pocket of her skirt, too. As her gaze swept in my direction, I leaned down all the way to the floor, unzipping my backpack and pulling out my music theory textbook.

I counted to ten. Then I sat up again just in time to see the girl gunning for my table, which she'd assumed was

21

unoccupied.

Worked like a *charm*.

When I popped up in my seat, she pulled up short, only a few feet away. Her neck turned red, and she blinked at me, trying to figure out how to play it. Her face said: *Damn it. Him again!*

"Well, sit down already," I chuckled, putting my book and my sandwich on the table, and pointing at an empty chair.

After a beat, she slid a salad container and a Diet Coke onto the table.

"I don't bite," I said. "Unless you're a turkey and coleslaw with Russian dressing on rye."

With her face flaming, she did as she was told. "I swear I'm not a stalker."

Smiling, I unwrapped my sandwich. "No kidding. Stalkers don't usually look so horrified to see the person they're stalking."

She shook her head. "It's just... never mind. Weird coincidence."

"So..." I said, taking a bite. She looked cute with her cheeks pink. I wondered what else I could say to make her blush like that.

"So..." she picked up her fork.

"Are you going to stick with both the statistics and the music?"

"Probably," she said. "But one of those two classes will be a joy, and the other one will probably kill me." Her eyes were an interesting hazel color. She was really attractive, but not in a bombshell way. There was something a little more serious in her expression than the sort of girl I usually went for. But it worked on her.

Not that I was sizing her up or anything. What would be

the point?

She took the first sip of her soda and then licked her lips, her pink tongue darting out distractingly. And for a moment I forgot what we had been talking about. Classes. Right. "That's where I stand, too."

"Right?" she agreed. "Statistics is going to be tricky, but I need it for pre-med. I thought I'd get it over with."

"Ah," I smiled at her. "You're a First Year, then. How's it going so far?"

"Well, this is day number two. So I'll have to let you know."

"Roommates okay?"

She made a face. "I suppose it could be worse."

"Look on the bright side. In two years you can have a single."

"Something to look forward to." She picked at her salad. "So are *you* going to keep both classes?"

"Sure. Statistics is a no brainer. I just haven't fit it in until now. I'm not so sure about the music theory. My schedule needs a Tuesday and Thursday class. And I thought it sounded easy. But now I'm not so sure. All that talk about intervals and semitones. It's like he forgot to speak English."

"Um, seriously?" She leaned back in her chair, which made her top ride up a little bit. I tried not to peek at the strip of smooth skin exposed at her waist. "How is it possible to understand stats and not music?"

"I'm worried that music is one of those things that you can *ruin* with too much examination. Like astronomy. I used to love to look at the stars. And now when I do, I have to wonder whether I'm looking at a red dwarf or a white giant."

"It won't be like that," she said. "You won't suddenly hear your favorite song and think — 'this would be so much

23

better in C minor.' The opposite is possible, though. You'll hear things you didn't before. You'll understand why the key change makes you feel differently about the middle of the song."

"Fair enough. But some things are beautiful whether or not you understand them."

She smiled then, and the effect was powerful. It took her from seriously pretty to dazzling. "Okay — beautiful whether you understand it or not... You mean like art?"

"Sure. Or, the female body." I grinned, waiting. And there it was — another flush in her cheeks.

She swallowed. "Okay...But aren't those things even more beautiful when you do understand them?"

"I'm going to have to think about that, Stalker."

She rolled her eyes at me. "Please don't call me that."

"But I have to. Because you haven't told me your name."

That made her blush even deeper. "Right. It's Scarlet."

Just like her face. I reached across the table to shake her hand. I could at least *pretend* to be a gentleman. "It's a pleasure to meet you, Scarlet. I'm Bridger."

"Bridger..." she frowned as we shook. "Are you a hockey player, Bridger?"

"Maybe I used to be." But the question had surprised me. It wasn't like I was the star of the team or anything. "Why? Are you a fan of hockey?"

Her face closed down then. "Maybe I used to be," she said, echoing me. "Hockey hasn't been good to me recently."

I picked up my sandwich. "Maybe you mean that a hockey *player* hasn't been good to you recently?"

She gave me a funny smile. "Something like that."

"Fair enough. Listen, I'm thinking we can make a deal here. If I'm drowning in music theory jargon, you can throw me a rope. And if you need any help with stats, I'll see what I can do."

That killer smile lit her face again. "You have a deal, Bridger. But I think I'm getting the better end of this bargain." She stabbed an olive with her fork.

After that, Scarlet loosened up a little. I gave her part of my story — the nice part. I told her I was a junior, and doing concurrent bachelor's and master's degrees in biology. "I wanted to go to med school, but I don't think I can swing after graduation." Of course, I didn't share my ugly reasons. "I'm hoping the master's degree will help me get a job."

"Sounds smart," she said.

"We'll see. The course load is kicking my ass."

She told me she was from Miami Beach, where I had never been. Naturally, she asked where I was from. "Sunny Harkness, Connecticut," I said.

"Nice commute," she offered.

"Sure. But at least you get to leave here once in awhile. I seem to be a lifer." Hell, that made me sound like a whiner. I was grateful to have a spot at Harkness College. Most townies never even got a tour of the place.

My watch beeped, reminding me that I had to pick up Lucy from school. "Duty calls," I said, balling up my sandwich wrapper. "I'll see you in class on Thursday?"

Scarlet gave me a smile — a big one, like the sun coming up over the beach. "I'll be there," she said.

Now I had something to look forward to. "Awesome. Later." I picked up my stuff and jogged out of the student center.

Chapter Three: *It Sunk In All Right*

— *Scarlet*

I got through the first week without any grave disasters. I memorized the dining hall hours, and I figured out which library was which.

I learned that the other nine students in my introductory Italian class were nice, but that the teacher was a dick. It was an immersion-style class, so no English was allowed inside its walls. And any accidental non-Italian words emerging from a student's mouth were met with a snarl from the ornery grad student who taught it.

"The… oops!" a petite girl with boxy glasses clapped a hand over her mouth across the conference table from me.

"EN ITALIANO!" Eduardo barked.

I gave the frightened girl a friendly wink, which brought one of Eduardo's glares in my direction.

Whatever, dude. My entire town snarled at me for all of last year. *You go ahead and do your worst.*

There was one more college rule I learned the hard way, on Thursday night. I'd gone to the library for an hour to go over my statistics notes. And when I returned to our suite, I pushed open our bedroom door without a second thought. And it took my brain a long moment to process what I saw inside. On Katie's bed was a body on all fours. But the broad, naked ass I saw there did not compute. Was I in the wrong room? No. But those buns couldn't belong to the very svelte Blond Katie. And wait… that was a *hairy* ass?

Not one but *two* heads whipped around to catch me staring. And that's when my feet got the hint. Quick as you please, I spun around and closed the door. Not sure what to do next, I went over to our window seat and dropped my book bag. As I stared out the window, I heard two noises start up. One noise was the smack of fat raindrops against our antique windows. Even as I watched, the sky darkened and the rain came down in sheets.

But over that sound was the muted, rhythmic grunting of a guy who was just about to…

Ack!

Quickly, I cracked the window open an inch, which let both the sound and the fresh smell of the rain into our room.

Even though it wasn't me in that bedroom, I felt an inexplicable slap of shame come over me. I wasn't a baby, and the idea of my peers having sex shouldn't disgust me. Even so, I felt shaken, like a little kid who had just walked in on her parents.

Come to think of it, I'd never happened upon that.

I needed to think about something else, and soon. It was really pouring outside now, so leaving wasn't a great option. I jammed my ear buds into my ears and cranked up a playlist of guitar solos I'd been hoping to learn. And tried really hard not to think about Blond Katie and Hairy Ass getting it on in the other room.

In some ways, I was a more jaded First Year than anyone else around me. I'd read about more criminally lewd acts in the past year than anyone ever should. But the normal nineteen year-old variety of sex was a mystery to me. At my house, we'd never talked about sex. We were New Englanders. We talked about sports and the weather.

I'd learned the basics of human reproduction, of course. From health class and from copies of *Cosmo* I read in the salon, I knew the mechanics. But I had no context. And what's more, I was ashamed of my own curiosity. But when you spent your senior year completely ostracized by your peers, there wasn't any time for learning the ropes. While other girls my age were experiencing their first loves, and hook-ups, I was alone in my room playing Jordan.

It's no accident that I'd named my guitar after a boy. He was as close to a boyfriend as I was likely to get.

I wished I had Jordan right now. But he wasn't available to me, since I kept him under my bed, which was just a few feet away from...

Gah.

An hour later, I pretended to be absorbed in my music when that bedroom door opened up again. Blond Katie showed her guest out into the hallway before coming back into the common room. She planted herself in front of the window seat and gave me a glare. "Didn't you see my flag?"

Pulling out my ear buds, I turned my eyes toward our bedroom door. Sure enough, a red bandanna was hanging on our doorknob. So *that's* why that was there. I thought she'd just left it there by chance.

"Sorry. It didn't sink in."

She chuckled. "Oh, it sunk in all right." At that, she retreated to our room, while I sat there, my face burning.

Later that night, the Katies were discussing a frat house formal they planned to attend. But there was a crisis — they needed new stockings, and didn't have any way to get to the mall.

Right across the street, my car sat waiting in its $300 per month parking spot. But I didn't feel like offering to take them.

When Saturday came, I did a chore that I'd been avoiding. I got in the new car that my parents had bought and drove to an address in the neighboring town of Orange, one that I'd looked up in the white pages.

Pulling up to the house, I saw a car in the garage and another in the driveway. So at least there was a good shot she was home.

As soon as I rang the bell, Coach Samantha Smith came to the door. "Why, Shannon!" she exclaimed, her smile wide. "What brings you out here?" She came out onto the wide porch. "Have a seat. It's so nice out, I should be outside anyway."

I sat joylessly in a wicker chair. The truth was that I'd driven out to Coach's home because I couldn't stand the thought of walking into the rink to find her. It would probably make me cry. "Well," I cleared my throat. "I'm not going to play. And I wanted you to know right away."

Her face broke open with surprise, and not in a good way. "But..." she sputtered. "We admitted you *anyway*!" And then she bit down, realizing that she shouldn't have said what she did. "Anyway" meant "in spite of your father's arrest and indictment."

"And I'm really grateful for that," I said quickly. "A lot of schools dropped me like a hot turd."

Her eyes were wide and liquid, waiting for me to finish.

"But I can't play. I love hockey, but..." There was an enormous lump in my throat. "I changed my name," I blurted out.

She sucked in a breath. "Okay..." she shook her head. "I'm trying to understand. But Shannon..." she cocked her head.

"Scarlet Crowley," I supplied.

"Scarlet Crowley, we are going to kick *ass* this year. And we really need some help in front of the net. You're good enough to start games."

"I know," I said in a small voice. "I just can't... I can't *be* her anymore. I... apologize."

Coach put her chin on her hands. "I'm really sorry you feel that way. But wouldn't playing in spite of them just prove to everyone who you really are?"

That sounded good on paper. But Coach hadn't lived the year I'd just lived. She really had no idea how bad it could be. "I'm so sorry," I whispered. "I wanted to play for you. I really did."

Her frown turned into resignation. "I wouldn't say this to a lot of players, Scarlet. But if you stay in shape, you could come back in a year or two. My gut says there will always be room for you."

I let out a long breath. "Thank you, Coach. Thank you."

There weren't any more words to say. So I got up and drove home.

Without hockey practice to keep me busy, I was at a loss for what to do with myself. Even though I'd vowed that this year would be different from last year, I found myself practicing guitar on my bed in the evenings. I could *almost* play the opening riff to Eric Clapton's *Layla*, which had bedeviled me for months.

And hey — there weren't any news trucks sitting outside. So that was progress.

Also, I had Tuesdays and Thursdays to look forward to. They quickly became the best days of the week, because Bridger and I were becoming friends. The moment I walked into statistics class, I always checked to make sure he was there.

He always was.

In stats, I'd learned to sit in the row in front of him.

31

Otherwise, the temptation was just too great to watch Bridger instead of the professor. My grade in that course could not withstand my wandering eyes. And I planned to do very, very well at Harkness. College was my lifeline, and I wasn't about to risk it with a poor performance.

After stats, the day got even better. With some careful timing (a goalie was good at this sort of maneuvering) I always managed to fall in with Bridger on the way to music theory.

"Stalker! What music do you think we'll hear in class today?" he would ask.

Except for the dreadful nickname he'd given to me, everything about Bridger was fun. I'd make a few guesses about what we'd get during music theory, all the while trying not to fall headlong into his green-eyed gaze.

After class, we usually ate lunch together in the student center. We'd hang around for a little while afterward, too, helping each other with the work from the courses we shared.

I learned plenty from Bridger. I learned that statistics wasn't as scary as I'd thought, once you got past all the new terminology. And the homework was more interesting than anything I'd ever done for a calculus class, because all the examples were practical, concrete things. In stats class, the world was not biased and abstract. Every mystery could be ordered, graphed and explained.

In addition to math, I learned that Bridger had pale freckles on the back of his hands, and that his smile was slightly lopsided. And that when he leaned back in his chair, his t-shirt stretched across every glorious muscle on his chest.

Each time we hung out, his watch alarm went off at exactly ten minutes past two o'clock. "Time to go to work," he'd say, shoving his books into his backpack.

"Where do you work?" I'd asked.

"Where *don't* I work?" was his retort.

Once, his alarm beeped when Bridger was right in the middle of helping me understand the Z-distribution. "Crap," I said. "Is there any way we can take this up later?" It was a purely selfish question, of course. I was nursing a big crush on Bridger, even though I was sure he was out of my league.

"If you need help, call me," he said. "Give me your pen." He scribbled his phone number on my notes. "But this is the only time I can study with you." He shrugged on a jacket. "I make expensive coffee some afternoons, I drive a forklift at night, and on the weekends I have a babysitting gig."

"*Seriously?*" I asked. "You work three jobs, and you're getting a master's degree alongside your bachelor's?"

"There's no rest for the wicked," he said. Then he gave me a cheeky wink and strode out of the library.

Only once did I see Bridger outside of our Tuesday / Thursday time slot. One warm Saturday, just as September segued into October, I went jogging. After four miles, I decided to stop torturing myself and buy something to drink. Panting in the back of a little Organic market on Chapel street, I was eyeing the choices in the cooler when I heard a familiar voice.

"I don't think so, Lucy," Bridger said in his warm baritone. "The bunny crackers cost twice as much as the ones we usually buy. Maybe another time." I turned my head just in time to see him pass by the end of my aisle and out of sight.

Now, it shouldn't have surprised me to see that Bridger was there with a girl. But this particular girl was about four feet tall, and wearing a pink bicycle helmet. And even though she passed by in a blink, there was no mistaking the chestnut colored ponytail flopping along behind her.

Bridger had mentioned a babysitting job. But that little girl had to be a relative.

It would have been easy to catch up with him and say hello. And I wanted to. But I was sweaty from my run. And even more importantly, I didn't want him to imagine I'd followed him here. So I let my gaze linger on the beverages. When I finally chose one, paid, and emerged from the store, they were nowhere in sight.

— Bridger

I survived September without any disasters, but that was no cause for celebration. My life was a house of cards. I woke up every morning wondering whether this would be the day that the slightest breeze blew everything down.

Classes. Lucy. Work. Repeat. That was my life. (Oh, and *worry*. There was always time for that.) It only took a couple of weeks before my friends stopped texting me. Since I never replied to their updates and invitations, it wasn't that surprising that they stopped trying.

Except for one. Hartley texted me every day, making me feel like a real jerkface for never replying. The first Wednesday in October, he came into the coffee shop during my shift.

"Dude!" he said, leaning on the counter. "Where the fuck have you been? And why don't you answer your phone?"

"Working," I said immediately.

He was quiet for a second, studying me. I hadn't seen him since move-in day, for Christ's sake. "How bad is it, Bridge?"

Shit, he cut right to the chase. I rifled through my short stack of excuses and came up dry.

"Why are you working so many hours that you don't even come into the dining hall at dinner time?" Hartley pressed.

34

I probably winced. Hartley and I had been friends for a long time. We'd played hockey together for years. Even last year, when Hartley was off the team for an injury, we'd somehow stayed tight. There really wasn't an excuse in the world good enough to convince him that my life wasn't circling the drain. I was pretty famous for working hard and partying hard. And my new living arrangement meant that I hadn't been able to show my face at a party since July.

"Hi, Hartley!"

My friend turned his head to see my sister waving at him from the cafe table where I'd parked her with two cookies and a Nancy Drew paperback. "Lucy! What up, girl?" He wandered over to get a high five.

Saved by the eight year old. Hartley couldn't grill me about my so-called life so long as Lulu was part of the conversation. As long as she didn't spill the beans, I should be okay.

I didn't even want to think about all the secrets I'd asked Lucy to keep this year. It can't be all that good for the third grade psyche to live a double life. But there really was no choice.

I had to make three froufrou espresso drinks for some sorority girls before Hartley and I had another chance to talk. "Do you want coffee, or did you just come in to see my pretty face?" I asked him.

He grinned. "Can I have a small French roast?" Even though Hartley had more cash in his pockets than he used to, he hadn't given up his cheapskate habits. He and I had grown up with an instinct for the cheapest thing on any menu. The soup at a diner. The dollar menu at a fast food joint.

The small French roast.

"How's Theresa?" I asked as I poured for him. "Is she

still freaking out about having to do homework?"

Hartley grinned. "Yeah, it's pretty funny hearing her complain about a pop quiz." Hartley's mother had just started nursing school. After twenty years of just scraping by as a single mom, she was finally getting her turn.

I loved Theresa, and I'd crashed at their house more times than I cared to count. I'd thought about calling Hartley's mom to ask her to take Lucy in. Hell, I thought about it every damned *day*. And I knew she'd do it. But I also knew she'd quit school to bail us out. I could not let that happen.

"How's *your* mom?" Hartley asked, taking his first sip of coffee.

I was ready for the question. "The same," I said. Although it was a lie twice over. Because things had gone *very* far South over the summer. Her drug addiction and her creepy friends had pushed me into taking Lucy off her hands. These days, I didn't even *know* how she was faring. I hadn't seen her in a few weeks.

And neither had Lucy.

Hartley studied me. "Do you have Lucy a lot?" he asked.

"Not usually," I lied. "She's in an after school program on Wednesdays, and it was canceled today for some reason. I told Mom she could hang with me at the coffee shop. So how's the lineup this year, anyway?" That's how desperate I was to get off the subject of Lucy — I was even willing to bring up hockey. This was precisely why I'd been avoiding my friends for a month. With me, there were only painful topics.

It was Hartley's turn to flinch. "The team looks damned good, honestly. Wish you were there. The frosh don't get my jokes. And half of them don't speak English."

"Ouch."

"I know. Coach wooed a handful of Canadians who were

tired of riding the bench in the semipros. Twenty-one year-old French speakers. I don't know how they'll pass their classes until the tutoring kicks in. But they sure can skate."

I put my elbows on the counter. "So that's it for us Connecticut kids, isn't it? If the Ivy League can pull in the ringers like that."

Hartley shrugged, putting two dollars down on the counter. "Maybe you and I already got the best of it."

"Maybe. But your final season could be pretty exciting." Hartley was a year ahead of me.

"We'll see."

"How's Callahan?" Hartley's girlfriend was another good friend of mine. Christ, I really missed hanging out with the two of them.

"She's good. Did I tell you that she's a student manager for the women's team this year?"

"No shit? That's bad-ass." Callahan used to play hockey, too. Until an injury put her on crutches for life.

Hartley shrugged. "She seems happy. The women's team looks really good this year, too. Except they lost a goalie recruit over the summer."

"Bummer. That's not an easy position to fill."

"I know. The girl was J.P. Ellison's daughter. You know, that coach who was arrested for…?" Hartley zipped his lip just in time, with a guilty glance over his shoulder toward Lucy. But Lucy was reading her book, oblivious.

"Yeah. Nasty story. I didn't know he had a daughter."

"She was supposed to mind the net this year. But she didn't turn up. Speaking of which…" Hartley checked his watch. It was time for him to go to practice. Shit, I wished I was going with him. He reached across the counter and punched me in the arm. "Call me, would you? Or I'm going to hunt you down, and drag you to a party."

Good luck with that. "I will."

Another lie.

Friday morning I blew off my neuro bio lecture to do an errand I'd been avoiding. I biked off campus, past Lucy's elementary school. She was in there somewhere, learning fractions and spelling rules. (Since I was the one who checked her homework these days, I was quite the third grade curriculum expert.) The further I traveled from campus, the smaller the houses became. On my childhood street, I coasted to a stop before I reached our ranch house. An unfamiliar car sat in the driveway. And the front door was standing open.

I pulled my bike under the bus shelter with me and watched the house.

A few minutes later, a scrawny man emerged, a box in his arms. He wore a loose-fitting denim jacket, and his hair had not been washed any time recently. He put the box in the back seat of the car. Then he walked back up on our small stoop and spoke to someone inside.

My mother shuffled into view, and the sight made my chest tight.

He led her by the arm. But even so, her gait was shaky. She wore rumpled, baggy clothes, lank hair and a completely blank expression.

Shit.

My mother was tucked by the greasy asshole into the passenger seat of the car. And then they drove away together. When the car passed me, I made myself look away, studying the bus schedule as if the secrets of the universe were written there.

They weren't.

Even after the car had gone, I didn't move for a couple of minutes. I watched our house, wondering who else might be inside. But I only had an hour, and things looked quiet over there. So I walked my bike up the drive, leaning it against the side of the house where it couldn't be seen from the street. I dug my keys out of my pocket, only to spot a new lock glinting on the back door. *What the fuck?* I tried the knob. Locked.

A cold dread expanded in my gut as I forced open the kitchen window. This had been my means of entry many times during high school, if I'd left my keys at home by mistake. The sill was chest height, since it was over the sink. But I still had it, ladies and gentlemen. I could still boost my ass up there without too much trouble.

It was the smell that hit me first.

God, the kitchen *reeked*. There was garbage on the counter tops, and abandoned dishes in the sink. I put my foot down on the counter and leapt to the floor. The sight of something moving just about stopped my heart.

A rat. Only a rat.

I stood there for a moment, heart pounding. It wasn't long ago that this kitchen was spotless. I used to sneak through here after curfew on Saturday nights. The worst smell back then was maybe a little cigarette smoke — a habit my father never managed to break. But the surfaces used to shine in the moonlight as I tiptoed towards my room. I would hear my dad sawing logs from his side of the bed. Sometimes my mother fell asleep in the living room, the TV watching her instead of the other way around. I'd put my hand on her shoulder until she woke up — Mom wasn't much of a stickler about curfew. At my urging, she'd rouse herself enough to go to bed.

Lucy was little then, still sleeping in a crib when I was fifteen, her red hair looking like a lion's mane when she woke up in the morning. My father was still alive, his van parked in the driveway. *McCaulley Plumbing and Heating* was painted on the side.

The ghosts of happier times were all around me. I took a deep breath to try to force them back. But all that did was to pull more of the stench into my lungs.

Fuck.

I moved from the kitchen into the dining room. The smell was less here, but that didn't make it better. Because the dining room table was covered with strange accoutrements. There was a stash of glass jars lined up in a row, and two small propane tanks. On the floor was a stack of crushed boxes that had once contained blister packs of an over-the-counter allergy medicine.

Somebody had been busy here, making something both illegal and dangerous. My first impulse was to pull out my phone and take a photo. But then I thought better of the idea. I wanted no part in this.

Leaving that shit behind, I walked toward the bedrooms. I already knew that there was nothing of value left in mine. There were some sentimental things, though. In fact, when I got there I saw that my treasure box — a big shoebox I'd begun keeping in my closet when I was nine — had been raided by some opportunistic shithead. But I found a handful of photographs scattered inside. I shoved these into the front pocket of my hockey hoodie and left the room.

Lucy's room hadn't fared much better. It smelled as if someone had been sleeping in there. There were still a lot of books and toys on the shelves. But I couldn't carry much back to campus. I tucked the box set of Harry Potter books under my arm. Then I went into her closet and grabbed a stack of sweaters off the shelf. I'd brought a plastic shopping bag, which I pulled from my jeans pocket. I crammed five sweaters into it, until it was so full that the loops would barely fit over my hand.

For winter, she'd need a coat and boots. What else? Long pants. Warm socks. We would just have to buy those things. Last year's probably wouldn't fit anyway.

Fuck it. I had to get out of here.

Thirty seconds later, I walked out the back door, leaving it unlocked. Then I was back on my bike, pedaling down the street with a box of books under one arm and a bag around my wrist. I made it almost all the way back home before it really hit me. And then the wave of sadness was so strong that I stopped in front of the hospital, dismounted and put my hands on my knees.

I *knew* it would be bad. Six weeks ago, I wheeled Lucy's bike out of the garage and told her to just come home with me. We'd put some of her things into her backpack and mine. And we pedaled away from there together. By taking Lucy, I'd basically given my mother permission to fall all the way apart. And she'd taken me up on it.

Six weeks. Not one phone call from her to ask if Lucy was okay. What kind of mother does that? So I'd already known that shit was hopeless. But... *Christ*. That house. That *smell*.

My brain began to spool through the usual What Ifs. What if I'd staged some kind of intervention? What if I just called the police right now? I'd thought through it all before, so this time it didn't take very long to arrive at the only answer.

No way.

Because anything I did to save my mom would put Lucy into the system. Even if I spent another night Googling "addiction treatment Connecticut," we didn't have any other family. If my mom was in rehab — or jail — Lucy would go to foster care. And I wasn't going to let that happen.

You can't save everybody, I reminded myself. The trouble was that I wasn't sure I could save anyone at all. Not even myself.

I straightened up, forcing a few deep breaths into my lungs. It was Friday. I had a bio lab in forty minutes. I had a shift at the coffee shop. And I had to pick Lucy up from her after school program by five. Her schedule was different every day of the week, and so was mine. I'd written a spreadsheet to track everything. I could do this.

So long as nothing ever went wrong.

Shoving off again, I pedaled toward campus. This weekend I'd take Lucy to her soccer game in the park, and then we'd go out for pizza together. We'd both do homework. And then the week would start again, with its schedules and deadlines.

And on Tuesday I could see Scarlet. She was my happy thought — with those perfect cheekbones and thoughtful, hazel eyes. I blew out another big breath and tried to pump the stress out of my lungs. It almost worked.

Chapter Four: *If You Want God to Laugh*

— Scarlet

On a busy October morning, the phone rang at a most inconvenient time. And — stupid me — I answered it.

"Shannon," my mother's voice hissed into my ear.

My old name already sounded foreign to me. "What is it, mom? I'm so late for class." I had overslept, and already statistics was beginning without me. Pinning my phone under my ear, I raked my hair with the brush.

"Whatever you're late for, Shannon, it isn't nearly as important as the things I need to say."

With a sigh, I sat down on my bed. "Then say them."

"There's no need to be rude. Your father's lawyers need to interview you."

"No," I said immediately. "I won't do it."

My mother's anger was audible. "Honey, you *will*. We're not even asking you to drive up here for the meeting. They'll come down to meet you in a conference room somewhere. It will take only a couple of hours. You'll answer their questions, and that will be the end of it."

"I'm not answering anyone's questions," I insisted. "The trial has nothing to do with me."

"Shannon! This is a small thing you can do for the father who raised you! There is no reason on *God's green earth* for you not to help him." My mother's voice reached its familiar shrill pitch.

"Mom, if it's so important, why doesn't Dad ask me himself?"

Her sigh could have burned the paint off of walls. "He shouldn't have to ask his only child for help. We are family and this is what families do. You should be sitting here in the kitchen, *volunteering* your time. Instead, you changed your name and left the state. How do you think that looks?"

It *looked* like something a person would do when she was desperate. But I couldn't say that to my mother, because she really didn't give a damn. She didn't care that my teammates had turned their backs on me. She didn't care that my textbooks had been defaced, that my gym locker had been filled with… with things that were supposed to be flushed down toilets. Just at the memory of it, I tasted bile in my throat.

But that was my mother — always concerned with the way things looked. She didn't care if my life was intolerable, as long as we held up the facade.

"You will answer their questions," my mother repeated.

"My answers won't be useful."

"That's not for you to decide."

"Mom," I said, and my voice shook. There was nobody on earth who had the capacity to make me angry quite like she could. "I can't be part of this process. I need to study, and get good grades, and move on."

"That's just selfish, Shannon. None of us moves on until your father can walk away from this bullshit with his head held high."

Later, I would remember to be shocked that my mother used a curse word. But at the moment, I was just too stunned by the threat she made next.

"If your father loses the cases against him, do you really

think there will be tuition money for you next year? You think you've run away from it all. But you can't. Do the interview, or I will not be responsible for your tuition check going astray next year."

The truth of my situation settled like a weight on my chest. I was never getting out from under the things that my father did.

Allegedly did.

Probably did.

God.

I didn't run out the door right after that phone call, even though I probably should have. Instead, I began Googling "compelling a testimony" and "children of the defendant." I didn't have a clue whether the law required me to talk to my father's lawyers, or whether I could be put on the witness stand. And there was nobody I could ask who would tell me the truth.

My phone rang again, and I picked it up the way you handle a poisonous snake. But the incoming call wasn't from my mom or a lawyer. It was from Bridger.

"Hello," I said, my voice husky.

"Stalker! Where are you? Sick?"

I cleared my throat. "I'm okay. There was some… family drama today. I wasted a lot of time on the phone with my mom. But it's no big deal."

"Huh," Bridger said. "I wonder how you're going to get the notes for today's classes?"

"Bridger," I smiled for the first time that day. "Maybe there's someone who will be nice enough to help me out with that?"

"Are you missing lunch, too?"

"I guess so."

"That's no good. I'm bringing you a sandwich. What kind should I get?"

"You don't have to do that," I stumbled on the words. But of course, I wanted Bridger to bring me a sandwich. What a swoon-worthy idea.

"What do you like? I'm not in line yet, so just give me a genre. Turkey? Italian?"

"Get whichever sandwich special looks good," I said quickly. "And a cookie wouldn't go amiss."

"I'll be there in ten," he said. "The Turner first years live in… Vanderberg, right? You can show me the guitar thing you were talking about last week." He ended the call.

For the next twenty minutes, I ran around tidying up my room. The common room was in decent shape, but I had to make my bed and kick a bunch of Blond Katie's clothes under hers.

My phone buzzed with a text from Bridger. KNOCK KNOCK.

I ran down the stairs and opened the entryway door. "Hi!"

He walked in, a take-out box in his hands. "Hi, stalker." His green eyes studied me. "Are you okay?"

Damn. I should have tidied myself up as well as the room. The way he stared, my eyes were probably red.

"Sure," I said, my voice as bright as possible. "Come on up. Thanks for bringing lunch."

And then he was actually walking *into my room*, something that had figured prominently into several of my recent fantasies. I very nearly sat down in the common room, but it occurred to me that one or both Katies might show up at any moment. And I didn't want to compete with them for

Bridger's attention, because surely I'd lose. So I walked right through the common room and into the bedroom, just as casually as if guys followed me in there all the time.

Bridger didn't seem to find that strange. He tossed his coat down and sat on the foot of my bed, setting the take-out box down on Blond Katie's trunk. "Let's eat." I sat on Katie's bed, to make things a little less weird. He popped open the box. "It was chicken and avocado day," he said.

"Score."

"Exactly." He spread a napkin on his lap. Then he took two sandwich halves and passed me the box.

"Ooh, stick-tap for remembering to bring chips!" I said.

He looked up quickly, a smile on his face. "You're welcome."

That's when I realized that I'd used a hockey reference. A stick-tap was the sort of thank-you that only another player would understand. Crap! My mother had put me off my game today. And I'd almost blown my cover the first day we'd met, too, when I'd recognized Bridger's name from the team roster. "It was nice of you to bring lunch," I said.

"It's nothing," he said, his voice gruff. "Are you going to be okay? Is it anything you want to talk about?"

I shook my head. "Nobody's dying, if that's what you mean. It's just… drama. Makes me happy to be many miles away."

"Well," he leaned down to steal a few chips out of the box. "I know drama. Everybody's got some."

We chewed in silence for a minute, and I thought Bridger was going to let the subject drop. But he didn't. His voice was wistful as he spoke again. "This year I seem to be punching above my weight in drama. Last week, I really let it get to me."

"But not anymore?" I asked. Our voices were hushed, by

47

some mutual agreement that this was not a typical conversation for us. "Because if you know any tricks for sliding out from underneath it, I'm all ears."

He cleared his throat. "My trick is understanding that there aren't any tricks. You just have to wade through each moment as it comes."

"Well I'm definitely doing it wrong, then."

He barked out a laugh. "Why?"

"Well…" I nibbled a chip. "I've always liked to plan things out, so that I know what to expect. But last year, that was impossible, and I never really got over it."

"There's a saying. If you want God to laugh, tell him your plans."

"I should have it tattooed on my person."

"Which part of your person?" His green eyes lifted to mine with a sparkle that I sincerely hoped was intentionally flirtatious.

A girl can dream.

"So," he said when the lunch was eaten. "Where's this guitar I've been hearing about?"

"Move your big feet and I'll show you." I pulled Jordan out from under the bed, and snapped open the case. It occurred to me that I could not tell Bridger my guitar's name, because I'd named Jordan after the hottest player in the NHL. And the real-life Jordan was a *ginger*, just like Bridger.

Biting back a smile, I sat down right next to Bridger on the bed, holding the guitar across my lap, and turning to face him.

He reached across to brush his fingers against the strings, each one making a watery sound as he plucked them.

I grinned. "Man up, Bridger. Like *this*." I strummed, and

the sound filled the room.

"Did you just call me a wuss?" Those jade eyes challenged me as he reached over again, this time plucking one string hard.

"Atta boy." This was the most fun I'd had in a long time. "Okay, so I promised to teach you about intervals. So, that's the D string you just plucked. Sing it with me." I sang a *la* on the note of D.

"Christ, Stalker. You didn't mention anything about singing."

"It's one note. Come on, give me a D."

His ears turned pink. But then he sang the note with me. "Yes! See, that was easy. Now we're going to raise it an octave." I sang a higher D, but Bridger faltered.

"A real man can't sing that note," he complained.

"Nonsense. Eric Clapton can sing it. And he has his Man Card. But never mind — can you *hear* that it's one octave higher? Still a D?"

"Sure. I hear it."

"Good. Now see this dot?" I pointed at the inlay on the fingerboard. "That divides the string exactly in half, from the bridge to where it's wound around the pin. So first listen..." I played the open D string. "Now put your finger there."

Bridger pressed down the string onto the fret at the half way marker, and then I strummed again. The sound was an octave higher.

"Deeee..." I sang and then knocked his finger off the fret. "Deeee," I sang the lower one. "Half the string, twice the rate of oscillation. Music theory is just a bit of simple math."

He regarded me, the room quiet around us. "That's very cool, Stalker. And so much more lucid than our shitty textbook. But now I need to hear you play."

"Play… what?"

"A song. I want to hear one."

"Um… maybe. If you can do me a little favor."

He crossed his arms, and I became momentarily distracted by the curved shape of his forearm muscles. "Favor? What's this going to cost me?"

"Well… could you stop calling me Stalker?" I knew my objection to his nickname was a little silly. But the past year had made me sensitive to anything even remotely creepy.

His eyebrows went up. "Sure. That's it?"

I nodded.

"No problem, Miss Scarlet. Now play me a song."

My hands felt a little sweaty, and I had to wipe them on my jeans. I shouldn't have been nervous, because I spent a lot of restless hours last year playing the living crap out of my guitar. When nobody at school will speak to you, and there's a full drama playing inside your house, there is really no better way to spend time than practicing music. But still, I was anxious to impress.

I cleared my throat. "Okay. What do you like? Give me a basic genre."

His smile lit up the whole room. "Classic rock?"

I put the guitar strap over my head, checked my tuning, and then launched in to Lynyrd Skynyrd's *Sweet Home Alabama*. With its distinctive opening riff, I knew it would sound impressive. And I'd played it a hundred times before.

I kept my eyes on the fret board, not because I needed to look, but because I felt shy. After the first few bars I began to relax, the music pulling me in.

When the song was done, I waited until the last note died away. And then I couldn't avoid his face any longer. Bridger was looking down at me with big eyes, dark green, the color of the sea before a storm. "Damn, Scarlet," he whispered. "You amaze me."

My cheeks did their thing, becoming hot. I busied myself with removing the guitar strap from around my neck. But I fumbled it, twisting my hair in the strap. "Ouch," I swore.

Bridger reached up to untangle me, and I felt my status tumble quickly from "possibly cool" right down to "dork." But just as I was beating myself up about it, I noticed something peculiar. After Bridger pushed my tangled hair off my shoulder, his hand stayed there, warming my skin. Then, his fingers cupped my cheek. My gaze flew to his, and I found him studying me.

Ever so slowly, he leaned in. Then his lips barely whispered across mine, and I felt myself break out in goosebumps. But he didn't kiss me properly. Instead, his lips came to hover over the corner of my mouth, a spot on my body which I'd never guessed was so sensitive. "Is this okay?" he whispered, his lips so close that I could feel the words vibrate on my skin. "I find you a little hard to read."

Hell yes. But I didn't trust my voice to answer him. Instead, I turned my face the tiniest distance towards his, hoping he'd understand. My heart slammed against my ribs as his mouth found mine. Bridger's lips were gentle and soft. As he pressed his mouth onto mine, a happy warmth bloomed in my chest.

One of his arms slipped around to encircle me, but then his mouth withdrew. "I've wanted to do this," he whispered, "since the first day you sat down to lunch." When he kissed me again, I slumped into him. His lips parted, and then his tongue slid slowly over mine. A little mewl of pleasure escaped from the back of my throat. I decided to be embarrassed about it later.

In my happy haze, I barely noticed when Bridger moved the guitar from my lap onto Katie's bed. We were still sitting side by side on my bed, but Bridger scooped a hand under my knees, lifting them over his, so that we could almost face each other. His broad hands warmed my lower back as he kissed me again and again. I let my fingers explore the hard muscles of his shoulders, the velvety skin on the back of his neck, and then wander into his thick hair.

And then his alarm went off.

Bridger broke off our kiss with a groan. He pressed a button on his watch to silence the beeping. Then he wrapped his arms around me, his chin on my shoulder. "And then real life intrudes," he said in a low voice.

I said nothing, just threaded my fingers together behind his broad back, holding on tightly.

"I have to go," he said.

I swiveled to slide my legs off of his. "I know."

"Not that I want to…" He stood up. "Can I call you later?"

I nodded up at him.

He bent down, gave me a tiny kiss on the lips, and then turned and left my room.

Alone, I flopped back on the bed, a quivering, grinning mess of a girl. My lips were swollen from his kisses, my palms damp.

At least something went right that day.

He called at nine thirty. I made myself wait until the second ring to answer. "Hi," I said, suddenly shy.

"Hi Scarlet." His voice was hushed. "Are we still cool?"

"Yes," I said. "In fact, we'd be even cooler if you came back over here." And after I said it, my heart took off galloping like a pony. Because there was always a chance Bridger was about to say something that started with "about this afternoon... I didn't mean to do that."

But he didn't. Instead, he gave a warm chuckle into the phone. "I wish I could."

"You're at work?" I asked. "At the warehouse?"

"Always. You know..." There was a pause, as if he was deciding whether or not to say something. "Scarlet, I really like you. But I'm not around very much."

"I know," I said quietly. "You've got a lot on your plate."

"This year... I've been told that being friends with me is kind of a drag."

"I never thought so," I said.

"Not yet anyway," he sighed. "I'll see you Thursday?" he asked.

"I'll be there."

Thursday's statistics lecture was about ten years long. Bridger ran into the room at the last minute, sitting somewhere behind me. It was a torturous ninety minutes spent squinting at the professor's hastily drawn examples and wondering whether things would be awkward with Bridger now.

When the infernal class finally drew to a close, I leaned down to put my notebook back in my bag. *Just be cool*, I coached myself. If only I knew what that meant. I had very little experience with boys. I was a bit of a late bloomer, with hockey dominating a lot of my early high school years. It's difficult to figure out the boy/girl scene when you're driving to Concord or Bedford every weekend for a game.

And then came senior year. And while other girls were planning romantic prom night festivities, I was alone in my room, hiding from satellite TV trucks three deep in front of my house. I spent those months honing my guitar skills and ticking off the days until I could escape to college. The result was that I knew the chord progressions for a great many songs, and almost nothing about how to act casual around a boy I liked. A lot.

But when I stood up after class, he was right there waiting, a slightly lopsided smile on his rugged face. He held out his hand, palm up. "Shall we?"

I took his hand. And when the warm fingers closed around mine, I wanted to do a happy dance.

After music theory, where we sat next to one another, he held my hand on the way to lunch, too.

"So, where'd you learn to play the guitar, Scarlet? Are your parents musical?"

This made me laugh. "God, no. I'm self taught. There's nothing a girl can't learn at the University of YouTube."

"Did you play in a band?" he asked. His thumb stroked my palm. I'd never thought of my hand as a sexual organ before, but the sweep of his skin across mine felt positively electric.

"A band?" I tried to keep it together. "No. I guess I'm a solo act."

"You are a very interesting girl, Scarlet," he said. Then he let go of my hand so that he could pull out his wallet at the lunch counter, and I missed our connection immediately.

"You never say very much about Miami Beach," Bridger said as we lingered over our coffee. "Or your family."

I didn't bother to hide my flinch. "Miami Beach is the best. My family... not so much. I don't really talk about them. It isn't a nice story." The truth was, I didn't want to lie any more than necessary to those deep green eyes.

Bridger's face flashed with sympathy. "Okay. It's exactly the same for me, but I didn't expect that. Because you *look* like someone from a family with a nice story."

"And you don't?" I countered.

He put one hand on his own cheek and covered mine with his other. "You make a good point. Maybe there's no look. I should probably stop thinking that everyone else in this room has it easier than me."

I turned my head, and together we both scanned the laughing, eating, bustle that was the student center at noon. It sure looked happy out there. For just a moment, I was a goalie again, analyzing the play, scouting for trouble.

"Nah," I said finally, turning back to Bridger. "I still think most of them have it pretty good."

Bridger grinned. "This is the cynical table," he said, tapping his fingertip on the wood grain.

"Party of two," I agreed.

Chapter Five: *Where There's Smoke*

— *Scarlet*

I was *happy.*

Now there was a word I hadn't used in the longest time. Even though I knew that Bridger and I would probably still only see each other twice a week, my entire attitude brightened. For the next few days I walked around in a giddy fog.

Which is probably why I didn't see it coming.

On my way out of the dorm on Monday, someone called to me. "Shannon! Wait!"

My head snapped up at the sound of my old name. I saw Azzan, my father's security man, leaning against a statue of Abraham Harkness. Running toward him so that he wouldn't call me "Shannon" again, I was already wondering what I'd say if anyone had heard.

"What do you want?" I snapped.

"Good morning to you, too," he said. His smile was thin and not the least bit welcoming.

"I have a class now," I told him.

"You need to set up a time for your interview. Soon."

"No, I don't. I don't have anything to say."

"That's for your father's lawyer to decide," Azzan said, dropping any pretense of a smile. "You name the afternoon, and we'll have the whole thing over in two hours."

"I can't be involved," I insisted, hiking my backpack higher onto my shoulder. "I don't know a thing, and I won't do the meeting."

"Shannon, you *will* do the meeting. If you want to be a rebellious teenager, pick a different way. This is nonnegotiable."

Unfortunately, I felt the same way. "I have class," I repeated. It was hard to believe that Azzan had driven more than ninety minutes to talk to me. That meant he wouldn't be shaken off very easily.

"You have one week to call me to set up a meeting." At that, he turned and walked away.

I was happy to see him go. But he hadn't said what would happen if I didn't call. I had a feeling that I would soon find out.

The encounter darkened my weekend, and then a newspaper article positively blackened it. It was on the front page, above the fold. There were three brand new complaints against my father.

"A year later, they're still coming out of the woodwork." I scanned the story, the familiar ache of dread in my heart. Like the others, the new accusers were young men who'd taken part in my father's charitable foundation for underprivileged boys.

I squinted at the low-resolution photo on the news website. Only one of the victims was pictured. He had a strong face — cut cheekbones, a prominent forehead. Had I seen him before? I didn't think I had. Or was that just wishful thinking?

For more than a year I'd been doing this — staring at grainy pictures, trying to jog my own memory. There were some days when I could convince myself that all of it was bullshit. I'd never seen my father do anything strange. Also, I'd spent a lot of time in locker rooms. They were big, echoing places where people were constantly walking in and out. How could a semi famous coach in his fifties spend a lot of time with fourteen year olds, and nobody noticed?

And yet...

My gaze was always drawn back to the boys' photos. This picture showed a young man's face. He was nineteen now. According to the teachers interviewed for the article, he'd become aggressive and self destructive during his early teen years. Nobody knew why his grade point average slipped from A- to barely getting by.

He told his mother that one of the hockey coaches was scary. But when pressed, he refused to explain.

He stopped eating.

God.

The newspaper accounts made my father look very, very guilty.

Unlike my mother, I could never be satisfied by the idea that the boys invented their stories. Even if there was a potential paycheck involved, my gut said that the cost to a young man for making these accusations was just too great. Even after everything that had happened to me last year, I wasn't jaded enough to think it was all a conspiracy.

The articles always portrayed my father (accurately) as an egomaniac. There was an endless supply of old photography of him screaming at his players, or alternately grinning with victory.

In real life, Coach Ellison was the most closed-down, silent, prickly person that you'd ever meet. He doled out affection with an eyedropper, always saving his approval for well-played hockey games.

The man had very few character witnesses rushing to his defense.

Today's article featured a press photograph from the Sterling College hockey program. In the photo, my father wore a designer suit and a smile.

My father *never* smiled, unless a photographer asked him

to. Or unless his players won a tough game.

The Steel Wings charity had gotten off the ground when I was five, right after we'd moved to New Hampshire. A group of NHL players contributed the seed money for ice time and the equipment. Hockey was an expensive sport, and Steel Wings gave boys who would otherwise never own a pair of skates a chance to play.

But now the world knew that the charity's founder may have had a sinister goal in mind, too.

Last year, not a single person ever asked me the obvious question. *Did you know?* Nobody asked it out loud, which is too bad, because I would have liked to answer.

No, okay? *No.* I had no idea.

What I wouldn't like to admit, though, is that I often found myself puzzling over the inconsistencies. If Coach Ellison did all these things, why did it take ten years before he was caught? This bothered me. And what's more, I was bothered by the fact that it bothered me. Because it wasn't out of love that I hoped there could be some mistake. And if my father did all these terrible things, I hoped they'd throw the book at him.

But how could I have missed it? Was I really that stupid? Or selfish? Or unobservant? If he did everything they said he did, what did that make me?

I threw the newspaper face down on the floor.

The last line of the article had said that the jury would be seated in December, and that the trial would begin immediately afterward. My parents had already told me that I was expected to sit there next to them in the courtroom.

The very idea made my stomach go sour.

— Bridger

Tuesdays and Thursdays were the best part of the week. They were my little vacation from reality. I lived for those few hours with Scarlet.

She and I abandoned the pretense of studying together. Our time after class was too valuable for music theory or statistics. We used the time to eat lunch and hang out.

And make out.

On Thursdays — when her roommate Katie had a noon seminar — we often ate a take out lunch in Scarlet's room. Sometimes, she played her guitar for me. But invariably, we would end up tangled up with one another on her bed.

It was always up to me to make the first move. Scarlet was shy. Her idea of a "come hither" look was to study me out of the corner of her hazel eyes. And then her cheeks would flush, and she'd look away. But when I pulled her into my lap and kissed her neck, she melted like warm butter. And when I laid her back on the bed, she reached for me, kissing me as though she was dying of thirst, and I was the last drink on earth.

And when two o'clock came around, my watch would chime. Then I'd apologize and leave, always with regret.

We never got any other time together. Sometimes she asked leading questions like: "so, what are you up to this weekend?" And I would have to make my usual empty excuses. "My babysitting gig is Friday and Saturday nights." Then I always changed the subject. She took the hint and left it alone. Scarlet wasn't a clingy person, thank Christ. I think she understood that I was giving her all I could.

It was a strange arrangement. But it was *our* strange arrangement.

One cool October day, carrying our lunch back to her room, we got caught in a downpour on Fresh Court. The sky opened up as we walked past the big oak trees, their leaves golden on the stone path. When the first giant drops hit us, we ran. But it quickly built to a deluge, and running became pointless. Soaked to the skin already, we stopped in the center of the courtyard, the heavy drops slapping the slate flagstones underfoot.

Laughing, I caught Scarlet by the hips and kissed her, my mouth hot, the rain cool. The storm had chased everyone else away, leaving just the two of us there, lip locked, on the flagstone pathway. When I pulled her body in tight, she groaned.

"Let's go inside," I said, my voice husky.

We ran, holding hands, up to her room. Our soggy bags and take out lunch got dropped to the floor, and we fell, laughing, onto the bed.

Then, in a move that surprised me, Scarlet gathered the fabric of my sodden t-shirt into her hands and peeled it upward. I ducked my head to get it off. And when I could see her again, I got a look at Scarlet's face. The expression said: *Sweet Jesus*. And then her hands began to skim over my body eagerly.

My pulse soared. With hands that were actually trembling, I eased her top over her head, too. Kissing her, I unclasped her soggy bra. And then I put my hands on her shoulders and pushed her back onto the bed.

"Mmm," she said as my mouth burned a trail from her jaw down her neck.

"Scarlet," I whispered. "You have the most beautiful body." I climbed on top of her, cupping both creamy breasts in my hands. And when my thumbs brushed her nipples, she almost shot off the bed.

"Jeez," she gasped.

"What?" I had been feeling a little out of control, but in a good way, or so I thought. But now I lifted my head, checking her expression.

Scarlet took a shaky breath. "Jeez, that's *nice*," she eked out.

Okay, then. I bent down, dropping open-mouthed kisses on her neck and down her shoulder. Scarlet was practically panting in my arms. She raised her arms, raking her fingers through my hair. She trailed them down my neck.

Scarlet had velvet skin, the sort I could touch all day long and never get enough. My lips explored the warm geography of her breasts. And when I began to bathe one nipple with my tongue, I heard her suck in a breath. Her body went completely still. This time, I didn't mistake her responsiveness for disapproval. Smiling up at her, I sucked the peak of her into my mouth. This elicited a breathy little moan that shot straight to my already throbbing dick.

Damn, this girl was going to kill me. And it wasn't because I hadn't had sex in a ridiculously long time. It was the way she glanced down at me that was so hot — her expression a blend of surprise, wonder and lust.

Releasing her swollen nipple with a pop, I nosed over to the other breast. As long as she kept making those hot little sounds, I could do this all day long.

— Scarlet

Holy hell. I had no idea there were so many nerve endings in my chest. What I didn't know about sex could fill volumes. Bridger's fingertips skated up my ribcage while he kissed me, his touches light and feathery. And the weight of his body on top of mine was delicious.

Before Bridger, I had never enjoyed fooling around. My previous experience had involved surreptitious make-outs at tenth grade dances. It was all very sloppy and pointless. Hockey had consumed most of my junior year, with away games squelching the opportunity for any serious time with boys. And then? My senior year — while everyone else was pairing up and hooking up, I was a pariah.

The loveliness happening here on my bed was all brand new. I was so inebriated with pleasure that I didn't hear the door open.

"Well, *hellllo*," Katie's voice rang out. "That's what bandannas on the door knob are for."

When the door clicked shut again, Bridger laid his head on my chest and laughed. "Whoops."

"That was… embarrassing," I said. My skin began to feel flushed.

"Nah," he said. "People have been caught out much worse than that, right?"

"Sure," I said. But that only made me wonder how many girls he'd been caught with over the years.

And then, as it always did, Bridger's alarm went off.

He took a moment more with me, sliding up my body, kissing me warmly on the mouth. "I have to go," he whispered after melting my knees one more time.

"I know," I whispered back. "Listen to me not complaining."

"And I do appreciate it," he said, reaching for his t-shirt where it lay on my floor. He handed me my bra. "Cover yourself, or I may not make it out the door."

"This is me, resisting the urge to fling it out the window instead…"

I saw him studying my nakedness again, before he threw back his head and sighed. "Damn, girl. That's potent."

I laughed. "Why?" It was so hard to believe that I had anything he hadn't seen before. Besides, even though I was no longer an athlete, I had an athlete's body. Nobody would mistake me for a Playboy bunny.

He shook his head. "You just do it for me, that's all. You're a *strong* kind of sexy, like you could take on Katie in a fight, and win. But also delicious."

I hooked my bra and swiveled it around my chest, ready to slip my arms back into the straps. But something in his face made me pause.

He knelt in front of me then, leaning in to kiss each breast once more. And his touch practically melted me into a liquid. I wanted to leap at him again, but he stood up.

When I hugged him goodbye, he said, "thank you, Scarlet."

"For what?" I whispered. "For being your Tuesday and Thursday girl?"

His eyes bored into mine. "For all seven days. Because I think of you on all of them." He leaned down to give me one more kiss, then turned to go.

"Take a sandwich," I called. "We never ate lunch."

Chuckling, he took one out of the box on his way. He closed the bedroom door behind him, but I heard his voice say "afternoon, ladies" before the outside door opened and shut.

I lay on my bed for a while, replaying the encounter in my mind. Taking off my clothes with a guy wasn't something that I was very comfortable with on paper. But Bridger made my inhibitions fall away. The warm look in his eyes, and the affection in his touch made everything feel okay.

Still, it was half an hour before I dared walk into the common room. Unfortunately, both Katies were out there, waiting for me. But if I had expected ribbing, I didn't get any. The expression in their eyes was something entirely different from what I'd expected. It was *awe*.

"So," Blond Katie said. "That was Bridger McCaulley, right?"

"Um, yeah?" I hovered near the window seat.

"Interesting choice," Ponytail Katie said. "He is *so hot*. I heard he used to be a real player. Both on and off the ice. But then this year he disappeared."

"What do you mean?" I asked. Why would anyone say he disappeared? I saw him all the time.

"They say he used to be a legendary partier, but he doesn't go out anymore. I heard a bunch of rumors, but they can't all be true." She ticked them off on her fingers. "His dad died, or he got some girl pregnant. Someone said he has a *kid*..."

"That all sounds pretty farfetched," I said. "But he does take a sick load of classes, and he works a lot."

"So where does he live?" Blond Katie wanted to know.

She had me there. I knew he was a member of Beaumont House, so I'd always assumed he lived there. But possibly he lived on or off campus. I just shrugged.

Ponytail Katie smirked, but Blond Katie looked thoughtful. "Just be careful, Scarlet. I don't know why there's so many rumors about that guy, but where there's smoke..."

There's a fire.

"Right..." I'd heard enough, so I stomped back into our bedroom. God, I wanted to shake anyone who used that expression. I'd heard it a thousand times during the months before charges were formally filed against my father.

Meanwhile, all that smoke tore my life apart. Reporters camped out on our sidewalk. My teammates disowned me. The boy I'd just started flirting with at school never spoke to me again.

If my life in New Hampshire was meant to burn out, I would have preferred a quick conflagration to the smoldering, choking curtain of smoke which ruined everything.

Chapter Six: *Popcorn vs. Schnapps*

— Scarlet

When I checked my phone after Italian class the following week, a new voicemail waited, from an unfamiliar New Hampshire number.

That couldn't be good.

I tapped the screen and held it to my ear, expecting to hear Azzan or a lawyer chewing me out for my lack of cooperation.

A woman's voice got right to the point. "I am trying to reach Shannon Ellison, also known as Scarlet Crowley." Ouch. She made it sound as though I had a criminal alias. "This is Madeline Teeter, assistant district attorney for the district of New Hampshire. Would you please give me a call at your earliest convenience? There are a few questions I'd like to ask you…"

My heart skittered even as she rattled off the number. Because I'd expected to get called by lawyers. But not the *prosecution*.

When I tapped my phone to delete the message, my fingers were shaking.

If my parents — and their lawyers — were unhappy with me now, they would be ten times angrier if I ever spoke to the district attorney's office.

I shoved the phone deep into my pocket.

Even before my world blew up, I'd sometimes spent time trying to figure out what my parents wanted from me. In many ways, my father was easier than Mom. Win a hockey game, and you were his favorite person. Lose, and you were invisible. A straight A report card and a spot on the girls' all-state hockey team was all he wanted from me. Luckily I was able to deliver most of the time. Because the man could be terrifying if you disappointed him in public. He was "that" dad, the one who screamed from the sidelines, letting you know exactly how badly you'd screwed up.

So I tried never to screw up.

My mother was far more complicated. She wanted a tricky mixture of gratitude and reverence and success. She cared about appearances, too, in ways that I never quite understood. It was okay with her that I was an athlete — she didn't try to dress me in skirts and heels. But in her mind, even sporty girls should be fashionable. She bought me Lululemon workout gear, and pink sports bras. She got huffy if I wore my most comfortable pair of gray track pants out of the house.

To Mom, it wasn't worth doing unless you did it in style. And when the TV trucks began to pull up in front of the house, she didn't fall apart. No — if anything, she upped her trips to the salon, determined to look stylish and confident every time they filmed her coming out of the house.

If I wanted to give her the benefit of the doubt, I might reason that hers was the pathetic response of a person with no other way to contribute to her husband's cause. But it was hard to be generous to a woman who had refused to acknowledge that my father's legal troubles weren't just a minor inconvenience.

Every day I thanked the gods of the Harkness Admissions Department that they'd sent me a fat envelope. Before the scandal, several schools had begun recruiting me for hockey. But nearly all of them dropped me when the story broke. Only two schools admitted me — Harkness, who was probably just too confident in its 300-year-old history to care about scandal. And Sterling — the college where my father coached. They probably admitted me out of obligation.

Thank God I wasn't sitting in New Hampshire with nowhere to go. I planned to stay as far from my father's trial as I could possibly get.

Normal people lived for the weekends. But I was not a normal person. Friday night loomed, and with it the usual poor set of options for entertaining myself. At times, I'd tagged along with The Katies to parties, but they always left me cold. I hated small talk and warm beer. Apart from deafening music, parties seemed to offer little else.

This Friday, I thought I'd stay in and watch some reruns on my laptop. But after dinner, as Blond Katie made plans on the phone, she kept eying me. "I'll ask," she said before hanging up.

Then she turned to me, and I readied my excuses on my tongue.

"Before you say no," Katie began, "it *isn't* a party."

She was *so* on to me. "What, then?"

"The freshmen football players we've been dating have a friend in town," she said.

"And you want me to be your third? For what?"

"A game!" she said. "Harkness versus Brown. Please? It starts in an hour."

I looked out of our rapidly darkening window and wondered what Bridger was up to. Working, of course. I hated to admit it, but his unavailability was starting to get to me. There was no chance in hell that the Katies' football friends would be as interesting as Bridger. They'd probably be several notches down the evolutionary chain. But I was sick of staying home on Friday nights, practicing the guitar and texting Bridger at work.

"Okay," I sighed. "But if the guy tries to grab my butt,

I'm leaving."

The Katies' boyfriends' visitor had a neck the size of a ham, and introduced himself as Spunky. Surely his parents had given him another name, but whatever it was, I never found out. I caught myself wondering who would give himself a weird new name on purpose.

And then I realized that's exactly what I'd done, too.

We trudged along in the cold and I tried to stay on top of the conversation. But there wasn't much of one. Anything the girls said caused the football players to grin, and then one of them would declare it "dubious."

For example:

A Katie: "And then the bartender *swore* that he knew how to make a Flaming Salamander. Even though I'd invented the name of the drink just to stump him!"

A Football Player: "That is *dubious.*"

And so it went, until the moment I realized where we were headed. "Hang on," I protested, stopping on the street corner. "I thought we were going to a football game?"

Ponytail Katie spun around and pinned me with her gaze. "They wouldn't be joining us then, would they? Duh! Tonight is a hockey game. The preseason scrimmage against Brown."

Oh, crap. "But... I don't go to hockey games," I whined.

"Scarlet," she protested, hoping I was not about to bail. "We're *here* already."

And so we were. Defeated, I followed them into the arena where I'd always expected to compete.

It made for a much more depressing evening than I'd bargained for, to say the least. And that's the only reason I drank from Spunky's flask whenever it was passed my way. It was filled with some kind of fruity schnapps, a flavor so sweet that it made my teeth itch. I thought it was weird that football players would want to get drunk on a sissy thing like schnapps. At least, it seemed weird until I got toasted on it. And then I figured out that's probably why they'd brought it.

Tonight I was really not on my game.

The Katies bought popcorn, and I ate a bunch of it to try to cushion the schnapps. The Harkness men's team was skating really well, and it made for a very exciting game. Tied at 1-1 for most of the first two periods, Harkness came out swinging in the third. The team captain sent a Howitzer right over the goalie's glove and into the net, and I was on my feet with the rest of the cheering crowd.

This had once been my whole life — watching the puck whip across the ice, critiquing the plays, and scanning for a breakaway. I missed it. Terribly.

Given the chance, I would have distracted myself with a little conversation. But in spite of his name, Spunky wasn't a talker. And I couldn't even fidget with my generation's favorite escape — my phone — because I'd left it behind in my dorm room by accident.

With four minutes left, Harkness drew a penalty, and the entire stadium leaned forward to see whether Brown would be able to make anything happen during the two minute period when one of our defensemen sat in the sin bin. Both teams amped it up, skating fast, checking hard.

We survived it, the Harkness players ragging the puck until their man was freed. And when the buzzer rang, Harkness had won, 2-1.

By the time we stood to leave, I was drunk on schnapps and the achingly familiar sound of the puck smacking the boards. Tipsily, I followed The Katies and their thick-necked men toward Hannigan's Bar, where the doorway was jammed with hockey fans. I waited with my roommates, wondering how they planned to get past the bouncer. None of us was twenty-one. Maybe that didn't matter?

But when the crowd before us cleared, Blond Katie stepped up to the bouncer. As I watched, she and all the others pulled IDs from their pockets.

Fake IDs.

Crap! This was going to be embarrassing. I didn't have a fake ID, nor did I have a clue where to get one. On the other hand, I now had the perfect excuse to leave without them. I leaned over to Ponytail Katie. "Sorry, I can't get into this place. I'm outie."

Then, just as I turned to go, my eyes swept the bar. As the crowd moved, I caught a pair of familiar eyes looking back at me.

Bridger was there, sitting on a barstool.

My mouth fell open. I wanted a closer look, but shifting bodies blocked my view of his end of the bar. Feeling awfully drunk, I wondered for a half a second if I had imagined it.

"Let me see some ID, miss," the bouncer demanded of me then.

"I…" Shaking my head, I turned for the door. What had just happened? Bridger, who was too busy to ever see me on the weekend, was chilling at the bar. I felt as if I'd been slapped.

The wintry air outside was bracing. I stopped just beyond the bar, trying to get a grip on myself. I felt my pocket for my phone, once again remembering that I'd left it behind. If I texted him right now ("Hi Bridge, how's work?") I wondered what he would reply.

Betrayal made my throat feel hot.

"Where are you going, pretty girl?"

I looked up to find Spunky the football player. "G... gotta go," I choked out.

"You could stay here with me," he said, taking a big step forward. In response, I took a staggered step backward, my bottom colliding with the brick building. The guy put his big hands on my shoulders, pinning me there. "It's early," he whispered. "Don't run off."

Now I was actually trapped, and feeling afraid. The rush of hockey goers had filtered into the bar, or down the streets. There was nobody but me and the big galumph holding me to the wall.

Great.

I squirmed to the side, but he stopped me. He put his feet between mine. There was no way to finesse this, other than the obvious. So I put both my hands on his chest and gave a mighty shove. "Back off," I said.

"Be nice," was his response. He leaned in to kiss me. I gave another great shove and craned my neck away from his alcohol soaked breath. He only grabbed my arms and pinned my wrists against the building.

That's when I really began to panic. "OFF ME!" I screamed.

And then he was gone. I felt the cool air of freedom, and registered the sound of a heavy body falling to the sidewalk. "Aaaarrgh, fuck!" the guy hollered. When I looked down, he was curled up in a ball, holding his nuts.

And Bridger was standing over him. "What part of *off me* did you not hear?" he growled. He wound up for another kick, but the guy rolled away, flopping over onto his other side, still protecting the family jewels.

"Bridge," I gasped, tasting bile in my throat. I was still stunned to see him. If only the world would slow down for a few minutes so I could catch up with everything that had just happened.

The sound of my voice seemed to change his focus. He wheeled away from Spunky and stood before me. Bridger took my hands in his, inspecting my wrists. He pulled me into a hug. "Did he hurt you? Jesus, I'll kill him."

That's when the tears began running down my face, and Bridger wiped them away with his thumbs. But I wasn't really afraid, just overwrought. About everything. And Bridger had no idea. Angry, I pushed him away. "No. Don't touch me."

He stepped back, shock on his face. "Christ, Scarlet. Tell me what's wrong."

"You," I squealed. "Why are you here? Why were you *there*, in that bar? With who? I'm just your Tuesday and Thursday girl…"

I broke off, gasping now. Even as my sobs gathered steam, I knew I was making an ass of myself. But I was too drunk to reign it in. I stood there, right on Elm Street, having an ugly cry.

"Where is it, Scarlet?"

Bridger was trying to ask me a question, but I was too busy sobbing to hear him. I wiped my nose on my sleeve.

He wrapped an arm around my back, and I let him. I allowed it, because crying while very drunk wasn't as easy as you'd think. The ground beneath my feet had begun to sway in unpredictable ways. But Bridger held me tight, and it felt so freaking good. And that only made me cry harder. Damn. It. *All*.

"Your *phone*, Scarlet. Did you lose it?"

"At home," I gulped. "Why?"

"Because I've been calling you for *hours*," he sighed. "I got an unexpected free pass tonight. So I started calling you before seven, right up until the minute I saw you in that bar. Go look at your phone. You'll see."

"Ohhhh," I moaned, the word long and shuddery.

Bridger pulled me to his side and started to lead me down the sidewalk. "How did you get into such a state? Do you always get wasted on Friday nights?"

I shook my head violently. "Never. Which is why I feel so... urgh."

"Let's get you home, then," he said, steering me across the street. "You have your key card?"

I nodded with my whole drunken body. The way a horse nods.

"Okay," he chuckled. "Come on."

We'd almost made it home when a war broke out in my stomach. As we walked across Freshman Court, the schnapps began fighting the popcorn, and I couldn't tell who was winning. But I, for one, was losing. "Bridger, I think... ugh." I swerved away from him, took two staggered steps, and managed to aim my vomit into the shrubbery. "Oh," I wailed, as much from the humiliation as from the discomfort.

Bridger gathered my hair together and held it for me. "You'll be okay," he said, with actual humor in his voice. "We've all been there."

"Not me," I said. "I don't do this."

Behind me, he let out another enormous sight. "Okay, you know what? We're going to write off this entire night."

"Are we?" I stood up again, fishing through my pockets for a tissue. No such luck. The best I could come up with was a receipt for a cup of coffee I'd bought. So that's what I used to wipe my mouth.

Sexy.

"Henceforth," he said, "we shall refer to this as The Most Pointless Night Ever. It's just one more example of my good luck. Getting this one night's reprieve…"

"And me not answering the phone," I mumbled. "It's all my fault."

"Not at all," he sighed. "I should have known about tonight before, but I didn't read the… never mind. Let's get you upstairs before that happens again."

"Again?" I whimpered.

"Probably."

Since the Katies were still at the bar, my room was dark and quiet. Bridger walked me into my bedroom. "Where are your PJs?" he asked.

Not willing to act helpless, I grabbed my sweats from a drawer. Bridger turned around to give me privacy, and I couldn't decide whether or not I appreciated the gesture. In my recent fantasies, he was less of a gentleman. Maybe I was such a repulsive drunk that he didn't want to look.

Getting out of my jeans was proving very difficult for some reason.

"Scarlet," Bridger said as I flailed in the dark, "you should probably take off your shoes first."

Right. That would help, wouldn't it?

"Okay, all set," I was finally able to say. "Now I want to brush my teeth."

"I'll bet you do." He picked up my bathroom caddy and pointed at the door.

The fluorescent lights of the bathroom were an assault on my eyes. "Ouch."

"Ouch," Bridger agreed, handing me my toothbrush. There was toothpaste on it already.

"Thank you," I sighed.

"Now, hop in there," he said a few minutes later, pointing at my bed. Bridger had filled a cup of water, which he set on my nightstand.

"Only if you'll stay for a minute," I whined. Even as I said it, an ache began to creep across my temples.

He tossed his coat onto Katie's bed and kicked off his shoes. Then he actually dropped himself over my prone body and into the space between me and the wall. He put his nose in my hair and his arm around my waist.

"Nice," I said.

He kissed the back of my head in reply.

It was dark, and Bridger was in my bed. In spite of my foul stomach and the beginnings of a nasty headache, I craved his touch. Wiggling in the tight space, I flopped onto my back and then turned to face him. His chest was warm and firm under my hands. I stroked the scruff of his whiskers, then pulled his head towards mine.

He gave me the gentlest of kisses, and then pulled back.

Unsatisfied, I hoisted my floppy body onto an elbow, leaned forward and planted one on him, square on the lips. If only to defend himself from my assault, his big hand landed on my ribcage, his thumb grazing my breast. This time, Bridger gave in and kissed me back.

The dark, his warm body, and a drunken lack of inhibition all crested at once. When our tongues met, a jolt of desire shot through me. The moan I let out was probably not very ladylike, but it had the intended effect. Bridger deepened our kiss.

Suddenly, it was no longer okay with me that I was trapped under the comforter and he was not. I slid out of the bed and then dropped back on top of it again, climbing onto

Bridger as he rolled onto his back. Kissing him, I settled onto his hips. His big hands cupped my bottom, pulling me in tight. Spread out over his warm body, each point of contact made me tingle. I could feel him under my breasts, my knees, my thighs. My... *everywhere*.

And he felt it too. Never mind that he was still kissing me in a way that was more polite than I wished. His body gave him away. As unfamiliar as I was with male desire, there was no mistaking the solid form of him, pressing against the fly of his jeans, lying just between my legs. My hips, acting without my conscious consent, rolled closer to him. My body wanted contact, right now.

Bridger groaned deep in his throat. Then he rolled me off of him, putting some space between us. Panting, he said, "let's stop."

"Don't want to," I said. The room was spinning. But I managed to find the fly of his jeans with two hands.

"Oh no you don't," he sighed, catching my hands in his own. "Not tonight, Scarlet. Not when we're both drunk."

"You're drunk? I can't tell."

He laughed. "I'm better at it than you. But seriously, we can't."

"*Why?*" I'm pretty sure it came out as a whine.

He pushed my hair away from my face, and the gesture was so sweet that I felt my eyes tear up. "Because," he whispered. "When we do, *if* we ever get to, I want you to remember it the next day."

"Don't say *if,*" I cried, the tears falling.

"Sorry, Scarlet. But in my life there's a big fat gap between what I want and what I can actually have. And I don't see how that's going to change any time soon."

"It just sucks," I shuddered.

"It does," he agreed. "It absolutely and totally sucks."

Bridger left soon after that. And, coming down off my adrenaline rush, I felt ill again and ran to the toilet. Eventually, I took the two Advil he'd left out for me, and slept about ten hours, only to wake to the most crushing headache I'd ever experienced.

When I finally turned on my phone, around noon, it was to find that Bridger had peppered me with texts and calls for three hours. Just like he'd said he had done.

Disgusted with myself, I tossed the phone aside. Then buried my aching head in my hands.

— Bridger

Sunday morning I woke up halfway when Lucy began to wiggle on her mattress, which lay on the floor beside my bed. Keeping my eyes slammed shut, I rolled into my pillow. We'd been sharing a room for more than three months now, so the week had a rhythm to it. On the weekends, my sister woke up at seven, which was just the same time she woke up on school days. So while I ignored her, she would get up to putter around, sneaking extra time for cartoons on my computer while I pretended not to notice.

I was just dozing off again when her little voice quavered up to me. "Bridge…?"

"Hrrmff," I said.

"I don't feel so good."

My consciousness buzzed to life in a hurry then. Because Lucy was not a complainer. I opened my eyes, startled to realize that it was still dark in our little room. It wasn't even morning.

"Bridge…"

And then I heard a telltale gurgle, and was on my feet

81

even before my brain caught up. In the dark, I jumped over the corner of Lucy's mattress to grab the wastebasket from under my desk. But Lulu had also taken action, lurching toward the door. She made it as far as the door handle before bending over to hurl on the floorboards.

Diving forward, I caught the second heave in the trashcan. Lucy began to cry before she even stopped puking.

"Aw, buddy," I sighed, pulling her hair out of her face. "You're okay. It sucks, but it'll stop." This was the second time in forty-eight hours that I'd comforted a puking female. Go figure.

"I... threw... up... *on your shoe,*" she sobbed.

Christ, she did. Fuck my life.

"It's okay." I kicked the offending shoe aside and opened the door. "Quiet, all right?" I whispered. Not that anyone else was going to be awake at five o-fucking-clock on a Sunday to hear us. I steered her into the bathroom. "Rinse out your mouth, but spit, okay? Don't drink the water, even if you're thirsty."

"Why?"

"Because your tummy is pissed off right now. Trust me."

"You said a swear." Her voice was small.

I turned on the tap for her. "You can say one, too. Anyone who's throwing up gets a free swear."

"Shit," Lucy said.

"Good one." I cleaned out the trashcan, which took a few minutes. But now I had to see to the floor inside my room. "Lucy, stay here for a minute, would you? Just in case it happens again."

Obediently, she slid down the tile wall until her little butt hit the floor.

"Be right back." I reeled several long sheets of the coarse

brown paper towel out of the dispenser on the wall and went to take care of some business. To be perfectly honest, it wasn't that bad. When you'd drunk as much as I had the past two years, a little puke wasn't that big of a deal.

When I came back into the bathroom, Lucy was leaning over the bowl, hands on the toilet seat, her little body heaving. There were tear tracks down her face. But her crying was silent.

Even puking her guts out in the predawn hours, Lucy knew the rules. She was supposed to stay quiet. Because children weren't allowed to live here.

"Rinse one more time," I said when it finally stopped. "And let's wash your hands." Seeing her hands on a toilet seat shared by four guys gave me the willies.

Afterwards, I steered her back into the room. Fishing one of my clean t-shirts out of my dresser drawer, I said, "strip." She yanked her P.J. top off, and I dropped the men's size large over her little shoulders. The shirt hung past her knees.

"Lulu, the trash can is going to be right here, okay?" I set it beside her mattress. "Let's try to get a little more sleep. Your stomach might leave you alone now." Weary, I stretched out onto my bed.

Lucy sunk down onto her mattress and wrestled her covers. "Bridge?" Her voice was shaky.

I sat up quickly. "Do you need the bucket?"

In the dark, she swung her head from side to side. And then her small shoulders hunched over and I could hear her crying again.

"Come here."

About one point five seconds later, she was in my bed, her skinny arms latched around my neck. I tucked her head under my chin, and began to think uncharitable thoughts.

Namely: *For the love of God, don't let me catch this flu. Because we will be so very screwed.*

As if we weren't already.

"Shh," I said. Because that's what you say to a crying child when there's no other comfort you can give. Her tears were beginning to soak through my t-shirt.

And then she opened her mouth and cut me in half. "I want *Mama*."

Lucy hadn't mentioned Mom for weeks. She was a smart little girl, who had followed me out of the only home she'd ever lived in without a backward glance. And I'd thought she was okay with it. But didn't that just prove that I was an insensitive ass? She was *eight*. She wanted Mommy to hold her when she was ill. "Of course you do," I whispered against the tightening of my throat.

Because you can't help what your heart wants.

"We should tell her I'm sick," Lucy muttered into my chest.

I waited for the familiar surge of anger I always felt when I thought about Mom. But instead of an anger tsunami, all I got was a sad little ripple. "It's the middle of the night," I explained, congratulating myself for providing a semi-logical excuse. Because I couldn't tell Lucy the truth. That her mother was a drugged up bitch who didn't give two shits about us.

The panicky, ill Lucy wanted to believe that Mom would somehow wake from her self-induced nightmare and pull herself together on account of a virus. But I knew she wouldn't. And in the morning, Lucy would probably know it, too.

My sister fell asleep without saying anything more. But I just lay there, watching as the gray light crept in through the leaded windows. This year was just so fucking hard. And it wasn't going to get any easier.

Being with Lucy wasn't the hard part. I was thirteen years old when she was born — a surprise to my parents. But things were going well for my father's plumbing business, and so we moved out of our apartment and into the little house on the outskirts of Harkness.

Because of Lucy, I've always been good with kids. I was the fifteen year old holding the toddler in the grocery store while my mother shopped. Lucy let my father teach her to tie her shoes, but she wanted me when it was time to take the training wheels off her bike. Her preschool graduation was on the same day as my high school graduation. There's a picture somewhere of the two of us, both wearing caps and gowns.

She was easy company. Even at her worst — sick in the night — she wasn't any trouble. But money was tight. Time was tight. And hiding her from everyone else was fucking killing me.

The stress monkeys began climbing around inside my head, swinging from problem to problem. Luckily, Lucy slept.

Chapter Seven: *The Monkey Nutter*

— Scarlet

When I saw Bridger again on Tuesday, he was pale and quiet. "Are you okay?" I asked him during Calculus.

"I feel off," he said. "Though it might be nothing."

But then, after music theory, he was still looking peaked. "I don't think I can do lunch," he said. "My head is killing me."

"I have ibuprofen in my room," I offered. "Do you want a couple?"

He sighed. "You know, that would be great."

Bridger climbed the Vanderberg stairs at half his usual speed. He sat on my bed, and I brought him a cup of water and two pills. "You look exhausted," I said as he swallowed them. "If you put your head down for a few minutes, I promise not to jump you."

His smile was weak. "I shouldn't be here, Scarlet. There's a 24-hour bug going around. I wouldn't want you to catch it. Christ..." his eyes closed. Even as I watched, he grew paler. "Fuck a duck," he said. Then he stood up and strode purposely out of the room. I heard the bathroom door open and shut. He didn't return right away, although I heard the plumbing groan as he flushed the toilet a couple of times.

Eventually, he walked slowly back into the room, his face a gray color.

"You poor thing," I said. "Is there anything I can get you?"

He shook his head. "I have to go."

"Okay," I said. "But you don't look like somebody who's ready to dash out of here. Give yourself a minute."

He nodded, miserable. "I'll just rest for a sec." He

slumped onto my bed, his head at the wrong end, his knees tucked up as if someone had punched him in the gut. He was the picture of misery.

"I'll be out here if you need anything," I said, taking my laptop into the common room.

Our suite was quiet that afternoon. So when Bridger began to snore, I could hear him. I lost myself in some research for my history paper until his watch began to beep. But unlike every other time, he didn't shut it off. I got up and tiptoed to the threshold of the bedroom. He lay there asleep, his strong chest rising and falling while the timer complained.

There was no way that boy was going to make it to work — not in that state. I just couldn't make myself wake him. And as I stood there hesitating, the alarm gave up too, silencing itself.

I went back to my homework. But thirty minutes later there was a groan from the bedroom. I heard a rustle, and then Bridger sprinted through the common room and into the bathroom again. Once more came the probable sounds of abdominal dismay, the flushing and washing and spitting. When he came back in, I opened my mouth to ask him if there was anything I could do. But that's when he looked at his watch. "Shit!" he cursed. He stumbled back into my bedroom and fumbled with his backpack.

"Bridger," I started. "You can't go to work like that." I stood in the doorway watching him saddle up. "Your hands are shaking."

"No choice," he said. He rose to his feet unsteadily.

When he came to the door, I was in his way. Putting my hands on his chest, I made him look me in the eye. "Stop," I said. "Give yourself a break."

"Let me go, Scarlet." The cold sound in his voice was

nothing I'd heard before. "I'm so very late, and it's not okay. I have to run. *Literally.*"

Chastened, I moved out of the way. "Can I drop you anywhere at least? My car is just across Chapel." I didn't expect him to take me up on it. But I had to offer, if it was so effing crucial that he get to work. I'm the one who let his alarm go off without waking him.

He surprised me. "Could you? I wouldn't ask if it wasn't important."

I grabbed my keys off the desk and plucked my coat off the chair. "Let's go."

"*This* is your car?" Bridger asked.

"Yes," I said quietly.

"You drive a brand new Porsche Cayenne with a turbo engine? In Harkness?"

"Sure," I said, my voice testy. "But only if you tell me where to drive it."

He pinched the bridge of his nose. "Make a right. *Please.*"

The tone he took made me want to cry. *He's just grumpy because he's sick*, I coached myself. *And stressed out about work.*

There was no way for me to explain to Bridger that the car was just another farce in my life. I'd overheard my parents' lawyer advising them to put assets in my name. In New Hampshire, I'd driven an aging Toyota Camry. But when my mother told me which car they'd picked out for me to keep at school, I wasn't exactly shocked. The Porsche was a way for them to hide something like seventy thousand dollars from the families who would eventually sue my father in civil court.

I could either explain this to Bridger, or merely let him

think I was ridiculously wealthy and out of touch.

Is it all that surprising that I chose the latter?

Bridger's face was still a ghostly color as he directed me toward a distant corner of town. We were in a residential area, where old wooden houses sat close together. Some of their porches sagged under the weight of time, while others had been spiffed up within the last century.

"Just let me out here, thanks," Bridger said stiffly.

"Bridge, there's nothing *here*," I complained. "Except these houses. And that school."

Oh.

The school.

Bridger put his hand on the door, but I accelerated. I followed the U-shaped driveway of the elementary school, remembering the little girl with the pink bike helmet. When I came to a stop in front of the glass doors, Bridger opened the passenger door and got out without a word. At that moment, one of the doors opened up and the little girl with the chestnut ponytail came flying out.

He shut the car door behind him, but I could still hear their voices. "I'm sorry I'm late!" he said, his arms wide. She ran to him, and I saw his body sway from the impact as she flew into his midriff. He steadied himself.

"Everyone else was gone!" the little girl said. "Mrs. Rose waited with me."

"I'm so sorry, Lulu. I'm not feeling well, and I fell asleep."

"Oh NO!" she said. "You got it too?"

"Yeah, but don't worry."

"You can throw up on my shoe, and then we'll be even."

"If I throw up on *both* your shoes, do I win?"

She giggled, and tugged on his hand. "I'll get my bike."

When she skipped toward the bike rack, Bridger turned around. He mouthed *thank you* into the window of her car, and gave me a little wave. Slowly, he walked toward the little girl, who was putting on a bike helmet. I took my foot off the brake and idled the SUV around the school's drive circle. At the stop sign, I braked again, and put on my blinker. Even though there was nobody coming, I waited.

A minute later, the little girl rode up to the corner and stopped. One foot on the ground, she turned back.

I watched in the rear view mirror as Bridger walked toward the corner, his gait painfully slow. He forced a smile onto his face, but his misery was evident. When finally he approached, I put my car in park. Then I pressed the button which automatically raised the tailgate door of my overpriced car. I gave the horn one minuscule beep.

He stopped on the sidewalk and looked at me. Then he limped over to the car. I lowered the passenger side window. "Bridger, put the bike in the back."

"I'm okay."

"You're being a dumbass."

He leaned on the door of my car, not because he wanted to but because he needed the rest. "I don't take help from people," he said. "Even you, Scarlet. But I have good reasons."

"I'm sure they're excellent," I hissed. "But unless you want her to watch you pass out on the sidewalk, get in the *damned car*."

His eyes slid closed from exhaustion. When they opened again, he turned to the little girl. She'd been watching us the entire time. "Come here, Lucy," he said. "My friend is going to give us a ride."

"Let me get it," I said, hefting the bike. Bridger was done

arguing. He opened the back door, and after the little girl climbed in, he slid in next to her.

"I'm so sorry, Lulu," he said as I got back behind the wheel. "You must have been freaking out."

"It's okay," she said. "Mrs. Rose told me some knock-knock jokes." Her voice sounded little, reminding me of a Muppet. "Where are we going?" she asked.

"Home," Bridger said.

"Which is…?" I asked.

"Beaumont House," he said stiffly.

"Seriously?" I swiveled around to face him.

He gave me one sad nod and then looked out the window.

No freaking way. He was keeping a child in the dormitory? That broke about ten different rules. I stole another glance into the rear view mirror.

He had leaned back, his head against the headrest, his eyes screwed shut. "Homework?" he inquired.

"Just a math sheet. And spelling words for Friday."

"That's it?" He squirmed uncomfortably against the leather.

"Yup!"

"God is merciful. How was the day?"

"Gregory pinched me, but then he got caught! And Mrs. Rose made him write 'I will not pinch' on the board. And it was library day, and I got an American Girl book out. A new one."

"Awesome," he said.

The drive was only a few minutes long, but that was long enough to break my heart into pieces listening to the two of them.

"Did you like the bananas on your peanut butter

sandwich?" he asked.

"Yep. What are we going to call that one?"

"The... monkey nutter?"

"Hmm..." she considered. "Maybe. I'll have to think about it."

Bridger wouldn't look me in the eye when I got the bike out of the back.

"Hope you feel better," I said.

"Thanks," he said stiffly.

"Let me know, okay?"

He didn't answer. Instead, he walked slowly toward the courtyard gate, where the little girl waited, still wearing her pink bike helmet.

That night, I was supposed to be working through a problem set for statistics. But my head was swirling with questions about what I'd seen.

Lulu had to be Bridger's sister, or maybe his niece. They looked so much alike. From the looks I'd snuck at her, she would be about eight or nine years old.

As manly as Bridger was, it seemed unlikely that he'd conceived a child at age twelve.

My phone buzzed at ten-thirty, and I was relieved to see that the text was from Bridger. *You still up?* He asked.

I dialed him. "Hi," I said carefully when he answered.

"Hi," he whispered. No wonder his voice was always hushed when I spoke to him at night. Because he wasn't alone in the room.

"She's your little sister," I guessed.

"Yes, she is."

He didn't volunteer anything more, but I wasn't ready to let it drop. "You don't drive a forklift at night, do you? You're home with her."

"You have it all figured out." His voice was so soft that I almost couldn't hear. "Well, go ahead. Tell me I'm a prick for lying to you."

My eyes were instantly hot. "I'm not going to say that. You told me you had good reasons, and now I know it's true. You're afraid of getting caught by the college."

"Scarlet, It's not just the college. My life is a house of cards. It's her school, and most of all child protective services. I don't have custody."

My heart contracted. "Where are your parents?"

"Our dad died three years ago. And Mom is indisposed."

"Indisposed to take care of her daughter?"

"Indisposed to stop manufacturing crystal meth on her dining table."

"Oh my God," I said.

"Exactly." His voice in my ear was warm and lovely, in spite of our depressing conversation.

"So you took her in."

"No other choice," he said. "It was either me or child protective services. And I'm not sending her away."

"She'd go to a foster home?"

"Right. And some of them are... I shouldn't really talk about this right now."

I blew out a breath. "Is your stomach feeling any better?"

"I'll live. Haven't thrown up for about four hours."

"Oh, Bridger. I'm sorry."

"I'm sorry too."

"You know..." He probably just wanted me to drop it. But I couldn't help myself. "I wouldn't have told a soul."

He sighed into the phone. "I *know* that, Scarlet. That's not why I didn't tell you. With you, I just don't want to be *that* guy. That guy with all the issues."

That made me suck in a breath. Because I'd done exactly the same thing — made exactly the same choice. He didn't know a thing about me, because I didn't want to be *that* girl.

"Are you still there?"

"Yes," I said.

"Does that make sense?"

"It makes more sense than you'll ever know," I said.

I didn't know if I'd see Bridger in class on Thursday, but he came in right on time, flopping into the seat next to mine. Wordlessly, I put my hand on his lap, palm up. And he took it, stroking my thumb with his.

"You take her to school in the morning?" I asked quietly.

He nodded. "She starts at eight thirty, which is why I gave myself nine o'clock classes every day of the week."

"She's so cute," I said, squeezing his hand.

"Yeah, she is." He squeezed back. "What are you up to this weekend?"

"I'm writing my psychology paper. And probably watching some fascinating reruns of Dancing with the Stars. You?"

"I'm doing a bunch of chemistry homework. And attending a fascinating puppet show at the public library."

As always, it was a struggle to tear my eyes away from his handsome face when the professor began class at the front of the room.

"I'm sorry to keep asking questions," I said later, picking at my salad in the student center.

"Fire away," he sighed. "Like I said, I didn't want to be *that* guy. But I *am* that guy. And it's a relief not to lie to you anymore." He took a bite of his burrito.

I love you, I thought, watching him, happy to see him eating again. Out loud I said "so, what brought about The Most Pointless Night Ever?"

He laughed. "That is an excellent question. Okay, so Lucy was invited to a birthday party, and she was so excited. And I got her over to the other little girl's house right on time, with a wrapped gift — just like you're supposed to."

He flashed me one of his killer smiles, and my heart melted a little more, just thinking about this hunky guy wrapping up a nine-year-old's party gift.

"...But when I got there, the mom says, 'where's her sleeping bag?'" Bridger put a hand to his forehead. "It was supposed to be a *sleepover*. And I'm totally on the spot, because I didn't read the invitation carefully. And the mom is like 'never mind, she can use one of ours, she can borrow pajamas.' So I looked like an ass. But then all of a sudden I was alone for the night."

I shook my head, as if I could erase the whole debacle. "Could we bribe that mom into giving another slumber party?"

"Believe me, I had the same thought." His green eyes flashed at me.

"How do you keep your grades up?" I asked.

"That's actually the easy part. Because I'm home every night in a silent room from eight o'clock on. I have a clip-on light I use on my books, or I work on my computer."

"What's the hard part?"

He shrugged. "Hiding her. If I didn't have to hide her, nothing would be all that difficult. And the money. Feeding her isn't expensive, but when the spring term ends, I'll have to find us some place to live."

"There must be people in your entryway who have

noticed that she's around all the time."

"Oh, there are," he said, swigging back some milk. "The guy across the fire door from me is the only one who knows the whole truth. He's propped the door open a couple times when I've had to run out at night, babysitting for me."

"That's handy," I said. Fire doors were a strange feature of the Harkness dorms. They were unlocked, wooden doors connecting one room to another, so that every room had two means of egress.

"The guys on my floor — there's three of them — they've seen her in the bathroom too many times not to notice. I tell them 'she's visiting,' but they're probably not stupid. Luckily, nobody seems to care."

"It's not like she's throwing loud parties."

His smile was rueful. "I actually make her be quiet. Even if she's singing some happy little third grade tune, I tell her to keep it down. It's like she's in prison."

I felt a pit in my stomach. "How long can you keep this up, Bridger?"

From the exhaustion on his face, I knew I'd asked the toughest question. "As long as I need to. If I lived off campus, I wouldn't be afraid to be caught all the time. But I have a full ride at Harkness, and that pays for the dorm, not an apartment."

"And there's no such thing as a part-time student here."

He shook his head. "No such thing. So, I already did the math on transferring to UConn. But it would cost so much more. You might not know this, but nobody does financial aid like Harkness. And they give me the full package, because they get to check a box next to my name under 'local success story.' Seriously, they care about that. The city keeps track of how many locals they let in."

I could only shake my head. "You amaze me. You have so much more on your shoulders than most people."

"Don't be too impressed. If the wrong administrator wanders by my dorm room while she's singing along with *Frozen*, I could be out on the street."

I put my hand on his wrist. "What can I do to help you?"

He winced. "Nothing, Scarlet. It's my mess to deal with." He reached across the table, catching my hand in his larger one. "Just be with me, okay?"

"That's easy." I squeezed his hand.

Chapter Eight: *You're Making Me Look Bad*

— Bridger

"So, we have a stats midterm coming up," Scarlet said the following week as we walked away from the student center's cafe take-out counter.

"Are you ready for it?" I was only half listening, because my eyes were focused on the way her jeans hugged her long legs.

"Nope," she shook her head. "I'm not even close."

"Ah," I sighed. "Has your tutor been slacking off?"

Scarlet cleared her throat, a tint of pink appearing on her cheeks. "Only on the statistics."

I felt a little pang of guilt, then. Because my mind was absolutely not on statistics. "Right. Okay. Well, let's find a seat here and not in your room. Because your tutor is easily distracted."

She led me to a sofa by the windows, where I sat down and patted the spot just beside me. "Let's see your notes," I said, pulling a sandwich out of our bag.

As much as I hated to waste any of my precious Scarlet time on homework, she needed a little help with time series regression. An hour later, I had finished both the tutoring and a chicken parm.

I had just stood up to throw away our trash when someone called out in our direction. "*Jesus*, Bridge! I've been thinking about putting your face on the back of a milk carton." Hartley was coming toward me, hand in hand with his girlfriend, Corey. I stared at them for a second, trying to figure out what it was that looked so different about them. And then I realized that Corey had ditched her crutches, and was walking almost smoothly, with nothing but a cane in one hand. It was wild.

I charged them, lifting Corey off her feet. After swinging her around in a complete circle, I set her down again carefully. "Christ, Callahan. I almost didn't recognize you."

"Because this is a new shirt, right?" she said, turning around in a circle.

"You goof," I couldn't stop smiling at her. "Seriously, you're looking great."

"Maybe if you showed up to see your friends more often, my accomplishments wouldn't be such a shock," she said.

"Really," Hartley added. "Where the hell have you been? I can't even catch you at breakfast."

I hadn't eaten breakfast all year.

I gave him my most casual shrug. "I'm working three jobs, guys. Entertaining you over meals doesn't pay enough." Seeing them right now — Hartley with the symbol for "captain" on his hockey jacket, and Corey walking almost as if she'd never sat in a wheelchair — it caused me almost physical pain. Because there was so much I'd been missing.

Moping over the carefree life I'd lost was totally pointless. But it hurt.

"Hi, I'm Corey," Hartley's girlfriend said, with a wave at Scarlet, who was now standing behind me. "If Bridger won't introduce me, I'll do it myself."

"No need to get impatient, Callahan. I was getting to that." I wrapped an arm around my girl. "This is Hartley, one of my oldest friends. And Corey Callahan, who's a pain in my ass. Guys, this is my girlfriend Scarlet."

There was a loud silence. Instead of saying something, both Hartley and Corey were openly staring, their mouths open.

Great.

Corey exchanged a loaded glance with Hartley. "Say it again," she demanded.

"C'mon, Callahan," I grumbled. "You're making me look bad, here." I snuck a glance at Scarlet, but she only looked amused.

Hartley recovered first. "It's nice to meet you, Scarlet." A smile tugged at his lips. "Now I know why we haven't seen Bridger since September."

Corey dropped Hartley's hand, so that she had a free one to shake hands with Scarlet. "Really, a pleasure to meet Bridger's *girlfriend*." Her eyes twinkled. "Wow. I can't believe that I have to sit down to a study session right now, after that bomb you just dropped, Bridge. Just promise me that we can all hang out soon."

"Sure thing," I lied.

"I'd better get over there. Nice to meet you, Scarlet!" She gave Scarlet a big smile, and me a wink. Hartley kissed her on the temple, and then she began to walk across the atrium toward the meeting rooms, planting the cane lightly with every other step.

My eyes tracked after her. "Damn, that's really impressive."

"I know, right?" Hartley agreed, flinging himself into a chair. "It's those new braces. There was a hell of a learning curve, but the results are pretty incredible."

"Is she... Will she get to skate again?" I sat down on the sofa, tugging Scarlet down next to me.

Hartley shook his head. "Nah. The motion's not the same. And it's too risky. If she broke a wrist, and couldn't hold the cane for a couple of months, that would be a disaster." He leaned over to punch me in the arm. "But, seriously, let's compare schedules. Hockey is kicking my ass for the next

101

three months. But there has to be a couple of hours somewhere. Preferably with a case of beer and a football game. But either way…"

"Sure."

"Gotta run," Hartley said. "I have a history lecture. But, *soon*, okay?"

"Soon," I echoed as Hartley got up and trotted off.

I watched him for a second before turning to Scarlet beside me. "So that was…"

"…*Fascinating*," she finished for me. "First of all, your *best* friends don't know you have Lucy?"

I gave my chin a single shake. "They're the last people I can tell."

"God, why?"

"Because they'd do anything for me."

Her frown deepened. "And that's a problem because…?"

"Hartley's mom waited two decades to go to nursing school. And I'm not going to wreck it."

"Damn," she whispered. "But maybe there's some way she could help you around the edges. I don't know… weekends or something?"

I shook my head again. "That's not how Theresa works. She puts other people first. I'm not going to be the one who fucks up her dream."

"Oh, Bridge," she put her head on my shoulder.

"Scarlet?"

"Yeah?"

"Is it okay that I called you my girlfriend?"

She was quiet for a second. "I liked it," she said quietly, "until I realized you only said it because you needed an alibi."

I slid my arm around her waist and pulled her closer. "No, I swear. It just slipped out, because that's who you are to me." I stole a single kiss before continuing. "I've never had a girlfriend before. I'm probably doing everything wrong. But I sure liked saying it."

She lifted her chin, and her hazel eyes sparkled. "Well, if you put it that way."

"I'm sorry my friends got so freaked out for a minute there. Last year…" I paused. And then I realized I had no idea what to say for myself.

Scarlet seemed amused by my discomfort. "The Katies told me that you never even dated anyone twice in a row. They told me to watch out for you."

"Well, ouch." I hated the idea that Scarlet's freshmen roommates, who I didn't really know, would talk about me like that. Even if what they said was mostly true. There were no secrets at Harkness. And now that I was carrying around a doozy of a secret, the gossip mill practically made me break into a sweat. "Maybe The Katies are right. I still haven't managed to date you two nights in a row, yet."

Scarlet punched me in the arm, and I kissed her on the lips. "Don't worry," she breathed. "I don't listen to everything they say."

I tightened my arms around her, putting my lips right beside her ear. "I wasn't looking for a girlfriend this year." I dropped my voice to a whisper. Because I'd never said this before. "Hell, I wasn't looking for a girlfriend *ever*. I never needed that connection before. But I like having you in my life. It's better with you here."

"I like being here," she whispered.

So I kissed her again. And then, because this is my life and not somebody's love song, my watch beeped.

Chapter Nine: *Never Much of a Basketball Fan*

— Scarlet

On Friday afternoon, I received a text from Bridger: *Please tell me you're free tonight. Giving you like 6 hours advance notice, here.*

I called him immediately. "Seriously? Where are we going?"

"Nowhere," he said. "Sorry about that. But we can watch a movie at my place together, for once. Come at eight-thirty, which is after bedtime."

"How…?"

"You'll see. I'm in the second courtyard — the little one."

I had no clue why it should suddenly work out for us to watch a movie in Bridger's room after Lulu's bedtime, but I was ecstatic. I brought popcorn and Cokes, texting him from the courtyard at exactly eight-thirty: *Knock Knock.*

A minute later Bridger's head popped out of an entryway door. "Hi," he said, smiling at me.

I couldn't keep the big grin off my face. "Hi." And then I kissed him right there on the doorstep. I was just so happy to see him.

"Mmm," he said. "Come upstairs, okay? But we're going to tiptoe through my room, and then through the fire door."

I followed him as he opened the door to his room — a single. Lulu was asleep on a mattress on the floor, which lay beside Bridger's bed. Her sleeping face wore a serious expression, her hair fanning out on the pillow. We tiptoed around her, then on through a wooden door, into the neighboring room. It was a single of similar proportions.

Bridger shut the door behind us. "My neighbor is on the basketball team," he said. "And they're away at Dartmouth tonight, for a preseason tournament. I asked him if we could sit in here and watch TV while he was gone."

"Brilliant. But what if she wakes up?"

He shook his head. "She sleeps like the dead. But also, I told her exactly where I'd be." He bent over his neighbor's bed, which was a tangled mess. Bridger straightened the spread as best he could. "He's such a slob. Hang on," he said. He slipped back into his own room and returned with his own comforter and pillows, arranging them on the bed. I sat down on the finished product, a pillow between my back and the wall.

The neighbor had a big flat-screen TV. Bridger flipped through the offerings, but there was nothing terribly appealing. "Let's just settle for that comedy," I said at last.

"Sure," Bridger agreed.

For about ten minutes we watched the movie, drinking Coke and snuggling against each other. But I couldn't keep my mind on the plot. The solid weight of Bridger's arm around me, and the feel of his thumb stroking my palm stoked my senses. I was all too aware of the heat of his body and the masculine scent of his soap. It was enough to make me want to launch myself at him. And I probably would have, if he hadn't gone there first.

Dropping his head, Bridger placed his lips on the side of my neck and began to kiss me. As it always did, the feel of his mouth on my body made me quiver with joy. It wasn't long before I rolled back onto the bed, pulling him down on top of me.

With a chuckle, Bridger muted the video. And then we behaved like crazy, frantic people. His kisses were those of a starving man, devouring me. I wrenched his t-shirt over his head as if was about to burn him. He threw my top and bra across the room as if they would bite.

We'd waited a long time for this, to be alone together. Every night when I climbed into bed alone, I lay on my side, just imagining him curled up beside me. I also had sexier fantasies. I dreamt of him hovering above me, his warmth weighing me down, his hands on my body.

I'd been wanting this, but I'd also been nervous about it. Yet now, skin to skin, our kisses were hot and urgent. There was no room in my heart for nerves. He laid on top of me, caressing my breasts, his hips sliding over mine. I felt warmth blossom everywhere he touched me. He felt so right, fitted between my legs. In spite of my lack of experience, my body knew just what it wanted from him.

Things didn't slow down until he rolled aside and put his hand on the zipper of my jeans. "Scarlet, is this okay?" His voice was thick with desire.

I nodded, reaching for his fly too.

In the movies, the clothes just fall right off. But the truth of the matter is that getting two people out of jeans and socks and underwear in one small bed was more awkward than I would have thought.

But never mind. In a couple of minutes we lay facing each other on the bed, nary a thread of clothing in evidence. One of my hands rested on Bridger's naked hip. His free hand caressed my sternum. "Tell me what you like," he breathed.

I had never been naked with a guy before, and the sheer beauty of him overwhelmed me. I was in way over my head, and it would have been *exactly* the right time to tell him that I was a virgin. But I didn't do it. Instead I said, "What I like is *you*."

As he leaned in to kiss me, his hand began a slow descent down my body. He paused at my belly to trace distracting circles there, before raking into the hair between my legs. And when his fingers found the wetness pooling there, we both gasped. Then I was paralyzed by the sensation of his touch, his fingers slicking an exquisite circle in a place where no man had ever touched me.

Oh. Oh. Oh. Oh and oh... My mind was a continuous loop of surprise and delight. Distracted, my hand slipped off Bridger's hip and onto his penis. "Mmm," he said as I grazed it. So I wrapped my fingers around it, surprised at how perfectly straight it pointed up towards his chest. It was hard and silky at the same time, and when I slipped my hand up the length of it, he made a happy groan from the back of his throat.

Heaven.

Before long, it was difficult to breathe, and touch him, and kiss him and not faint from arousal all at the same time. Something had to give. My head rolled back onto the pillow and my hand released him. And then I was down to just the breathing and the miracles happening beneath Bridger's hand.

He moved closer to me then, his lips on my neck, one of his knees bent across my thighs. I was drowning in sensation, and in the wonder of so much of his skin pressed against mine. Then I felt a sort of heady acceleration, like feet running too quickly downhill. And a wave of pleasure swept me under, shimmering everywhere he touched me. I felt my back arch up off the bed, my hips twisting involuntarily. And I was lost to myself.

The next thing I knew were Bridger's fingertips pressed gently to my lips, and his chuckle in my ear. "Shh... You'll wake the neighborhood," he said softly.

I sucked in oxygen as his words made it into my

consciousness. "Sorry!"

He nuzzled into my hair. "You have nothing to be sorry about. It's just too bad that I don't turn you on at all." He chuckled again.

Embarrassed, I punched him on the arm.

"Easy, killer." He folded me close to his chest, where I tried to slow down my breathing.

"Wow," was all I had to say for myself.

He cupped my face in his hands and stared into my eyes. "You sexy thing," he whispered, kissing me. I wrapped my arms around him, sliding onto his body. He felt so good underneath me, all solid muscle and taut skin. We kissed, and his hips rolled gently underneath me. His erection pressed into my belly.

That's when I finally began to feel nervous, because I wanted to make Bridger feel as wonderful as he'd made me feel. And I really had no idea what I was doing.

— Bridger

To say that I was raring to go would be a dramatic understatement. And it wasn't only because I hadn't had sex in a ridiculously long time. That was part of it. But the anticipation was sweeter than that. My life was shit right now, and meeting someone special had not been on my agenda. But it had happened anyway, somehow. And so here I was, skin to skin with the most amazing girl I'd ever met.

Scarlet slipped off my body so that we lay facing each other again. Tentatively, she curled her hand around my shaft, her soft fingers stroking me. *Damn.* I had to clench every muscle in my body to try to control myself. And then I kissed her again, because it was either that or I'd probably start moaning like an overzealous porn star.

I wanted Scarlet. Badly. Even though we'd never had the chance to have sex before in real life, in my fantasies she and I were already Division One champs. My imagination was pretty vivid, but the real thing was so much better. The way her soft hair slid across my chest made me crazy. And the intense, sexy look in her eyes just about undid me.

I felt like a cartoon bomb with a fuse that was already lit. It was only a matter of time before I detonated. My hips moved of their own volition. She stroked me, and sighed into my mouth. And life was very, very good. Maybe too good.

"Scarlet," I whispered, catching her hands in mine. "If we're going to have sex, you'd better stop that. But if you don't want to go there tonight, that's okay too."

She blinked, hesitating. And for a moment my body quivered with the fear that she was about to call everything to a halt. "I want to," she whispered.

Blowing out a breath, I made myself count to ten before I reached for the condom, which was in my jeans, somewhere on the floor. My body was on fire, but at the same time I didn't want to rush this. This was *Scarlet*. I wanted to do everything right.

"I never was much of a basketball fan until tonight," she murmured.

"What?" I asked, stupidly. "Oh!" I laughed. I'd forgotten the rest of the world existed. There was only Scarlet and I, and bare skin.

Rustling through our discarded clothing, I finally came up with the packet I sought. When it tore, the room filled with that telltale medicinal odor which foretold imminent gratification. I rose up and rolled it on, all the while feasting on the sight of Scarlet's lush body stretched out beneath me. I'd done this a hundred times before, but never with such sweet anticipation.

This girl, and this moment were both rare gifts.

Trying to go slow, I stretched out over her. "You're so beautiful," I whispered, kissing her. But even to my own ears, the words didn't measure up to the way I really felt. Every time she touched me, it felt as if she was saving me from something.

I nudged her knees apart with my own. And that's when I saw it — a flicker of hesitation in her eyes. And her body tensed.

Lifting my head, I paused. "Hey, are you okay?"

"Perfectly," she said. But her voice shook.

I propped myself up on one elbow and teased a finger around her nipple. "Scarlet, don't take this question the wrong way. But have you done this before?"

Again she hesitated. And then, slowly, shook her head.

"Christ," I swore. And then we blinked at each other for a moment, before I swung myself up and off her, turning to sit on the edge of the bed.

A warm hand landed on my lower back. "Bridger...? What's the matter?"

There had been many moments in my life when Scarlet's admission would not have even slowed me down. "Maybe we shouldn't," I said. God knows I wanted to. But for her, it wouldn't just be sex. It would be a Big Deal. And I didn't think my life could sustain any more drama. I was so tapped out. Which meant that I probably wasn't thinking straight. And Scarlet deserved better than that.

"Hang on." She scrambled up to sit beside me. "I think... I just became another thing you have to take care of, didn't I?"

I dropped my head. Because she wasn't far off the mark.

"Bridge, I didn't want to say anything, because I didn't want to make a big deal out of it."

"But what if it is a big deal?" I asked. Her first time shouldn't be on a stranger's bed, with a guy who's life was circling the drain.

"Why does it have to be? This was my choice. You asked very politely, and I said yes instead of no. And now you're rejecting me."

"Damn." I curled an arm around her back. "I'm not rejecting you. I could *never* reject you." I rubbed the space between her shoulder blades. "It's just that girls... some people think the first time is supposed to be... I don't know. Important. But usually it's just awful. Or maybe that's just me and all my dopey friends."

The tension bubbled out of her then, in the form of a giggle. Her soft skin shook against me as she laughed. Her head landed on my shoulder, that soft hair torturing me again. "So what's the solution? Because if you won't be my awful first, then you can't be my excellent second. And if by some miracle Harkness Basketball makes it into the NCAA tournament, we'll be stuck watching whatever movie is on."

Smiling, I dropped my head into my hands. "Have you *met* our basketball team?"

"Bridger," she whispered, her fingers lightly stroking my hip. "We can talk about basketball if you want to. But..." Her hands wandered onto my groin, just like they did every night in my dreams.

I held back a groan. "Does anyone ever win an argument with you?"

"Not often."

I turned to meet her eyes, and her gaze was steady. She didn't *look* nervous. Still, something held me back. "Seriously, Scarlet. How are you going to feel about it tomorrow?"

She leaned in, brushing her lips across mine. "You'll just

have to ask me tomorrow." Then she kissed me, both her hands massaging my pecs. It was potent stuff.

When she slid her tongue into my mouth, I pushed her down on the bed. "You're very persuasive," I said. "Wait for me a sec." I got up and stumbled into my boxers, then opened the fire door a crack. Lucy was out like a light, wheezing just a little with each breath. I grabbed something out of my desk drawer and then tiptoed back to Scarlet.

"What's that?"

"It's lube. Because I really don't want to hurt you."

She settled onto her back. But I didn't climb on top of her right away. I wasn't in a hurry anymore. If she wanted to do this with me, I was going to make it good for her.

I lay down next to her, smoothing her hair away from her face, trailing a hand down her belly. Kissing her. Touching her the way I had before.

"Nervous?" I whispered. Our kisses were as gentle as I could manage, under the circumstances. My dick was starting to remember that we were just about to get some. I was throbbing with need.

Scarlet shook her head. "I'm only nervous about... you liking it too. I don't know what I'm doing."

My lips paused on her cheekbone. "You never touched a guy before?"

"You're not going to freak out again, are you?"

I laughed. "No. I'm just going to wonder how in the hell it's possible that you never had a boyfriend in high school. You're *hot*, Scarlet."

"It... I had dates when I was younger, and always fought them off. Lots of grabby sixteen year olds tried."

I chuckled against the smooth skin of her neck. "If I'd met you when I was sixteen, I would have grabbed you too."

"But last year... can we not talk about this, actually?"

I wrapped both arms around her in a protective embrace. "Sorry. None of it matters, anyway."

"We already decided that," she whispered.

"Yes we did." I gave her the slowest, most controlled kiss I could manage.

"I want to make you happy, Bridge."

"You already do." I took her hand and guided it to my shaft. "Guys are easy," I breathed into her ear. "There's only one button to push." Her fingers closed around the condom. So I lowered her hand, and when her palm curved around my sack, I let out an achy breath.

There was no more talking for a while. I tended to her, touching her until she began to whimper with pleasure. And when I finally rose to kneel between her knees, there wasn't any fear in her face. I doused myself with lube, and while she watched me touch myself, her eyes were hooded with lust. "Still good?" I asked, and she barely managed to nod.

But now *I* was nervous. Taking myself in hand, I eased forward, pressing slowly onward. I watched her face for trouble. She frowned just for a second. Christ, she was tight. And I realized I was holding my breath. But then her face softened.

Holding perfectly still, I asked, "are you okay?"

"Better than okay," she whispered.

I eased back, and she smiled at me. And when I pressed forward again, she sighed, her breasts arching upward. And the sound of it rushed through me, tightening up my balls, pressing the small of my back.

Jesus.

I went slow, but it didn't cool me off any. The slide of my body against hers was delicious. Her eyes tracked me in a lusty haze, and the whole experience almost killed me. I put my elbows down on the bed and made the symbol for "time out" with my hands. "I need to talk about basketball for a second."

"What?"

I needed a moment to pull myself back from the action. And basketball bored the snot out of me, so it was the perfect distraction. Instead of admiring Scarlet's lush body beneath me, I tried to think about skinny men in baggy nylon shorts, their shoes squeaking on the gymnasium floor.

Must. Relax.

Scarlet reached up to put her hands on my face. "Is something wrong?"

I shook my head. "Everything is going a little too well. Do you know any basketball trivia? I just read that the shot clock is eleven seconds longer in college ball than in the pros. Wait... the shot clock is not the image I need right now."

Her lips curved into a smile. "Bridge, I wasn't freaking out before. But if you keep talking about *basketball* when your..."

I didn't let her finish the sentence. Instead, I took her mouth in a hungry kiss. She wrapped her arms around my back, and the kiss went wild. With my mouth locked onto hers, I couldn't hold myself back any longer. My hips settled into a rhythm, and my breathing became hot and tight. And Scarlet seemed to join the swing of things, meeting me on every stroke.

"Scarlet," I panted between kisses. "You make me so fucking happy. Every day you make me happy." I forced myself to slow the pace, circling my hips against hers. And Scarlet gasped with pleasure. "You like that?" I whispered. I did it again. And in my arms, she seemed to gather herself in.

"Bridge," she breathed, her eyes closed. I ground against

her, and then I watched as it took her under. She arched off the bed and moaned.

"Oh, fuck yes," I bit out. I covered her mouth with my own and jacked my hips. Straining with pleasure, I came like a freight train. She gripped me with her knees as I rode it out, sweating and wild.

Seconds later I collapsed onto the bed, pulling her closer. My eyes were slammed shut, but I didn't need to look at Scarlet to know that everything was okay. Her hands skimmed my body with a reverent touch, and her lips grazed my ear.

"So," I said, hoarse from exertion. "Good thing I got all worried about that."

"But you promised me it would be awful," she whispered.

"Did I?" Her hips fit perfectly into my hands. "Maybe next time."

— Scarlet

I could have stayed there forever, curled up with him. His arms encircled me, and I listened to the sound of his breathing. I waited for the slap of shame to come along and ruin it for me. *Look how J.P. Ellison's daughter spends her Friday nights.* But the dark thoughts just wouldn't stick. Bridger's arms were warm, and I could hear the thunk of his heartbeat under my ear. It was the most peaceful moment I'd had in weeks.

"We should get some sleep," he said eventually.

"I know. I'll go," I said quickly.

"We can stay here together," he said. "But I can't have us naked if Lulu opens that door in the morning. Let me find you something to wear."

Bridger fetched me a pair of flannel boxer shorts and a t-shirt for each of us. We curled up together again on the bed. And even though I was sure I would lay awake all night just

116

appreciating him, I fell asleep almost instantly.

There was barely any light in the sky when Bridger woke me the next morning, his fingers running up and down my spine. "I hear Lulu walking around my room," he whispered.

I sat up quickly. "I'd better go."

"Don't panic," he said. "I'm sure she's sticking a cartoon DVD in my laptop right now, and rooting for junk food. She's a bit of an opportunist."

Quietly, I got dressed. Bridger and I were sitting on the edge of the bed, cuddling our goodbyes when the fire door opened.

When I turned my head, Lulu looked from Bridger to me and back again. "Bridge, do we have any pop tarts?" she asked.

He held out an arm, chuckling. "Lu, come here a sec."

The little girl walked over and slid easily onto Bridger's knee. Set against his muscular shoulder, she looked tiny. Doll-like.

"Lu, in the first place, the pop tarts were a special treat, and they're gone. You can have Cheerios or yogurt. But how about a good morning? This is my girlfriend, Scarlet."

The little girl patted his arm absently. The gesture — her slim fingers on his big wrist — was so natural and trusting that I felt a lump in my throat. "Good morning," she said, scrutinizing me. "Scarlet's hair isn't red like ours," she pointed out. "So why are you named that?"

"Good point," I told her. "I guess I should have thought that through."

Bridger gave me a strange look, and I kicked myself for saying it.

"Do you have any brothers or sisters, Scarlet?" Lucy asked.

I shook my head. "No, and I always wished I did."

Then her face lit up. "Hey, is that popcorn?"

"You can have it," I said, nodding toward the bag.

"...after breakfast," Bridger said quickly.

Lulu slid off Bridger's knee and picked up the bag. "Thank you. I'm going to watch a video now." Then she turned on her heel and went back to the other room. I could hear SpongeBob's voice as the door shut on her.

"Sorry," I said right away. I meant to leave before Lulu saw me.

"Scarlet..." he whispered into my ear. "I'm not sorry about anything. You and I were just talking. She wasn't robbed of her innocence."

I flinched, because "robbed of innocence" was one of the phrases that regularly appeared in articles about my father.

"Listen," Bridger said, kissing my ear. "I don't even want to guess what things that kid saw in her so-called home."

"You never told me why you took her away."

He slipped his arms around my waist, his voice low in my ear. "It was summer term, and I was living on campus. I was starting to realize that my mom was losing her way. When I'd stop by, there were strange people in the house. Lulu seemed skittish..." He stopped talking for a second, pulling me closer. "It was freaking me out. And then I went over there one day and found they'd put a lock on the outside of her door. They locked her in there, Scarlet. And when I opened the door, she jumped a mile."

He took a deep, shuddering breath. "So I just took her. We packed up some of her clothes and a couple of stuffed animals, and we never went back. She hasn't asked about mom since September."

"My God," I whispered.

"So…" his voice was thick. "If that little girl sees you and I sitting here, saying nice things to each other — that's the *right* thing for a kid to see." He rubbed my back. "You're one of the good guys, Scarlet."

My eyes pricked with tears. "You don't know that."

He cupped my face in his hands. "Yeah, I do." Then Bridger kissed me with lips so soft and gentle that it nearly stopped my heart.

"I'm going to leave you two to your morning," I said afterwards, squeezing him one more time.

"It's very hard to let you go, you beautiful creature."

"Then I'll go fast. See you in class on Tuesday." I stood up and marched out his neighbor's front door.

Since it was only eight o'clock when I walked into my common room that Saturday morning, it was something of a shock to encounter both Katies. They were lacing up their running shoes. And staring at me.

"You are so busted," Blond Katie smiled. "Look at you, doing the walk of shame."

I giggled, my embarrassment complete.

She stood up to stretch her quads. "Tell us. Does Bridger have freckles on his dick?"

I put my hands in front of my eyes. "Jeez, Katie."

"Well? Does he?"

"It was *dark*."

Katie giggled too. "Get changed, Scarlet. Since you're up, you might as well join us on our run."

I was just about to decline like I always do. But I heard myself say, "you know, I think I will."

That afternoon I sat on the window seat, supposedly

doing my Italian homework. But I was also texting with Bridger.

BRIDGER: *Lu asking about you. Your favorite color, etc.*

ME: *Let's go with red.*

BRIDGER: *Favorite book?*

ME: *Ballet Shoes.*

BRIDGER: *Huh. Now she's your new groupie. She loves that book.*

ME: *My work here is done.*

BRIDGER: *She asks if I love you.*

Oh boy. With my heart pinging around in my chest, I tried to think up a breezy reply. But there weren't any. Silence was the only response that wasn't entirely loaded. Then my phone chimed again.

BRIDGER: *I said yes, obviously.*

ME: ***SWOON!*** *Tell her I'll pay her the 5 bucks tomorrow*

BRIDGER: *LOL! Signing off to read a chapter of Harry Potter.*

"You're grinning like a fool over there," Blond Katie observed.

"Can't help it," I sighed.

Katie clutched her chest. "Oh, you've got it bad. I can tell."

Sunday, Ponytail Katie had another fashion crisis. She'd been invited to a dinner party that evening at some fraternity or other. And dress was *not* casual. "I don't have the right shoes. Not even close. And there's nowhere to shop around here. I should have gone to Columbia. It's only a subway ride to Bloomingdales."

I laughed out loud. Today, the Katies' first world

problems were more funny than irritating. "I might be able to help you," I said.

"But all your shoes are sneakers," she moaned.

"True. But I also have a car."

"What?" the Katies yelped in unison. "Scarlet!" Blond Katie gasped. "You've been holding out on us."

"I don't ever use it," I admitted. "But I'll drive you to the mall, if you two will help me with a few questions on the way there."

"Deal!" they squealed.

Half an hour later, I drove out of Harkness, both Katies in tow. Hopefully neither of them would wonder why a girl from Miami Beach had New Hampshire plates on her car. Soon we were accelerating toward the big mall in Stamford.

"So what do you need help with?" Blond Katie asked.

If she hadn't remembered to ask, I probably would have chickened out. At just the thought, I felt my face heat. Best to just get this over with. "Birth control," I blurted. "Where do I go — and what do I ask for?"

"Oh, that's easy," Ponytail Katie said from the passenger seat. "The gyno department phone number is 4900, and you want an appointment with Barbara. The minute you set foot in her office, she'll ask you if you need birth control. Say yes. The end."

"Well, okay." I could do that.

"What else do you need to know?" Blond Katie asked from behind us. "I'll make you a list of my favorite sex toys. The Lelo corporation should name a wing of their corporate headquarters after me. I'm like their best customer."

"Omigod," Ponytail Katie laughed. "You're making Scarlet blush. That is *so* cute."

When I'd chosen my new name, my reasoning had nothing to do with blushing. But it might as well have. Because I was so good at it. "I'm not up to... those yet," I stammered.

"Pity," Blond Katie said. "What are you up to?"

"Well," I kept my eyes on the road, so I wouldn't have to look anyone in the eye. "Lots of things. Except I've never given, erm…"

"Given… a rim job? A prostate massage?"

Lord, I didn't even know what that second thing was. "A blow job," I blurted.

There was a stunned silence in my car. "Wow," Ponytail Katie whispered finally. "I'm so glad I wasn't home schooled."

"Right," I snorted.

"Girlfriend, there is nothing to it," Blond Katie piped up. "Do you like ice pops?"

"Sure?"

"That's all you need to know. Lick it. Suck it. Never use any teeth."

"Gotcha," I said as my face flamed away.

"Seriously, there's a whole lot of extra credit techniques you could learn on YouTube. But you don't need that, because enthusiasm counts for ninety percent of your grade."

"Good thing." I tried to imagine myself Googling "how to give a blow job." And failed.

We went to the mall, where I ate a giant pretzel from one of those evil kiosks that belches the irresistible scent of warm butter into the air. And I watched with amusement while the Katies shopped for lingerie.

I felt lighter that weekend. It was as if my new life had finally put down little roots. The Katies were less annoying to me all of a sudden. I'd been hating them for their self absorption. But now that I had a taste of living in my own little dreamland, my stomach fluttering every time I pictured Bridger leaning over me in bed. I was distracted. And happy. And whimsical.

It felt damned good.

Chapter Ten: *Exactly the Wrong Question*

— Scarlet

I got my graded midterm back at the end of statistics class the following Tuesday. As Bridger and I walked toward our music theory lecture, I held it up for him to see. On the top, "87%" had been penned in bright red letters. "See that?" I said, skipping down the sidewalk like an idiot. A *happy* idiot. "Do you have *any idea* how smart I am? That's why you hang around with me, isn't it? Tell the truth."

"You've got me all figured out, babe." Bridger reached over and pinched my ass. Then he took my hand. "Damn, your fingers are cold," he said, massaging them. Then he brought my hand up to his lips and kissed it.

God, I had it bad for this guy. But could you blame me?

November had arrived, and people began to talk about their plans for the holidays. I was relieved to learn that the dorms didn't close over Thanksgiving weekend. That meant that I could make it all the way to mid-December without having to go home to New Hampshire.

"You're not flying home?" Bridger asked when I brought it up.

The question confused me, because I'd forgotten for a second that I was supposed to be from Miami Beach. I shook my head. "I'm not going to bother. It's only four days, anyway. A long weekend."

"This place really empties out over Thanksgiving," he warned, his eyes studying me.

I shrugged. "That's okay. What are you and Lucy up to?" It had suddenly occurred to me that I might get to see him over break.

"Usually we go to Hartley's mother's house. But this year

he's going to be with his fancy dad on an island somewhere. So I thought we'd stay here," he said. "But then my fire door neighbor," He paused to raise his eyebrows suggestively, until I laughed. "He invited us to his place, which is about ninety minutes away. Lucy and I might stay for the weekend."

"That's so nice," I said, hoping to convey the proper amount of enthusiasm, even though I'd rather have him here with me.

"Yeah, it is. But you know how I feel about accepting help. And I don't want his parents knowing that Lucy lives with me. But I also don't want to ask an eight year old to lie. So I haven't decided what to do."

Stay here with me! I thought loudly. "What are you going to do about Christmas?" The vacation was three weeks long, and the dorms were closed. I'd already checked.

When I looked into Bridger's eyes, I saw that I'd asked exactly the wrong question. Because there was an exhaustion there that hurt me to see. "No idea. We'll probably go to Hartley's for some of that time. I'll try to find a house-sitting gig, or something."

I squeezed his hand, wishing I could offer any kind of help. But my options were as limited as his.

That afternoon, I didn't get to have lunch with Bridger, because Lucy's school let out early for an in-service. This seemed like very bad luck, at least until I got back to Vanderberg, where an unfamiliar voice called out to me.

"Shannon Ellison."

The sound of my old name stopped me cold. But I didn't recognize the petite woman in the suit who was waving me down beside the entryway. "That's not my name," I protested.

"I'm sorry," the woman said with a frown. "It's Scarlet now, right?"

I must be the biggest idiot alive. Because this woman had just gotten me to confess to my old identity. I looked over both shoulders, checking to make sure that no one was near enough to overhear. "Who are you?"

"I'm Madeline Teeter, assistant district attorney for your home state. I'd like to speak with you. And I figured you would be coming back to New Hampshire for Thanksgiving. Let's set something up now, and we'll meet next week."

It took me a second to process the idea that the D.A. had come all the way down to Harkness to ask me for a meeting. I almost felt sorry for her. "I *cannot* speak to you. And just to put your mind at ease, I wouldn't be any help anyway."

She shook her head. "We can subpoena you, Scarlet. We can schedule a deposition. You don't want that. That's a whole room full of lawyers and a sworn testimony. It would be so much easier for you to just answer a few questions voluntarily. Come in for the interview, Scarlet. If you have nothing for us, it will keep you off the witness stand."

"I *can't*," I whispered. Surely she knew that. My parents would have me boiled in oil.

To her credit, the prosecutor didn't look surprised that her ninety-minute drive would be in vain. She handed me a business card. "Take this. If you change your mind, my cell phone is right there. Think about it, Scarlet. A chat with me would be quick and painless."

I took the card between two fingers. "I'm not kidding. I don't know a thing."

She nodded, still calm. "I believe you. But it's my job to ask a lot of questions, and to learn what there is to learn. And there are boys who need me to ask. If you talk to me, you'll be helping some people who are in a lot of pain. Even if you think there's no point, do it for them."

Well, *ouch*. She was willing to play the guilt card. But it didn't really matter, because I truly knew nothing. I fished my key card out of my pocket. "I'm going now," I said. My voice only shook a little.

"Call me," she said, turning away.

I didn't watch her go.

Chapter Eleven: *Consonance and Dissonance*

— Scarlet

Now that I was in on Bridger's secret, and I'd met Lucy properly, he began inviting me to spend time with them. One chilly Friday night we all went out for pizza. "I like olives on my half," Lucy explained. "Bridger likes sausage. I guess we can ask them to divide it into three halves if you like it plain."

"Three halves, huh?" Bridger winked at me from across the table. "Maybe it's time we did a little work on fractions, Lulu."

Somehow his offhand comment hit me hard. I'd spent the afternoon trying to memorize a bunch of Italian verbs, and thought it was tough going. But Bridger was responsible not only for feeding Lucy, but for whether or not she learned math. My twenty-one year old boyfriend was somebody's only real parent. He just killed me.

"I like the Christmas lights here," Lucy said, pointing at the ambitiously early holiday display over the bar. "Bridge, we could have Christmas lights on our window."

"I suppose there's no reason why not," he agreed.

Since I'd seen some at the drugstore, I promised myself I'd buy a string of them tomorrow. "You'll be all ready for Santa Claus," I said. But then I wished I hadn't. Because I had no clue where Bridger and Lucy would go for Christmas — a full three weeks when the dorms were closed. And Bridger didn't have the cash or the space for a holiday gift fest.

But Lucy only rolled her eyes at me. "I'm not a *baby*, Scarlet," she said, as Bridger bit back a grin. "I used to believe in Santa, though," she said quickly, as if she might have offended me. "...Before. When I lived with my mom." She picked up her pencil and drew a tic tac toe board on the place mat.

My chest felt tight, just thinking of what this kid had been through, and what uncertainty awaited her. Yet she looked perfectly at peace, sitting next to her protector, doodling on the paper.

Under the table, Bridger reached for my hand and squeezed it.

On the Tuesday before Thanksgiving — our last day of classes that week — I caught Bridger staring at me during the music theory lecture. When I looked into those green eyes, he winked and looked away. But I felt his eyes on me again a few minutes later. And when I met his gaze, its intensity startled me. The way he looked at me was serious, but also warm. I don't think anyone had ever looked at me that way before.

Since we were seated in the back of a big lecture hall, nobody noticed when I reached over to pencil "what?" into the margin of his notebook.

He gave me a sweet smile before returning his attention to the professor. The day's lecture was about consonance and dissonance.

"A consonant chord sounds pleasing to the ear," the professor said, "while a dissonant one makes the listener uncomfortable. Traditional music is structured to take advantage of both comfortable and conflicted emotional tones. Listeners, upon hearing dissonant chords, crave resolution. They expect consonant tones to follow dissonant ones."

Bridger swiped my notebook off my lap. When he gave it back, the margin read: "my dissonance craves your consonance."

I drew an arrow pointing at his words, writing "DORK" under it. When I angled the notebook toward him, I heard him laugh. He snatched my notebook again, scribbled something and then handed it back.

Make love to me. Right now, it read.

Just reading it, my face and neck heated.

Beside me, Bridger flipped his notebook closed. He got up, hefted his backpack and walked out of the lecture hall.

When I stepped into the hallway a couple of minutes later, Bridger took my hand and began walking.

"Where are we going?" I asked.

"To my room, of course," he said. "I'm not used to bringing anyone there, because they'd ask questions about the extra mattress with the Hello Kitty sheets on it. But since you're already in on the secret..."

"And she's at school..." I said.

"Just once," he squeezed my hand. "We're getting an A in that class anyway."

My pulse went into overdrive, and I picked up our pace. We made it to Beaumont House in record time.

The moment his door shut behind me, Bridger braced me against it. His kiss began on my forehead, slid down my nose and landed on my waiting lips. His thumbs grazed the sensitive skin of my neck, before his hands moved down to cup my breasts. My own hands were busy unbuttoning this shirt, so that I could see that beautiful chest in broad daylight.

"For once, we don't have to rush," he said, unclasping my bra.

"But I want your hands on me," I breathed, yanking on his belt buckle.

131

Bridger moaned into my mouth. He tugged down the zipper of my jeans, then steered me over to the bed, where he covered me with his warm body. His tongue began to stroke mine, and I heard myself whimper in appreciation. Our kisses were so deep I could taste more of Bridger than myself.

Then he dropped his lips to my ear. "Scarlet," he whispered, his hand sliding between my legs. "This was the best idea I've had in a long time."

"Noted." His finger dipped inside me and I gasped with pleasure.

He kissed me, and we began touching each other everywhere. His body was so beautiful and strong, and the daylight meant I could see every curve of every muscle. I followed the ginger trail of hair down his belly and between his legs, sneaking looks at his... erm... equipment. I scooted down until I was eye to eye with it. I mean eye to...

Right.

Bridger propped himself up on his elbows, and looked down the length of his muscular torso toward me. There was a smoky gleam in his eye, and I realized that it was time to step up my game a little. I put both hands on his body, fanning out my fingers in the reddish hairs I found there. Under my touch, Bridger's hips twitched with anticipation.

Okay, penis, I steeled myself. *Let's get acquainted.* Anyone could do this, right? Time to think about ice pops.

Right.

I took a closer look. Long and jutting, it stood at attention in a way that body parts don't usually do. Interesting.

Sorry, penis. I shouldn't stare, should I?

Any time you're ready, it seemed to reply. *Don't give us a complex.*

Slowly, I leaned in, giving Bridger a tentative kiss right

where it counts. Above me, he let out a sexy hiss. So I did it again, sweeping my tongue all the way around the top. With a happy moan, my boyfriend let his head fall back on the pillow.

Okay, penis. We've got this. I channeled my inner Katie and went to town. I must have done something right. Because his stomach clenched, and his hips danced. And the unconscious growl he gave was so sexy I could hardly stand it.

Eventually he reached down, gently nudging me away. "Stop," he panted. "Or I'm going to come all over you."

When he said it, I felt a zing of excitement everywhere. I had always thought this would be a little demeaning. But instead, it was a power trip.

"Oh well," I said, reaching for him again. I loved having such an effect on Bridger — making him lose control.

Applying my newfound skills one more time, I heard him let out a monstrous groan. "Fine, if that's the way you want to play it. But you've been warned."

I backed off. "Where do you hide your condoms, Bridge?"

After suiting up, Bridger sat down at the foot of his bed. "Come here, Scarlet," he said, tugging on my hand.

"What?"

"Up here," he said, easing me into his lap, until I was straddling him. I hesitated, not quite sure I was ready to drive this bus. "You don't have to," he said quietly. "But I'll last longer. And you'll... Well, you might really like it."

I stared into his green eyes, which were lit with warmth. This wasn't me. It seemed impossible that I was really here with this gorgeous man, in broad daylight, climbing onto his naked body.

But I was. And I did.

It was a tad awkward lining him up underneath me. But when I got it right and sank down on him, I had a perfect view of his eyes squeezing shut with pleasure. He gave a big sigh and looked up at me again. "Damn, you make me crazy." Then he wrapped his big hands around my hips and pulled my body tight against him.

At first I was tentative. But after only a moment or two, I forgot to be embarrassed. Controlling our contact felt absolutely amazing. A decadent pressure began to build low in my core. I strained against Bridger, while his eyes became unfocused, and his head flopped back. "So good, Scarlet." He pulled on my hips to urge me on. The look on his face was precious to me — blissed out and trusting. For a year I had found it impossible to live in the present. But every moment I spent with Bridger was bright and fully realized.

And what a moment it was.

With my weight on him, every tiny movement created a sweet friction against him. I shifted my hips, experimenting, until I found an angle of contact that felt almost unbearably good. "Bridge," I warned. He moved his hands up to cup both my breasts, and I felt the wave begin to carry me under. I dropped my lips onto his and moaned.

"Oh, oh yeah," he panted, shoving his hips off the bed while my body quivered against his. And then he gasped, letting loose with a masculine growl of satisfaction.

All too soon, we lay coiled in a slightly sweaty heap, breathing hard and feeling happy.

"That was not on the music theory syllabus," I whispered.

"But you're a prodigy," he chuckled, stroking my hair with clumsy hands. "You make me feel lucky."

"That's because you just *got* lucky."

He shook his head. "That's just extra." We were quiet for

a few minutes, as my heart swelled with joy. "Scarlet," he whispered eventually. "Can I ask you to do something for me?"

"Anything."

"Would you look into getting some birth control pills?"

"Sure," I said, my voice hoarse. The Katies had already told me what to do. I just had to make the phone call.

He raised himself up on an elbow. "I don't mind using condoms, but it would be nice to have some backup."

"Okay," I touched his face. "We sure don't need any more drama."

"So true." He pulled me in for a kiss. "But the universe must not hate me too much."

"Why?"

"Well, it dumped a lot of shit on me this year. But it also gave me you."

"The universe and I are on similar terms," I said.

At that, his face became serious again. The intensity I'd seen earlier was back. "I hope you know," Bridger said, his lips brushing my forehead, "you can tell me all your shitty stuff too."

I held him even more tightly. "I know I can," I whispered. "But I don't want to."

"I can take it, Scarlet. Whatever it is. You know that, right? You might feel better if you got to talk about it."

The very idea was terrifying. Even thinking about it made my stomach twist. Bridger's secret — caring for a helpless child — only made him more attractive. No matter how crazy or ill timed, the purity of his motive was clear.

My family secrets were only ugly.

I pushed up and out of his embrace. "We should get up."

"*...She said, quickly changing the subject.*" Bridger

snaked an arm around my bare waist. "Stay here a little longer. I won't interrogate you. I promise."

I obeyed, of course. There was nothing in the world so good as snuggling into his embrace. I stared at the side of his face until he turned his head to look at me.

"What?" he asked.

"I love you," I whispered, leaning in to kiss his jaw.

"Thank you, universe," he said.

Later, I was trying to finger-comb my hair when someone knocked twice on the fire door.

Bridger glanced in my direction to make sure I was dressed, before calling out, "What's up, Andy?"

As the door opened, I was busy worrying that Bridger's neighbor had overheard us having sex. But then I got a good look at the neighbor's face, and I realized that I had a much bigger problem.

He was just as tall as I remembered, but he had filled out. His face was broader, more mature. And the Harkness Basketball sweatshirt was an improvement over the Star Wars t-shirts he'd always worn to our high school.

Andrew Baschnagel.

I forgot to breathe. For a second, we stared at each other. Then he laughed. "Shannon Ellison. How's your slap shot these days?"

I opened my mouth to say something, but no words came out. Bridger's head swung in my direction, and my chest was suddenly tight. I took a step backwards, and then two more. When my back hit the door to Bridger's room, I fumbled for the knob. As I wrenched it open, I heard Andrew's puzzled voice. "What the hell did I say?"

I fled.

PART TWO

"Shame, Despair, Solitude! These had been her teachers - stern and wild ones - and they had made her strong, but taught her much amiss."
— *The Scarlet Letter by Nathaniel Hawthorne*

Chapter Twelve: *The Baschnagel Boy*

— *Scarlet*

I ran down the stairs and out the entryway door. Beaumont College was a beautiful Gothic labyrinth, and I had to run beneath three pretty granite archways to reach the outer gate.

"Scarlet!" I heard Bridger's voice behind me somewhere. But I couldn't talk to him. I didn't want to see the look on his face when he realized who I was, and how much ugliness there was in my life.

I'd tried to be someone else. For almost three months, it had worked.

I hustled up the sidewalk toward the gate to Fresh Court. Ahead of me, the door of a shiny black car opened onto the sidewalk, and I angled to avoid it. But the passenger — a man in a suit — lunged forward and grabbed my hand.

Startled, I whirled to face him. It was Azzan, my father's bodyguard.

"Shannon, come with me," he said.

I yanked my hand back and tried to propel myself away. But a second man blocked me, allowing Azzan to get his hands onto my lower back and steer me toward the car. The other guy — a driver I'd seen before — opened the back door.

"No!" I said, confused. I did not want to get into that car.

"Yes," Azzan said simply. He gave me a gentle shove, but it was enough to send me pitching toward the leather of the back seat. His hand came down on the top of my head, which probably kept me from scraping my scalp against the frame of the car during my graceless entry.

Azzan pushed me further into the car as he slid in beside me. And just as it occurred to me to reach for the opposite door and climb out into the middle of the street, his hands grabbed me. "Drive," he said to the other man, who had already closed his own door and started the engine.

"What are you doing?" I asked as the streets of Harkness began sliding by. My heart was pounding and I tasted bile in my mouth.

"Happy Thanksgiving, Shannon. We're your ride back to New Hampshire."

"But I'm not going!" I wailed. Except it seemed that I was.

My phone began ringing.

"Don't answer that," he said immediately.

I checked the display. It was Bridger. "Why not? Afraid I'll say you just kidnapped me off the street?"

"Don't be cute."

"I don't need to be. My boyfriend just *watched* you stuff me into a car and take off. He's probably calling the police right now. Maybe he's the sort of guy who writes down license plate numbers."

He swiveled quickly, slapping me. The sound of his hand

hitting my face was almost as surprising as the sharp sting of pain. "I said don't play cute."

I tasted blood in my mouth where my teeth had caught on impact. But the slap actually did me a favor, shaking off my confusion. I felt a steely calm settle over me.

Not that I had a plan. Only a clearer head.

The only person within a fifty-mile radius I could trust was Bridger, even if he was in the process of discovering my ugly secret.

The phone bleated again. "He saw you drive off with me, and he wants to know why."

"There was nobody with you," Azzan said.

"He was about ten paces behind." My voice was icy calm. With the phone on my palm I held it out to him. "If you don't want me to answer, I won't. But you might be hearing from the cops."

He sighed. "Tell him you're fine, and you're on your way home for the weekend."

I hit *ANSWER*. "Hello?"

"Scarlet," he gasped. "What the fuck just happened?"

"Well," I cleared my throat. "My father's bodyguard decided to drive me home for Thanksgiving."

"What? That's sure as hell not what that looked like. I got the license plate number. Are you really okay?"

My heart contracted. "I think so."

"That's not good enough. When are you coming back?"

"Azzan," I said. "He wants to know when I'm coming back."

"Sunday, just like every other kid in America."

"Every other kid in America plans her own trips home."

"Shut up, Shannon. Get off the phone now. You're going to lose him in the tunnel anyway."

"I got all that," Bridger said into my ear. "Scarlet, we have to talk."

"I'm sorry." As I said it, the car rolled into the West Rock Tunnel.

"No — I want you to know..." Bridger said. And then the call was cut off.

I was staring at my phone when Azzan grabbed it out of my hand. "Give that back," I complained.

I heard my phone chime twice. "Aw, what a guy." He held up my phone so I can see the text.

BRIDGER: *I love you no matter what.*

"I'm going to hang onto this for the weekend," Azzan said, pocketing my phone. "You can have it back after you do the meeting with the lawyers, and eat turkey with your family."

I spent the next hour and a half breathing through my nose, trying not to cry.

The media presence outside our house was down to a skeleton crew, because jury selection was still a month away. I counted only two TV vans.

Azzan's driver pulled the car into the driveway, but he stopped well shy of the garage.

"Get out here, Shannon," Azzan said. He wanted the bored TV people to see that I'd come home for the holiday.

I think I surprised him by not arguing. Instead I jumped from my seat and ran into the garage. I didn't stop to wonder whether anyone snapped a photo or not. I'd been photographed countless times already, as the press rushed to cover every angle of the story about the famous hockey player and philanthropist who was secretly Satan.

My mother opened the mud room door as I approached it.

140

"Come in, sweetie."

I pulled up short in front of her. "Was this your idea?"

"You haven't answered my calls in a month, honey. How were we supposed to discuss it?"

"He slapped me," I said, pointing over my shoulder toward Azzan. "And he threatened me."

Her lips pulled tight. "You look all right to me, so why don't you come inside."

I heard Azzan's footsteps behind me, so I walked past her and into the dining room. The top of my father's head was visible in his chair by the TV. Turning away from him, I ran up the stairs to my room.

My mother — her wheels were always turning — didn't even try to coerce me into sitting down to family meals. The first night, she brought me a bowl of chili in my room. "You should say hello to your father," she said.

But I'd had two hours alone in my little suburban cage, stewing in my misery. And I didn't have it in me to be civil. "Let's not pretend this is an ordinary visit," I said. "When am I sitting down with the lawyers?" I'd realized that agreeing to meet the lawyers was my only move. And since I knew nothing, it would get them off my back.

"Friday," she said, setting the tray down on my desk. "The day after Thanksgiving."

"I want to go back to Harkness afterwards."

She shook her head. "Azzan will take you back on Sunday. This could have all been easier, Shannon, if you'd driven yourself home for the holiday. If you'd spoken to your family."

I said nothing, because there was nothing to say.

Somehow I passed twenty-four hours there by myself. I

used the time to catch up on my sleep. But the waking hours were awful. It was hard not to obsess over Bridger. He'd had an entire day now to catch up on the newspaper articles about my family.

I didn't even have Jordan to take my mind off things.

After a long shower on Wednesday night, my mother knocked twice on my door and then pushed it open. "I got a phone call for you about fifteen minutes ago."

"Really? Was it Anni?" I doubted that my only remaining friend from High School would make the trip from California just for a long weekend.

She shook her head. "It was the Baschnagel boy. He wanted to tell you that he was going to the hockey game tonight. He asked if you were going."

"Andrew Baschnagel," I repeated stupidly.

"He's at Harkness too?"

"Right. He's a junior."

"I'm glad you're making friends, Shannon. There's no reason why you shouldn't enjoy the game. They're playing Quinnipiac."

I laughed. "There's no reason I shouldn't go? Do you think they'll even let me in the building?"

"Don't be catty," she sighed. "In a few months, when this is all over, your father will have his team back. Go to the game and hold your head up high. Or not. It's your choice." She turned away.

"Mom?"

"Yes?" she paused.

"I need my phone back."

"Sunday," she said. Then she went downstairs.

I was their prisoner. And they weren't even trying to hide it.

Brushing out my wet hair, I didn't know what to think. Andy Baschnagel's phone call was a surprise. Yesterday, I'd literally run from the room when he'd said hello to me.

Only ten days ago (although it felt like millennia) Bridger had told me that his fire door neighbor had invited him for Thanksgiving. My heart wanted to jump to all sorts of romantic conclusions. And even though optimism was probably a bad idea, I found myself staring into my closet at seven o'clock, taking an inventory of the clothes I'd left behind.

On the top shelf I found what I was looking for — a baseball cap with my high school's mascot on it. I also put on a baggy hooded sweatshirt, shoved my wallet in my jeans and went downstairs.

My father, the source of all my life's misery, was pouring himself a scotch. "Hi," I said. My voice sounded scratchy and underused.

"Well hello there. How's school?" His gray hair glinted in the kitchen lights. He touched his finger to a drop of scotch, which had escaped down the bottle, and then licked his finger. The lines around his mouth had lately become canyons and valleys. And his pants hung off his butt in a way that they never had before.

The most demonized sports star in network history was looking older and more pathetic by the day. Even his voice sounded wobbly. Looking at him, it wasn't pity that I felt. And not revulsion, exactly. It was confusion.

To encounter my father in the kitchen was to experience the same disconnect I felt every time I looked at him now. *Did he do it? Probably. But then why didn't I notice?*

And these familiar questions were chased by an equally familiar answer. *You're guilty, too. Only a self-centered idiot could miss something that.*

Clearing my throat, I answered his question. "I like everything about school."

He looked up at me for the first time. "That's really good, kid. I'm glad to hear it."

"I'm going out for a little while. I'll see you later?"

He nodded. "You need any money?"

"I'm okay. Thanks."

He nodded one more time, picking up his drink. Then the man — who was either the world's worst pedophile or the most wrongly accused man in sports history — shuffled back to the den.

Before I got out the door, my mother came through. "You're going to the game?"

"Yes."

"Did you speak to your father?"

"Yes I did."

She squinted at me. "Do you want a ride...?"

"No," I said quickly. "And I have my house keys. Bye."

Out in the garage, I pulled the hood of the sweatshirt up over the baseball cap, and pulled the brim down low. Azzan and the other goons were nowhere in sight. I left the garage via a side door, into the darkness of our double lot. When I was seven, my parents bought the house next door and tore it down, granting us the biggest yard in the neighborhood. My father had built a small ice rink there at the side of our house. It wasn't quite cold enough yet for my father to fill it, and now I wondered whether he'd bother this year.

I sprinted around the rink, heading for our side property line, and away from any TV cameras that might be camped out front. Nobody chased me, but still I ran. As a kid, I'd never liked the distant corner of our big property, and I felt a latent childhood chill as I crashed through the shrubberies and onto the sidewalk beyond.

It was a ten minute jog to the arena, and I didn't stop until I'd reached the drive circle. Walking the last few yards to catch my breath, I eyed the brightly lit building. I hadn't been inside since the college placed my father on leave pending an investigation. If I had to pick a spot in town where I would be least welcome, the Sterling Hockey Arena was clear winner. But curiosity about who I might find in there, coupled with a desperate wish to get out of the house, were enough to make me step over the threshold.

I bought a ticket at the window and went inside.

Scanning the crowd for Andy really wasn't that easy, because I didn't know what he was wearing, or whether he'd donned a hat. I walked slowly around the top level. There were dozens of familiar faces in the crowd. My dentist was in his usual spot behind the penalty box. My middle school hockey coach was sitting with her husband near the student section.

Not one of these people would be all that happy to see me, or anyone else from my family. Last year I'd spent hours attempting to make sense of their blanket hatred. And I'd come to understand that my father's Stanley Cup ring made everything worse. The people in my town couldn't live with the fact that maybe they'd boasted to their friends that they knew J.P. Ellison, or that they often saw him in the coffee shop.

They'd been duped by someone they'd praised. And they felt guilty for admiring him. My face was just a reminder of it.

Of course, I'd been duped, too. But there was no room in their disapproval for nuance.

Because old habits die hard, I found myself checking the scoreboard. It was 2-1 in Quinnipiac's favor, with the first period just half over. *Time for a comeback*, my brain said before I remembered that I really didn't give a damn.

— Bridger

When I saw her, I'm ashamed to say I didn't recognize her right away. There was a girl standing atop the mezzanine walkway, scanning the crowd. She wore a baseball cap and a hoodie, in which she seemed to drown. I almost disregarded her. But then she moved, and the gait was pure Scarlet — shoulders back, spine straight. There was something strong about her that even sloppy clothes couldn't hide.

I tracked her around the edge of the arena, prepared to wave if she would only look our way. But when she finally spotted me, the look on her face made my gut twist.

It was *fear*.

For a second, she just stood there, shrinking inside herself. I shook off my surprise and beckoned to her. And as she began to accelerate toward the bench where Andy and I sat together, I felt the first whiff of relief. I'd called her all last night to no avail. I'd texted. I'd emailed. And she'd said nothing. Today, Andy had finally pulled out the old high school directory and offered to call her house, just to put me out of my misery.

And now here she was, picking her way past a few people to come over to us. Biting her lip, she sat down on the other side of Andy. It was way too far away. And my throat picked that moment to close up. "Scarlet," I choked out. "Thank Christ... you have no idea what I thought. When I saw them... that car." God, I was going to lose it if I wasn't careful. But the image of that asshole pushing her into the sedan was burned on my brain. It was just the way things happened in nightmares —

146

when the person you're trying to reach is suddenly snatched away. And then you're running, but the car is faster…

I had that dream all the time, actually. But usually Lucy was the star.

Andy made to stand up. "I'll just move…"

"No," Scarlet grabbed his hands and pulled him down again. "You're fine where you are." She looked skittish, and the sight of her looking over her shoulders made my skin prickle. "Where is Lucy?"

"At my house," Andy said. "Hanging with my sisters."

"Good," she said quickly.

I leaned toward her, and it was all I could do not to take her face in my hands. "You have to tell me what the fuck is going on. Why did they make you come home?"

She sighed. "They want things from me."

"What things?

"I don't want to talk about it, Bridge. The trial…" she shook her head.

I smacked my hands on my thighs. "Please don't be that way. I watched a couple of goons haul you off the street yesterday. What do they want?"

There was a blast of Queen's *We Will Rock You* from the PA system, and the players took the ice for the second period. "I'm getting popcorn," Andy announced, standing up. He climbed over me and went for the aisle.

"Scarlet, look at me," I demanded. She dragged heavy eyes from the floor and up to my waiting gaze. I didn't know how she was going to take what I had to confess. "I already knew," I whispered. "I knew who you were."

A wave of disbelief washed across her face. "You did?"

I nodded, feeling miserable. Because I'd meant to come clean about it since the moment I discovered it two nights ago.

But instead, like a caveman I'd dragged her home to my lair and had sex with her instead. "I figured it out Monday night."

"How?" she whispered.

"Well, sometimes I still hear the hockey gossip, you know? I heard that a kick-ass women's goalie who just happened to be J.P. Ellison's daughter was going to join the team, but she didn't show up this fall. And you seemed to know too much about hockey for a Miami girl, and I wondered why. But it wasn't until I saw another newspaper article about the trial that I put it together. So I Googled Shannon Ellison," I paused, taking one of her hands in mine. "…And your pretty face popped up on the screen."

"I'm sorry," she said, staring down at the concrete floor again.

I slid closer now, wrapping one arm around her back. "You don't have to be sorry, Scarlet. I understand why you changed your name."

"Do you? It didn't even work," she said, close to tears. "This is ugly. It's all *so* ugly, and I'm stuck in it. I tried hiding, but…"

"Deep breaths, okay? We'll get you through it." My lips grazed her eyebrow. "There's only one question I need you to answer for me right now. Just one." My hand tightened on her waist. "Scarlet, are you safe in that house?"

I could feel her body go absolutely solid at the question. And my own heart practically stopped beating, because I was so afraid of what she was about to say. Although I needed her to tell me. Even if the answer gutted me.

"Scarlet," I whispered. "I need to know."

"Yeah," she said. "I am." But even as she said it, her eyes filled with tears.

"Then what's the matter?" I asked, my voice close to

cracking. "This is important."

"Nothing, Bridge. Nothing is the matter."

But I still had a prickle of unease. There was no room for error here. Because if I thought there was any chance of her being hurt by anyone in that house, there was no way I was letting her go back in there. "Scarlet, have you always been safe in that house?"

"Yes," she said quickly.

"You would tell me if you weren't, right? It's important that I, of all people…" I didn't have any experience with this. But I'd taken Scarlet to bed. Twice. And if she'd been abused as a child, then it wouldn't have been easy for her.

She looked me straight in the eye. "I *would* tell you. Of all the issues I have, that's not one of them."

"Then why are you crying?"

She pushed the tears away with one hand. "Nobody ever asked me that before. They were all too busy running the other way."

Jesus fuck. The smolder of fear in my chest flared into anger. And it was stuck somewhere right near the center of my chest. Slowly, I took a few deep breaths. "I was worried maybe that's why you never told me your real name."

"That wasn't it. I promise."

Andy's shadow appeared. "This has turned into a pretty exciting game," he said, sitting down on the other side of Scarlet.

Trying to calm down, I checked the scoreboard. The game was now 3-3.

"Quinnipiac is on a six-game streak," Scarlet said, looking down onto the rink. "They've got great foot speed. But they're graduating a fuckload of players, including most of their blue line guys."

A laugh got stuck in my throat, and I pulled her a little closer to me on the bench. "What hurts the most is that I never got to hear you talk hockey before."

Andy grinned. "Shan..." he caught himself. "Scarlet owns this place."

"Used to," she corrected.

"You were such a queen bee in High School," he said.

"Gee thanks," She gave him a shaky smile. "If I was, I'm sorry."

Andy shrugged. "It's just high school. I don't get shoved into lockers anymore."

She stole a piece of his popcorn. "You missed it, Andy, but I got a taste of how the other half lives."

"You got shoved into lockers too?" He tipped the popcorn in her direction. "Have some more."

"Not exactly..." she broke off, eying a family was threading its way across the bleachers to sit down just in front of us. They settled themselves on the bench, and the mother began passing hot dogs to her two boys, who were middle school age.

Scarlet pulled her hood down and took off her baseball cap, shaking her hair free. Then she leaned forward to put a hand on the woman's shoulder. "Hi Mrs. Stein," she said, her voice cheery. "Happy Thanksgiving."

The woman turned with a neighborly smile. And then when she recognized Scarlet, her face closed up tight. Then her husband, sensing a disturbance in the force, looked first at his wife and then craned his neck to see my girlfriend. He cleared his throat. "I think we forgot the..."

"...Mustard," his wife supplied. "Boys?" She stood up, nudging her sons toward the aisle.

It was unbelievable. "Did they just..." I didn't even want

to say it out loud. "...*Move* their seats because of...?" *You.*

"Yeah, I think they did," Andy said, his eyes still following the family.

"I used to babysit for them," Scarlet said. She put her hat back on and pulled up her hood. "You have to understand the mindset around here. Those people are probably shuddering every time they remember leaving their kids with me."

"That makes no *sense*," I argued. "You're not..."

"*Him*," she finished my sentence. "To them, it doesn't matter, okay? They're freaked out, because they just figured out that monsters under the bed are real. They're out of their minds, wondering how everyone missed it. So our name is like a toxin. You can stop wondering why I don't have any friends, or why I changed my name, or why I remained a virgin until that night on Andy's bed."

Andy choked on his soda.

"I had *one* friend last year. Only one person would be seen with me, would sit with me at lunch. Andy — remember Anni Boseman? Blond, skinny?"

"Sure," Andy coughed.

"Well, she had a nervous breakdown right before graduation. All year long she stood up for me. And then in May she just couldn't get out of bed." She swallowed, then looked up at me and Andy in turn. "I'm trying to tell you that being my friend is not that much fun." She stole one more bite of popcorn. "You two are the only people in this four thousand seat arena knowingly sitting next to me. And if you both suddenly thought better of it, I wouldn't call you crazy."

I hated that there wasn't a thing I could say that would make things better for her. I could only flatten my hand against Scarlet's back, and rub circles of warmth into her skin. Scarlet closed her eyes in appreciation. When she opened them, Andy

151

was studying her. "What?" she asked.

"You must have been recruited by Harkness to play goalie."

She swallowed. "Sure. The coach was not terribly happy when I quit the first week of school."

"You and Bridger both," he said. "That sucks."

"We're the hockey quitters club, party of two," I said.

"That just leaves you more time for..." he cleared his throat. "Each other."

Scarlet put her head in her hands. "I can't believe I said that out loud."

Andy shook his head. "At least somebody has fun in my bed."

"We'll drop you at home," I said as we left the stadium after the game.

"I'm going to walk," she said quickly.

"Why?"

"Well, there are TV vans in front of my house. Can you just let me be the only one who's..." she stopped in the middle of the sentence, looking for the right words. "*Tainted* by the whole thing. Please?"

The parking lot lights illuminating her small face. "If that's really what you want."

"Trust me, it is. And hey — I can save you the whole meet-the-parents drama."

"Yeah? We can skip that at my house too." I held up a hand for a high five, and she slapped it.

"Will we see you this weekend?" Andy asked, his grin friendly. My neighbor was such a good guy. And my debt to him grew a little larger every day.

She chewed her lip. "I don't think so, actually. I might

not stay the whole weekend, if I can help it."

"Call me," I said, hugging her one more time. "It wasn't nice of you not to answer all afternoon."

"They took my phone."

I stepped back from her. "Seriously? How will I know you're okay?"

"I'll be fine," her face had closed down again. She looked as rattled as I'd ever seen her. "I'll jump through their hoops, and in a couple days, we'll all be back at school."

"You could ride back with us on Sunday," Andy offered. "There's room in the car."

"Thanks, I'll ask my overlords," she said. "And I'd fit, because it's not like they let me pack any luggage."

I kissed her quickly. "Everything about this stinks."

"Welcome to my world," she said.

— Scarlet

When I woke up on Thanksgiving morning, it was to the smell of onions and garlic. My mother had a rule — she'd always doubled the garlic in recipes. "For a good result, double the garlic," she'd said more times than I could count. I'd probably hear her say it today, too.

My mother was a piece of work. There could be a lynch mob on our front yard, burning a cross into the lawn, and she would stand in the kitchen with a perfect manicure and spout cooking advice.

By the time I made my way down to the kitchen, my mother had made stuffing and wrestled a turkey into the oven. "I could use your help peeling the potatoes," she said.

Peel the potatoes. Speak to your father's defense attorneys. Welcome to Thanksgiving at the Ellison residence.

I found a peeler and got to work. When my father

eventually wandered into the kitchen, he greeted me with a single question. "Who won the game?"

I bit back the litany of things I would have liked to scream. *Who cares? Why is hockey the only thing you've ever talked about? Why do I have to come home to the insane asylum for Thanksgiving? How on earth did it come to this?*

What I said was: "Quinnipiac, in overtime."

I peeled the vegetables and then went back upstairs. Walking into my room, my eye went straight to the corner where I used to keep Jordan. Without my favorite escape, it was so hard to pass the time. Exams were coming up, but of course I didn't have my books with me.

When you found yourself missing your statistics textbook, things were really going poorly.

Beneath me, the house was quiet. Thanksgiving had always been like this, just the three of us. My mother's parents were killed in a plane crash when she was seventeen. And my father's parents were out of the picture too. He'd grown up in Canada "under the thumb of that drunk," as he referred to his father. Apparently I'd met them once at a hockey game in Calgary when I was four. I don't remember.

Then there was my uncle Brian. He was six years younger than my father, and they'd never been close. We saw him maybe once a year when he came through town, usually during my hockey season. I'd heard my mother tell her friends that Uncle Brian was in jail when I was born. The last time I saw him was last fall, during the thick of the investigation. He'd come to the door unannounced, startling both my parents. "We have to talk," I'd heard him say. "You need to take my calls."

At that, my parents shooed me upstairs and closed the

door to the den. I heard about ten minutes of muffled shouting, and then he was gone.

Now I wished he was here to break up the stillness. There was a lot of thick irony over Uncle Brian's absence, now that I thought about it. He was never around because my parents — with their love of success and appearances — couldn't stomach having a felon for a family member. Uncle Brian was a perfectly respectable social worker now, from what I could gather. My mother had let that slip out once when I asked about him.

He lived in Massachusetts, which was not all that far away. But even so, he was never invited for Thanksgiving. And now my father was on his way to having the mother of all criminal records, a string of felonies after his name.

So much for keeping up appearances.

I did not dress up for my interview with the lawyers. When I went into the kitchen the morning after Thanksgiving, it was in a pair of jeans too baggy to have made it into the suitcase I packed for school, and the hoodie I'd worn to the hockey game.

"You look terrible, Shannon," my mother said, her eyes hard. "Have a little respect."

"Maybe if you'd let me pack for the weekend like a normal person, I'd have something nice to wear."

That shut her up. We spoke no more words until Azzan nodded toward the door. "It's time to go," he said.

I followed him out. Because I had no choice.

"Can I get you coffee, Shannon?" The female lawyer was impeccably dressed in a dove grey suit and pink silk shirt. She paused, her fingertips resting on the polished wood of the conference table.

"My name is not Shannon," I corrected. The objection sounded petty. But I didn't want them to think they could treat me however they wished.

"Sorry, Scarlet," she said smoothly. "My mistake. Would you like a beverage?"

"No thank you. Let's just get this done."

Two more people entered the room — another lawyer and a legal assistant. The assistant adjusted a video camera standing on a tripod in the corner, where a red light winked on.

"Why are you videotaping me?" I asked.

"In case we need to review," she said.

Lovely. "Okay, whatever."

She sat down in front of me, a yellow legal pad and a pen poised in front of her. "Could you state your name and address for the record?"

The questions started out slow and dull — facts of my life, birth date, how long I'd lived in my father's house. "Far too long," I said, wondering if I could shake them off by acting like a bitch.

"Measured *in years*, how long have you lived in your father's house?" the lawyer asked.

With a sigh, I told it to her straight.

Eventually, the questions got meatier. "Scarlet, has your father ever touched you inappropriately?"

"No," I said. "Never." It was an easy question. "In fact, he never touched me in any way — no pats on the head, no hugs. He's the opposite of affectionate."

The lawyer paused. "This works better if you just answer the question. No need to fill in details unless I ask."

"Fine," I shrugged.

"Did your father ever hit you?"

"Once," I said. "I yelled in his face, and he slapped me."

"When did this occur?" she asked.

"I was fifteen, and it only happened once. But two days ago, your guy Azzan slapped me after kidnapping me off the street."

I wanted her to break her pretty facade, but it didn't really work. "Please answer the questions you're asked."

"I thought you'd want to know what your employee did."

"You may take that up as a separate matter after this interview, if you choose. Did your father ever hit you on another occasion?"

"No."

"Have you ever seen your father hit, assault or molest anyone?"

"No." Not unless verbal abuse counted. "Not physically."

"Hitting, assaulting and molesting are all physical actions. Did you see your father do any of those things?"

"No."

"Have you ever seen your father touch his hockey players inappropriately?"

I shook my head. "There's a lot of butt patting in hockey, between coaches and players. But that's everybody, and there's about an inch of foam between players and their butts."

"I'll repeat the question. Have you ever seen your father touch his hockey players *inappropriately*?"

"No."

And so it went. Every question she posed produced a harmless answer. As the interview went on, I came to understand that they were using me to construct a family narrative that implied: *nothing to see here!* My answers painted what was actually a bland portrait of the man.

Of course, she never asked me if he screamed like a lunatic every time I missed a shot in practice, if his face turned the color of raw meat when he was angry. She didn't want to hear about that.

When all her questions were finished, I let Azzan drive me back to the house. I climbed the stairs to my room wondering what Bridger and Andy and Lucy were up to. I hoped they were all on a sofa somewhere, watching a movie. Or maybe they'd taken Lucy ice skating, or bowling. That's what normal people did on the Friday after Thanksgiving. People who weren't me.

Chapter Thirteen: *You Have a Future at the CIA*

— *Scarlet*

"Can I have my phone back now?" We were finally on our way back to Harkness. Azzan hadn't let me ride with Andy and Bridger. He insisted on driving me back himself.

"Maybe," he grunted. "There's something I need to ask you. In your call history, I found a missed call from the State of New Hampshire. The caller left a voicemail, which you erased."

My heartbeat went wild. "So?"

"The prosecutor's office called you."

"Well, Sherlock, did you check my outgoing calls too? Because I didn't call them back. It's not personal. I don't want to talk to *anybody* about the trial."

He smirked. "The thing is, Shannon, I believe you. I'm sure you'd like nothing more than to forget your family exists. But we're not going to let you do that. Your name is officially on the witness list, which will be filed tomorrow."

"It is?" *Damn it.*

"Yes it is. So I need you to listen to me right now. Don't talk to *anyone* about the case. And if the prosecutor contacts you again, I want you to call me immediately, and tell me who it was and exactly what he or she said."

"Okay." Instinct told me to agree with everything that came out of his ugly little mouth.

"They might promise you they only need fifteen minutes, they only want to talk about you personally. But that would all be a total lie, understand?"

"Sure."

"All you have to do is keep it together for a few months, sit in the courtroom a few times like a good kid, and this will all be over." He slipped my phone from his breast pocket and handed it over. "I put my number in your contacts."

"Okay Azzan." That's it. Play the good girl.

He leaned back in his seat. "It looks like it's pretty serious with this Bridger guy. He's the only one you ever call or text."

It squicked me out to think of Azzan sifting through the calls on my phone. "So?" I asked. "That only proves that I don't have many friends. Harkness is hard work."

"Uh huh. Who's Lulu?"

My mouth went completely dry. "Just another friend. What do you care?"

"You're right, I don't really. But you probably do."

"What's that supposed to mean?"

"Shannon, you do what your family needs you to do, and I won't have to go crawling up your boyfriend's ass, okay? With just his name and phone number, I can find out who he calls, who he owes, and whether or not he's ever had a parking ticket. Maybe a little bag of pot turns up in his dorm room if you're not a good girl. Think about it."

I tasted bile in my throat, and my view of the road began to go blurry at the edges.

"Breathe, Shannon," Azzan said. His laugh sounded like a stutter. "These are simple things we ask of you. Answer all our questions. Don't answer any of the other side's questions. Do it right, and everything will be fine with you and lover boy."

I forced myself to face him. "I don't think my father would like you threatening me."

He only smiled. "Honey, your dad is a washed up old

man with a weakness for fucking little boys up the ass."

My stomach clenched, and I struggled to keep my face impassive.

"See, I don't work for your dad. I work for his *lawyer*. And his lawyer took this shitty case knowing that everything had to go exactly right. And that's my job. Even if you go whining to daddy, it won't make a difference. He can't fire his lawyer right before jury selection." Azzan switched on the radio.

I spent the rest of the trip looking out the window, counting down the mile markers.

That afternoon, Bridger texted me repeatedly. *Are you back? Call me.*

But I didn't call him, because I was too freaked out. Bridger was the last person in the world who needed any of Azzan's bullshit. And I'd suddenly become ten different kinds of paranoid. I had to keep him out of it, no matter what.

That night, Blond Katie was in a really terrible mood too.

"What's the matter?" I asked her as she stomped around our room.

"I broke up with Dash," she said.

It took me a second to remember that Dash was the name of her latest football player. "I'm sorry."

"Don't be too sorry. All he wanted was a fuck buddy. And if he weren't a total asshole, I might have been okay with that."

"Sometimes hot just isn't enough," Ponytail Katie said, from behind a copy of *Vanity Fair*.

Blond Katie pointed a bright pink fingernail at me. "You, Scarlet, are the one who has it all figured out."

"Me?" *Whose life is a freaking melodrama?* "Yeah, I've

definitely got it all figured out."

"Well, don't you?" Blond Katie asked. "You have a hot athlete who actually loves you. How'd you do that?"

I sank down on our secondhand sofa, bone weary. My life was a dark tunnel, and I had the sinking feeling that Bridger and I wouldn't make it out on the other side. "Just luck," was my answer. *Bad luck.*

"Does he have any nice friends?" Katie asked. "There's a Christmas party coming up at the sorority that I'm pledging. But I can't think of who to ask."

"And you can't just go alone?"

She looked gobsmacked that I would even suggest such a thing. "No way. You need a date, and it *has* to be an athlete. Preferably an upperclassmen."

"Hmm," I said. "How do you feel about basketball players?"

Her perfect little mouth frowned thoughtfully. "I guess I wouldn't have to worry about towering over him in heels. Who is he?"

"His name is Andrew. He's a junior in Beaumont."

"Is he as hot as Bridger?"

"Nobody is as hot as Bridger," I pointed out.

Ponytail Katie looked up from her magazine again. "What's the team's record so far this year?"

"The season just started," I said quickly.

Blond Katie just shook her head. "Don't buy tickets to the final four. Have you *seen* our basketball team?" She sighed. "He's a nice guy?"

"The nicest," I promised. "You should invite him."

"Do you have his number?"

An hour later I got a text from Andy.

ANDY: *Um, thanks?*

ME: *Um, you're welcome? You don't have 2 go, U know.*

ANDY: *Oh, I'm going. But there could B dancing. I dance like an epileptic turtle.*

ME: *Man up, Andy. This isn't really about the dancing.*

ANDY: *UR just trying 2 get rid of me 4 the night.*

ME: ***BLUSHING***

ANDY: *Call Bridger before he gets any grumpier.*

But I was still too panicked to know what to do about Bridger. I needed to put some distance between us. So instead of calling, I sent him the world's least interesting text.

ME: *Home now and hanging out with the Katies.*

BRIDGER: *So I heard.*

I slept, very, very badly that night. For once, my nightmare changed. Instead of the puck falling into a hole, in this new dream it was my phone. I skated toward it as it skidded across the ice, never reaching the phone before it pitched into the darkness.

Eventually, I gave up on sleeping and spent the last predawn hour staring at the ceiling, worrying about Azzan's intentions. I had to assume that he'd read every text and email on my phone. His threat had been creepier than my nightmare.

I worried all through breakfast, and then through my morning classes. So I skipped lunch to answer a question that had nagged at me all morning. Mostly, the idea made me feel like a paranoid lunatic. But as the saying goes, just because I was paranoid didn't mean they weren't out to get me.

The guy behind the counter at the Nerd Patrol was a Division One level geek — complete with vampire pale skin and toothpick arms. "Hello and welcome to the Nerd Patrol," he said. "How can I help you?"

"Hi," I smiled at him. "I have a couple of strange requests."

The geek rubbed his hands together. "Awesome. What are we looking at?"

I set my phone down on the counter. "Okay, this has been out of my control for a few days, and — this is going to sound weird — I wonder if there's any way you can tell me if the phone's been altered?"

"What do you mean *altered*?" the guy cocked his head at me. He had the darkest eyebrows I had ever seen on a human being.

"Well, the man who had my phone is kind of stalkerish. I just want to know if he added anything that I can't see."

"Um, that would be icky," the geek said. "Let's take a look." He plugged my phone into his computer and began tapping on the keyboard. "When did you last have it to yourself? How far back am I searching, here?"

"I left it with him on Tuesday afternoon before Thanksgiving, and I got it back Sunday around noon."

He tapped madly at the keyboard, his Adam's apple bobbing. Then his face creased into a frown. "Well..."

"What?"

"And here I thought you sounded like a nut. But there *is* some weird software on your phone. It's like a spy program." He rubbed his chin with his hand.

"Seriously? What does it do?"

"Well, let's Google the title of it." There was more furious typing, and then he turned his monitor so that I could see.

He had pulled up an advertisement for something called *iTail*. "Instantly Tracks What Your Child Does and Where He Goes!" it read. "Quickly and Effortlessly!"

There was something about the cheery advertising copy that made my stomach turn. "So I'm not crazy? My phone is bugged?"

He shook his head. "It can't *hear* you talking. But it tracks your location, the phone numbers of calls made and received, email messages, texts..." he scrolled down the screen. "It uploads all that information to a site where your stalker can browse it remotely. Luckily, it will only take me three minutes to uninstall."

"Wait..." I put my elbows on the counter. "I think I need to leave it on there. At least for now."

The geek's eyes got big. "Sneaky!"

"Can I ask you something else?" I pressed. "Is there any way for me to make a recording of the calls I make on my phone?"

"Well, yes and no," my geek said, tugging on his sideburns. "You want to record the call without the other person knowing, right?"

I nodded.

"I know a trick, but it isn't, um, a sanctioned operating procedure." He looked around the room to see who might be listening. Then he looked at his watch. "My break is coming up in ten minutes. I'll look something up real quick, and then maybe I could tell you what I know over a cup of coffee?"

"Okay..." I wasn't sure if the geek was hitting on me, or if he really wanted to help. "I'll meet you outside in ten."

"My name is Luke, by the way," the geek said, holding out his hand.

"It's nice to meet you, Luke. I'm Scarlet."

"I'm a computer science major, in case you didn't figure that out," Luke said.

"I would have never guessed."

By the time I realized he was steering us into Bridger's coffee shop, it was too late. When Bridger lifted his eyes to mine, my heart did the same excited skitter that it always did when I saw him. For about a nanosecond, I was completely happy. And then I remembered what Azzan had done to my phone, and my stomach clenched.

"Hi," Bridger said, his voice tight.

"Hi."

"Thanks for letting me know you got back safely last night," his green eyes flared accusingly.

My mouth opened and closed like a fish. "Sorry." We really couldn't have this conversation here.

"What can I get you?" Bridger asked. "Since it's obvious you're just here for the coffee."

"I'd, uh, love a tall latte," I told him. "And this is my friend Luke," I said. "I'm treating him as payment for a technical glitch he's helping me work out."

"Okay," Bridger said, punching numbers into the cash register. "Your friend Luke drinks a triple shot cappuccino with a blackout cookie on the side."

"I'm so predictable," Luke sighed as I handed over a ten. "Thanks, Scarlet."

When Luke walked to the end of the bar for our drinks, Bridger handed me my change. And then he grabbed my hand in his. "Scarlet, what is the matter? When are you going to talk to me about your trip home?"

I closed my eyes and just let myself feel the warmth of his fingers over mine. "I'm not sure I can, Bridge. I think I have to handle this myself."

He squeezed my hand. "I'm *out of my fucking mind* with worry over you. Is that what you want?" His green eyes burned me.

"No. That is not at all what I want."

There were customers behind me then, making impatient noises. "Can I get a double mocha latte with caramel?" a voice called out. Defeated, Bridger gave me one more upset look. And then he let go of my hand.

I found Luke at a back table, breaking off a bite of the cookie. "Have some," he offered.

"Yum." My stomach rumbled to remind me that I'd skipped lunch.

"Please tell me your pissed off boyfriend over there didn't bug your phone."

I shook my head. "Nope. He's one of the good guys. And he's worried about me because of the bad guys."

"Do you promise?"

I held up a hand as if swearing an oath. "I promise."

He sighed. "And now you want to record phone calls?"

"Maybe. I'm trying to think of a way to beat them at their own game."

He grinned. "You didn't get this from me, okay? I need to keep my job."

"I understand."

"All right, I'll tell you what I know. If you search the app store for 'record phone calls,' you'll find several choices. The app you want is ten bucks, it's called Red Wolf, and the icon looks like... wait for it!"

"A red wolf," I supplied.

"Right. But wait, there's more," Luke said, sipping his coffee. "All these programs work using the conference call mechanism. After your call starts, you hit the app and it actually dials *another* phone number which is really just a recorded line. And that takes ten or twenty seconds, so there's a lag when you can't record. So you call whoever and then *stall*."

"Tricky."

"That's not even the tricky part. In order to stay legal, these programs make an announcement after you hit the 'record' button on the app. A voice will say 'this call is now being recorded,' which your caller will hear."

"Well that sucks."

"Right. But there's a way around it. When you're setting up the app, there's a choice for which language you want your announcement in. And you're going to choose Tagalog."

I stared at him. "Seriously? Tagalog?"

He nodded. "The blogs I've read say that one is actually silent. Try it. It's a ten dollar experiment. I bet it works."

"Luke," I said. "You have a future at the CIA."

He beamed. "I have a couple other tips for you, okay?"

"I'm listening."

"If your stalker is someone who can read your credit card bill, then buy this app with a gift card. And pay cash."

"Crap. Can they tell from the spy software that I bought the app?"

He shrugged. "I don't think so… but I can't guarantee it. What if you bought a whole bunch of apps at once? Try a new video game or two — or some productivity note-taking thing. Make it look like you're just bored and doing some shopping."

"Okay, now you're scaring me just a little bit with this spy stuff. Damn, dude."

Luke twirled his coffee cup around in circles to stir its contents. "Your guy is shooting us dirty looks right now. He wouldn't hurt a geek for having coffee with his girl, would he?"

I shook my head. "All those dirty looks are for me."

He knitted his dark eyebrows together. "Promise me you'll be careful? Because if I read in the newspaper next week that your mutilated body was found in a dumpster, I'm going to feel terrible that I didn't report this craziness to the someone."

"Thanks for the visual, Luke. But that won't happen. The people who bugged my phone work for my parents. They're jerks, but they don't want me dead."

"Yikes. Still, if you need anything, I'm the only Luke in Spanner House, and my number is in the student directory."

"Awesome. You've been a huge help." I slid out of my seat. "I have Italian class."

"Grazie per il caffè!" Luke called as I walked away.

"Prego!"

I walked around for the rest of the day feeling Azzan's eyes on me everywhere I went. Sitting in the dining hall with the Katies, I pictured Azzan staring at a dot on a screen. A dot that was struggling to finish her macaroni and cheese on account of the pit of fear in her stomach.

"Grumpy much?" Blond Katie asked.

"Sorry," I sighed.

"Man troubles?" she guessed.

"Well…" I swallowed. "Bridger's pissed at me."

"Shit!" she swore. "I'm so sorry. Did you cheat?"

"No!" I shook my head. "We've both just got a lot to handle right now, and… I haven't been very accommodating."

"Sounds like all is not lost," Ponytail Katie put in. "Maybe call him?"

I put another forkful of pasta into my mouth and thought it over. It occurred to me, even in the depths of my panic, that my spies would notice if I quit Bridger cold turkey. And I didn't want them to think that I knew about *iTail*. So I should call him, at least one more time.

Even though it would hurt.

After dinner, I found a missed call and a voicemail on my phone. Walking towards the dorm, I listened to it. "This is assistant district attorney Madeline Teeter for Scarlet Crowley. Scarlet, I'm going to be in your area later this week, and I'd like us to sit down together. It will only take a half an hour. Please call me back to set up a time."

Crap!

My pulse flew, because I realized I had to comply with Azzan's instructions right away. He would know if I didn't. Shakily, I found his number in my contacts and dialed him. He answered on the first ring. "Hello?"

"It's Scarlet," I said. "You told me to call if I heard from the prosecutor?"

"Yeah, Shannon, did they call?"

"She did. Sometime in the last hour. A 603 area code. Her name was Madeline something, and she said she would like it if we could sit down together."

"Don't call them, Scarlet."

"I won't. I'm just telling you, because you asked me to."

"Good girl. If she calls again, or shows up, I want to hear from you right away."

"Fine." I hung up.

Good girl, he'd said. But every day it got a little harder to figure out what that meant. Did a good girl help the prosecution, or duck them? Did a good girl lie to her boyfriend to keep his little sister out of harm's way?

Everything was just a mess. And I didn't have the first idea how to untangle it.

Chapter Fourteen: *Hester Baby*

— *Bridger*

My phone vibrated around nine thirty. As silently as possible, I rose from my desk and tiptoed into an uncomfortable position on the closet floor. Sealing myself into a makeshift phone booth, I answered Scarlet's call. "Hi."

"Hi," she breathed. "Can you talk?"

"Quietly," I said. "I'm in my closet."

I heard her laugh through the phone, and the sound of it made me ache from missing her. "Sounds cozy."

"Yeah, it's terrific. But I need to talk to you, and she's asleep, so…"

"How are you, Bridge?" she cut in.

"Not good, because you have me worried. What do your father's people want you to do?"

She sighed. "It's nothing illegal. They want me to testify, and I don't want to. And I'm supposed to sit in the courthouse when the trial starts after New Year's."

"You don't want to go, do you?"

"No." Her voice was low.

"Scarlet, did they ask you to lie?"

I could hear her hesitation coming through the ether. "I can't talk about this with you. It isn't as bad as you think, though. As long as I show up exactly when they want me to, and smile on cue, it will all be okay."

But there was something evasive in her voice. "Nobody

should lean on you for anything. I don't like it at all."

"Do you trust me, Bridger?"

Well, shit. "Of course I do. But…"

"Then you need to let me handle this."

"It feels like you're keeping things from me. Bad things."

"Bridge…" her voice cracked. "I can't talk about this."

There was a long silence on the phone. It was the sound of two people moving away from each other, and it made my chest ache. "Scarlet?"

"Yeah?"

"How did you choose your new name?"

"Oh, Bridge," she sighed. "I love that you asked me that."

"Tell me."

She sniffled. "The Scarlet Letter is one of my favorite books. The main character is so brave, and everyone hates her anyway."

"Wow."

"It's a tad melodramatic."

"No, it's awesome," I told her. "But… what was the woman's name in the book? She wasn't called Scarlet."

"She was Hester Prynne. But I just couldn't do that to myself. *Hester* is just so… not sexy."

Even as stressed out as I was, I laughed. "Hottie, I would have fallen for you anyway. Let's try it out." I dropped my voice to a growl. "Oh Hester, baby. Ride me, Hester."

There was a strangled noise on her end of the line, the sound that laughter made when there were tears in the mix. Eventually, Scarlet said, "I love you Bridger."

I gave my head a couple of little smacks against the closet wall. Because sometimes there was just no way to win. "I love you, Scarlet. That's why I can't stand how you're handling this. You're holding it against me. Cutting me off instead of letting me help."

"That's not it. I need a little room to maneuver through this crap."

"That's not how love works. You're supposed to share the crappy things as well as the good ones. You said so yourself."

There was a defeated silence on her end of the line. "But I can't do that with this."

"And you can't tell me why." I wasn't going to let it drop. I could wear her down until she told me. I could blow off music theory one more time, remove all her clothes and then make love to her until she knew how important she was to me.

Just as I began to really appreciate the fantasy, she said something even worse.

"Bridger, we're going to have to take a break while I sort this out."

"What? No way."

"I'm sorry, Bridge. I love you, but I need some time."

The closet seemed to get smaller then. "That makes no sense, Scarlet. I didn't push you away when you found out about my shitty life."

"You're a bigger person than I am," she said. "Goodbye for now." These last three words were squeaked out.

"Scarlet, wait…"

She disconnected the call. And I threw my phone into the pitch black of my crappy little closet.

— *Scarlet*

The next week was awful. I walked around with red eyes, and The Katies tried to ask me what was wrong. But I couldn't tell them, because I'd have to lie about our breakup and lie about the reason I couldn't see Bridger any more.

I was so, so tired of lying.

At first Bridger called frequently, and I didn't answer. Bridger texted me, and I did not respond. *Don't do this*, he wrote. *We can figure it all out.*

I could picture Azzan sitting at his computer, pulling up a log of my phone's activity. He was probably sipping a cup of coffee while spying on my life. Maybe our little spat made him chuckle.

That idea cut me right in half.

I didn't like drama. I wasn't that kind of girl. And the little voice inside my head was practically shrieking now. *Just tell him! Just tell him the problem.*

And I considered it. I really did. But if I told Bridger that Azzan was threatening him and asking questions about Lulu, Bridger would want to take my side. That's the kind of guy he was. Then he'd think it through, and come to the only logical conclusion — he couldn't. A desperate guy who was hiding an eight-year-old girl could *not* tangle with a bunch of rich, arrogant defense attorneys who had no moral compass and a whole lot of money on the line.

If I laid it all out, I'd be forcing him to choose Lucy over me. And he'd hate that. And I'd have to listen to him tell me he was sorry.

Thinking about it cost me another entire night's sleep. While Blond Katie snored off a night of playing quarters at some fraternity, I thought of a way to get Bridger to give up on me.

The next morning, when I got a text from him, my reply was ready. *Bridger, I met somebody else. And he has his nights & weekends free.*

I sent this little grenade at around ten in the morning. And he neither called or texted after that.

So, I'd won that battle. And lost the war.

If I thought I'd been depressed before, it was ten times worse after that. My heart ached, and my eyes watered, and all because I'd been drained of hope.

My mistake had been to think that I could change my identity the way The Katies changed from ballet flats to stilettos. Now that I knew it wouldn't work, I no longer felt brave and new. I no longer felt like Scarlet. Instead, it was Shannon who stumbled around campus, trying to focus on my coursework. Friendless Shannon made flash cards for memorizing Italian verbs. She studied in the library while others went to dinner. And she played her guitar on the bed while the others made plans for the Christmas Ball.

There was only one moment during those long, lonely days when Shannon made a welcome appearance. I rarely checked my snail mailbox in Warren Hall, because nobody writes to a girl with a brand new name, not even the J. Crew catalog. But on one of my rare trips to the post office, I pulled out a large envelope with the Harkness College logo on it. The return address said Office of the Dean of Student Services.

Slitting it open, I found a single sheet of paper and yet another envelope inside. The paper read:

Dear Ms. Scarlet Crowley,
Please accept our apology. The enclosed piece of mail stymied us for several weeks, since your name change was not correctly cross-referenced in our records. We have made the necessary correction, and should any more mail arrive for you, we are confident that a delay such as this one will not happen again.
Sincerely,

A.J. Roberts
College Postmaster

I inspected the envelope, which was addressed to Shannon Ellison, Class of 2017. The return address was Massachusetts Department of Children and Families, with the name Ellison scrawled above the printing.

Uncle Brian?

I slit the envelope with my thumb, and drew out another letter, dated September the twentieth, more than two months ago. It was handwritten on notebook paper, the words slanting hard to the right, as if in a hurry to reach the margin.

Dear Shannon — This will sound like a strange sentiment coming from a relative that you barely know, but I've been very worried about you. J.P.'s trial is going to be bloody awful. It is my misfortune to know a thing or two about criminal trials. They are long and dehumanizing, and I hope you are not too caught up in the proceedings.

Last year I tried to visit you to offer my support, but your parents weren't having it. Now that you're out of their house, I hope we can reconnect. Unfortunately, I don't have a phone number for you, so I really hope you'll give me a call. Please let me know if there's any way I can help. If you feel like you're in over your head, or if you just want to talk, don't hesitate to call or write. Any time. —Uncle Brian.

He left me his email, plus work and cell phone numbers. I wasn't about to call him from my traitorous phone, or even enter his contact information. Still, I tucked that paper into my pocketbook. It was nice to know it was there.

Chapter Fifteen: *A Ginger Streak*

— *Bridger*

"Look at that!" Lulu said, bouncing ahead of me.

I raised my eyes from the pavement to see what she wanted to show me. It was a giant, inflatable Santa Claus in the center of some poor slob's lawn. And there were animated reindeer mechanically bowing their heads beside it.

It was the tackiest thing I'd ever seen.

Lately Lucy had the big eyes that kids got when Christmas approached. She was old enough to know that Santa was a myth, but young enough to get carried away by somebody's cheesy lawn ornaments. "Fancy," I said lightly.

"Isn't it?" We both came to a stop at the pathway that led to the school. Kids were streaming past us now, because the bell was about to ring.

"You have your lunch in there, right?"

She patted her pack and nodded.

"All right. Then give me a hug." I bent over to give her a quick squeeze. She hadn't started blowing off the goodbye hugs yet. Though I knew my days were numbered, because she wouldn't let me hold her hand anymore when we walked through a crowd.

"Bye Bridge," she chirped over her shoulder as she ran off in the river of children.

"Bye!" I called after her. A moment later, her red ponytail had disappeared, and so I did a one-eighty and hoofed it back to campus.

We were down to the last week of classes, followed by a week of Reading Period, followed by exams. My classmates were waving in the end of the semester like flight controllers on the tarmac. But the end of the term only brought me trouble, because Lucy and I had nowhere to go. Her vacation didn't start until a week after exams were finished. So even if I fell on my sword and confessed to Hartley that we were effectively homeless, Lucy would miss a week of school if we stayed at his place. Because I had no car to get her to school from Hartley's house.

As usual, all my choices sucked.

Putting one foot in front of the other one, I got to Stats class on time. I sat in the front row and took good notes, even though I really didn't need to. It was hard to shake the idea that I wouldn't be helping Scarlet study for this exam. Her rejection had been burning a hole in my gut for days.

It should have made me feel better to see that she looked miserable, too. Whenever I passed her walking into class, she snuck looks at me. She was pale and tired, and those hazel eyes fell to the desktop every time I caught her seeking me out.

To tell the truth, I felt damned uneasy about the whole thing. She'd thrown me over in a way that left very little room for interpretation. But she didn't *look* like someone who was happy about having a new guy.

She looked like a wreck.

Unfortunately, being pissed at her didn't make me love her any less. And it didn't matter that I actually had more important problems to think about. I kept turning the events of Thanksgiving weekend over in my mind, searching for an explanation that never came.

Thursdays used to be one of my two favorite days of the

week. But now the morning was just pure pain. After stats, I walked alone into music theory, careful to take a seat far from Scarlet. Avoiding somebody was hard work. When she was in the room with me, it was like there just wasn't enough air for the both of us. My chest felt tight, and it was impossible to concentrate.

"Hi, Bridger!"

I looked up to see someone sliding into the seat next to mine. "Hi there," I replied, careful to keep my reaction polite but uninterested. Her name was Amelia, and she'd sat next to me during Tuesday's lecture, too. Amelia was in one of the a cappella singing groups. We'd hooked up once last year after a party in Corey Callahan's room. Actually, we'd hooked up *during* the party. And after. But it was just the once, and a year ago, too.

"We're going to review structure today," the professor said at the head of the class. He wrote some terms on the white board as he talked. *Sonata. Minuet. Concerto.* "First, let's go over the various musical notations which instruct the musician to *repeat* a portion of the piece." He wrote *D.C. al fine, and D.C. al coda.*

"Awesome," Amelia said beside me. "I like repeats."

Christ. *Subtle, much?* Ignoring her, I scribbled down everything the professor wrote, since I couldn't count on Scarlet to help me prepare for this exam. And I sure the hell wouldn't be asking Amelia.

I was taking a few notes about the format of a sonata when my phone vibrated in my pocket.

— Scarlet

The goalie's job was to see the whole rink, all the time.

So even if I didn't want to notice the pretty girl who'd sat down next to Bridger for the second time in a row, I couldn't help it.

In the newspaper that morning, I'd read that my father's trial was expected to last "two or three months." Even if that were true, there would be appeals. And after the criminal case was finally resolved, there would probably be a civil suit, too. By the time it was all over, Bridger wouldn't even remember my face.

When I sent my awful text to Bridger, I knew it would ache to see him afterward. But watching that attractive upperclasswoman flip her hair for Bridger's benefit gave me an outright stab of pain. I wanted to kill her with my bare hands.

Now there was a great idea. Another Ellison commits a crime. We could have our own wing in a prison somewhere.

Three cheers for gallows humor.

The professor droned on about concertos, and I didn't take notes. I'd read this part of the textbook already.

A goalie notices everything, whether she wants to or not. So even though my view of Bridger was obscured by the flirtatious girl beside him, I knew right away when he pressed his phone to his head. And when he trotted out of the lecture hall, panic on his face, I saw it all.

A minute ticked by, then two. But he didn't reappear. His notebook was still on top of the desk where he'd left it.

Finally, Bridger came shooting back into the room, his face red. I saw him trot over to his stuff, grab it up and turn back around in a flash. As he ran back toward the doors, I got one more look at his face.

Devastation was the only word to describe what I saw there.

As fast as possible, I shoved my things together and left to follow him. But by the time I got outside, Bridger was a ginger streak running down College Street. I jogged after him. Maybe Lucy was sick at school? But the look I'd seen on his face had freaked me out. Bridger didn't rattle very easily. News of a tummy bug would not have affected him like that.

Still in pursuit, I saw Bridger draw up to Beaumont House. Instead of continuing on towards Lucy's school, he scanned his card and pushed through the gates.

Weird.

By the time I got there, puffing from the run, the iron gates were shut already. My ID wouldn't open them, either, because Beaumont was not my House. All I could do was to stand there, doing a little dance of impatience, waiting for a Beaumonter to wander by and let me in.

"Hey there. It's Scarlet, right?" I turned around to see Bridger's friend Hartley waving his ID in front of the sensor. "Are you and Bridger going to have lunch in the Beaumont dining hall for once? Or do I have to put both your faces on the back of that milk carton?"

"Hi," I squeaked, grateful to be let in.

"Hey — are you okay?"

Actually, no. I stood there for a long moment, trying to decide what to say. Bridger had specifically kept Hartley out of the loop, and I understood his reasons. But even so, it had just occurred to me that I couldn't get into Bridger's entryway without help.

Screw it.

"I think something's wrong with Bridger," I said.

Two minutes later, I ran up the steps of Bridger's entryway with Hartley on my heels. Finding the door to Bridger's room open, I paused on the threshold. I was just in time to see Bridger kick Lucy's mattress across the wood floor. Even as I opened my mouth to say something, he leapt over to it again, picked it up and hurled it at his own bed. "FUCK!" he shouted. Then he picked up a pink bunny and whipped it at the window. Making a fist, he punched the back of his metal desk chair, throwing it to the floor.

"Stop it!" I screamed.

Bridger didn't even look up at me. He put both hands on the surface of his desk, and hung his head in defeat.

"What the fuck?" I heard Hartley whisper behind me.

"Bridger, please tell me what's happened." I walked over to the chair and set it up again. "Please."

His shoulders heaved, and his fists clenched. He was still breathing hard, and his eyes and his face were red. Even though I was a little afraid of him, I walked closer. I put a hand on his chest. "What's the matter?"

He took a shuddering breath, which I felt beneath my hand. "They took her out of school."

"Who did?"

His gaze was unfocused. "DCF—the social workers. They took her out. I don't know where she is." His eyes had the glaze of someone who was in shock.

"Who called you?" I asked.

"Her teacher," he said, his voice cracking. "They came to the classroom with the principal and asked for Lucy. When Mrs. Rose asked, 'what is this regarding,' they said 'her mother has passed.'"

"She *died?*"

"That's what they said."

182

"I'm so sorry."

His head drooped. "I'm really in the shit now." As I watched, his eyes welled.

With two hands, I rubbed his back. I was probably the last person on earth he wanted to touch him. But I couldn't help myself.

He shuddered. "I told her I wouldn't let her go."

"You haven't."

"*Strangers* have her. She must be out of her mind."

"I know, Bridge. We'll get this cleared up. You're going to have to ask for help."

"Fuck that. Nobody will help me. They'll tell me to let her go."

"We'll find someone who knows what to do. You just need to ask the right people."

At that, he stood up and shoved my hands away. "Ask for help, like *you* do, Scarlet? Thanks for the tip."

"Bridge?" Hartley asked quietly. I'd actually forgotten he was in the room. "Has Lucy been *living* here with you?"

"Yeah." His voice was flat.

"Dude, *why*?"

Bridger chuffed out a bitter laugh. "Why do you think?"

"I mean... why didn't you *say* anything? My mom would have..."

"I *know*," Bridger snarled. "Teresa, who worked her ass off for twenty two years and got nowhere, would put aside her new life to help us out. I didn't want that. And I couldn't have made it legal without risking losing her to the system, which is exactly what just happened anyway..."

Turning his back on us again, Bridger opened his laptop. When the screen blinked to life, he typed "Connecticut department of families and children" into the search line and waited.

"What are you going to do, Bridger?" I asked. "Call them? Go there?"

"What do you care, Scarlet? Shit." He clicked on *Contact Us*.

"I care a great deal," I said quietly.

"Bullshit! I'm out of my fucking mind over you, so I never saw *this* coming." His voice rose to a shout. *"And now you want to help?"* He yanked his phone off the desk and began dialing.

"Bridger," I whispered.

He pressed the phone to his ear and waited.

"Bridger," Hartley echoed.

"No," Bridger bellowed into the phone, as his face reddened with devastation, "I do NOT know my party's extension." He closed his eyes.

I stepped forward again, wrapping my body around him from behind, my face pressing into his back. "Shh," I said. "It's going to be alright."

"No," his voice was rough. "It isn't. I did everything I could, and it's all fucked up anyway."

Hartley walked over to the window seat and picked up the pink bunny. "We need someone who knows their way around the department of social workers, or whatever it's called. And we need someone who can help you with legal stuff."

"I think you should go to the Beaumont House dean," I suggested.

"No fucking way. That's who I've been ducking since the summer."

"Wait..." Hartley said, looking up at the ceiling, as if the answer was written there. "I think she's right. You were breaking the rules before, but right now you aren't anymore.

So now he can only help you. That's his job, anyway."

"I don't know. I can't think," Bridger said. I ran my hand through his hair. It felt so good to touch him again. Even if the timing was awful, I just didn't want to let him go.

"Look," Hartley said. "I'm going to duck into his office and see if he has an hour for you today. I'll tell him it's important, but I won't say why."

"All right." Bridger sounded numb.

At that, Hartley left the room and closed the door.

"Shit," Bridger cursed. "I don't know anything about the system. I don't know anything about social workers, except that I never wanted to meet one. I have no idea how it works."

Neither did I. But I realized that I knew someone who might. I set my bag down and dug out Uncle Brian's letter. I tapped his number into my phone, my thumb hovering over the "send" button.

I stopped myself just in time.

"Bridge, can I use your phone? It's important. My uncle is a social worker. He's not in Connecticut, unfortunately. But he might know what to do."

"Something wrong with yours?" He pulled his phone off the desktop.

"It's sort of bugged," I sighed. "My father's attack dogs know every call I make, and read every text."

"What?" His eyes got huge. "That's so fucked."

"Yes, it is. It's also why I haven't talked to you in ten days." I hit "send" on Bridger's phone and held it to my ear.

Bridger put his forehead in his palm. "You should have just told me."

"Hold that thought," I said, as I listened to a phone ring at the other end of my call.

On the fourth ring, and just when I was losing hope, a

185

man's voice answered. "This is Brian Ellison."

"Uncle Brian?" I said into the silence. "It's... Shannon." After all this time, my old name felt foreign on my tongue.

"*Shannon,*" his voice was rough. "Wow. I'm so happy to hear your voice. Is this your phone number?"

"It's my boyfriend's." Somehow I managed to prevent myself from checking Bridger's face when I called him that. But it wasn't easy.

"I wrote you a letter a couple of months ago. Did you get it?"

"Just last week. Because I changed my name, and everything got confused."

"Oh," he said, his voice quiet. "I didn't know that."

"Why would you, you know? But do you have a minute? There's a problem."

"For you, I always have a minute. What's the matter?"

"It's not my problem, but it's really important. I need some advice about how social services in Connecticut would handle a situation. There's a child — she's eight — and the mother has died. But her brother is an adult who wants custody. And it's urgent."

He was silent for a moment. "That sounds serious. Does this have anything to do with J.P.'s mess?"

"Not a thing. But it has everything to do with people I love." *Please*, I begged him silently. *Please help.*

"Can I come and discuss it in person?" he asked. "I could be in Harkness by... five o'clock."

Relief flooded through me. "That's an amazing offer. But won't the social services offices be closed by then?"

There was more silence on the line. "Why don't you tell me the story. Who is this little girl?"

"My boyfriend's little sister," I couldn't help looking up

186

at Bridger. His eyes were glued to me, but his face gave away nothing. "He took her out of his mother's home last summer. Because the mom had a drug habit and some scary friends."

"Shit," Brian said into my ear.

"She was living in his dorm room until this morning, when social services came and took her from school. Because their mother died. And they probably assumed that she'd been living at home."

"And the father?"

"Deceased."

"What a mess," Brian sighed. "I'm so sorry."

"I am too."

"Okay. What's your boyfriend's name? Can I speak to him?"

"Of course."

I handed the phone to Bridger. And while I tidied up the things that Bridger had kicked around the room, he spoke to Uncle Brian, filling him in on all the details.

Ten minutes later Bridger thanked my uncle and disconnected the call. He set the phone down and turned to me.

"What's going to happen?" I asked.

Bridger raked a hand over his face. "He's going to call around, and try to figure out where she is, and if I can see her. And then he's going to call back and talk to me about how to try for custody."

"Wow. Okay."

"Thank you for calling him." Bridger didn't even look at me as he said this.

I tried to swallow the lump in my throat, but it wouldn't go. "I would do anything to help you."

"If that's true, then where the fuck have you been?" He looked up then, his eyes cool. "I am so incredibly angry with you right now."

The disappointment on his face made me feel shaky with fear. "I know you are. But I needed to keep my head down, so my father's security guys would leave me alone."

"And how's that been working for you?" There was a sarcastic edge to the question that made my eyes burn.

"I'm *sorry*, Bridge."

"Your phone is *bugged?* Is that why you broke up with me with a text message?"

I nodded.

"You wanted them to see that?"

Again, I nodded.

"Can I assume there's some fucked up reason why that seemed like a good idea?"

I knew I deserved his anger, but it scared me anyway. "The asshole-in-chief started asking a lot of questions, pointing out that you were the only one I ever called. He actually *threatened* you. And then?" I swallowed. "He said, 'who's Lucy?'"

"*Fuck.*" Bridger's eyes got wide. "You should have just told me."

"Why? So you could have two people to worry about instead of one?"

"But I do anyway!" he shouted. "I'm so twisted up over you, I never saw this coming!"

"So this is all *my* fault," I spat.

His shoulders drooped. "I didn't say that."

"All the ugly in my life was bleeding into yours."

"...Where there was *already* a shit ton of ugly," Bridger finished. He lifted his eyes to me again, an unreadable expression on his face. My heart tripped over itself like it always did when he met my gaze. He was only three feet away, yet I felt like we were separated by miles.

The door opened as we stood there glaring at each other.

Hartley came in, clearing his throat. "Okay, the bad news is that the Dean is at a conference in New York today. The good news is that his assistant blocked out an hour for you tomorrow at noon."

"Thanks, man."

"And I'm coming with you," Hartley added. "Would you let me do that?"

Bridger turned to face his friend. "Yeah, that would be good."

"We're going to get her back, Bridge. We can figure this out."

"Yeah." His voice held zero conviction.

"What do we do next? We could borrow a car and drive to the social services department." Hartley shifted his weight from foot to foot by the door, and my heart swelled to see that Bridger had friends who were ready to help him.

Bridger jammed his hands in his pockets. "Actually, we're waiting for Scarlet's uncle to call us back. He's looking into everything."

"Okay. What else, then?"

"Go to practice Hartley. You'll help me tomorrow."

Hartley hesitated. "You sure?"

"I am, man. Go."

But his friend didn't move right away. "I guess I finally get why you quit hockey."

Bridger sat down heavily on the bed. "Yeah. Now you do."

"You moron. I'm pissed that you didn't tell me." Bridger looked up at me, and we locked eyes while Hartley continued his rant. "I'm sure you had some noble fucking idea about handling it yourself."

"I know." Bridger's voice was flat.

Hartley heaved a great sigh. "You were a lot of help to me last year. Kinda kills me that you didn't ask."

"I'm sorry."

"Me too. I'll see you tomorrow." Without another word, Hartley turned around and left the room, pulling the door shut behind him.

After a couple of beats of silence, I spoke up. "You just had the same fight with Hartley that you picked with me."

Bridger's answer was almost a grunt. "I noticed." For a moment he only rubbed the back of his own neck. And then he moved fast. One moment he was sitting across from me, but in the next he'd closed that gap. He put his hands on my hips and hoisted me into the air, catching me in his arms. Then he backed up again, dropping onto the bed, cradling me in his lap. "I wish you would have explained it to me," he whispered.

I couldn't answer him, because I was trying really hard not to cry. It felt so good to have him holding me again.

"I need you, Scarlet. Even when things are really ugly. Especially then."

Tipping my face into Bridger's neck, I took a deep breath of him. He smelled of soap and comfort. I'd missed this so much. "I need you, too."

His voice became raspy as he asked me a question. "Is there some other guy?"

I shook my head vigorously. "I don't even know any other guys."

Bridger only sighed into my hair, and gathered me closer. We sat there a long time, just holding each other. When Bridger's phone finally rang, I jumped off his lap.

He lunged for it. "Hello?" After he listened for a minute,

I saw his shoulders relax. "Of course. Thank you. Let me get a pen." When Bridger began scribbling something onto his notebook, I got up to look over his shoulder. It was an address in the neighboring town of Orange.

"I'll call them before we come. Yeah, Scarlet has a car here. Sure. Okay. Thank you."

Bridger turned to me, holding out the phone. "He wants to talk to you."

I took the phone from him. "You found her?"

"She's with a foster family who takes in emergency cases. Bridger is going to be allowed to bring Lucy some of her clothes, and visit her tonight."

My eyes went to Bridger, who was now rustling around, pulling small t-shirts out of a drawer. "Wow, thank you."

"It's nothing. But, listen — he's not the type to do anything stupid, right? She has to stay with the foster family until this shit gets sorted out."

"No, it will be fine. He wouldn't... snatch her or whatever you're thinking."

"Good. Because he'll be no help to her in jail."

"I'm sure he understands that."

"Emotions run high in these situations. People do stupid things when they're afraid."

Don't I know it.

"Look, Sweetheart, I want to drive down there tomorrow. I'll help Bridger figure out some things, but also I'll get to see you too."

"Wow. Okay."

"I think I can get to you about nine. Can you make time for me then?"

I could if I skipped my last Italian study session before the exam. "Sure."

"Great. Can you give me your phone number?"

I hesitated. "We'll just use Bridger's number, okay? Not mine."

"Shit. Are your parents tracking you?"

"Yeah."

He cursed. "Hang in there, Sweetheart. I'll see you tomorrow."

Chapter Sixteen: *Dolphin Breath*

— Bridger

"It's going to be that green one — with the porch," I said as Scarlet idled down the little residential street. The street looked okay. Hell, some of these houses were probably a little nicer than the ones on the street we grew up on. But that didn't mean that anything about this was okay with me. And if Scarlet weren't sitting beside me, I'd probably be a cursing, ranting mess. Instead, I settled for just shaking like a leaf.

She brought her car to a stop in front of number 118, and I stared at it for a minute. The house needed a coat of paint, like, two years ago. And there were toys scattered around the front yard.

Scarlet put her hand on mine. "That's not so bad," she said softly.

"Right." At least there weren't weapons and live ammo lying around the front yard. Or crack vials.

"I'm going to wait here," she said, giving my hand a squeeze.

But I barely heard her, because the front door opened, and a woman stepped out. Behind her I could see Lucy standing there, her face pale and stricken.

A half second later I was out of the car and up the walk. Lucy flew out and down the steps. She launched herself at me, landing full force in my chest. I dropped the bag I was holding to catch her, to lift her up.

She shoved her face into my jacket and howled.

"Whoa, Lulu," I said, fighting for breath. For some reason my lungs did not want to expand properly, and my vision went blurry. "Hey, now," I choked out, rubbing her back.

While Lucy sobbed, the woman picked up the bag I'd dropped, and nudged me toward the porch steps. Somehow I climbed them, carrying Lucy into the house. A cluttered living room was just inside. I staggered over to an ottoman and sat on it, holding Lucy tight. I took a few deep, slow breaths until I had myself back under control.

Lucy's sobbing had progressed to the drippy, hiccupping stage, and I wiped her face with my hands. She was trying to calm down, but her fingers still had a vice-like grip on my jacket. "I've got you," I said, even though it was only half true, and both of us knew it.

"She d...d...died," Lucy stuttered, still drowning in her own tears.

"I know, buddy. I'm sorry about that." My throat threatened to close up again, so I cleared it.

"We should have..." she choked on her own words. "...The hospital, maybe. We didn't..." Lucy shoved her face into my jacket again.

Oh, fuck.

I pulled her head out where I could look her in the eyes. "No, buddy. Listen to me." Those green eyes were wild and scared, and it took a second before I had her attention. "She was sick, but she wouldn't go to the hospital. This is not your fault."

"She wouldn't go?"

I shook my head rather than lie again. It was true that I'd brought up treatment to my mother many times, and she

194

wouldn't discuss it with me. Whether I could have made a difference by actually hauling her selfish, bitchy ass to some kind of facility somewhere, we'll never know. By the time I was sure she needed some kind of violent intervention, I had Lucy on my hands. There was nothing I could have done.

At least, that's what I was going to keep telling myself. Probably for the next sixty years.

My sister seemed to have worn herself out from crying. Now she just lolled against me, and I got the feeling that both of us were catching our breath.

"I'm Amy," the foster mother said after a few minutes. "Are these Lucy's things in here?" she pointed at the bag.

"Yeah." My voice still thick. "Lulu, I brought you some clothes, and your PJs. And I brought Funny Bunny."

"I don't want to sleep here," she said into my t-shirt.

"I know you don't." I closed my arms around her. "But it's just temporary, until I get a chance to tell the judge that I should be the one who takes care of you." I chose my words carefully, making no promises.

"Why does the judge care?"

"When somebody's parent dies, they want to make sure you have a good home to live in."

"We can move back into the house," Lucy said. "You and me."

It made me swallow hard to hear Lucy trying to come up with a solution. That's all I'd done all semester — mentally rearrange the cards, trying to come up with a winning hand. I'd never managed it. "You're going to stay here with Amy until I can figure out what we're doing," I said.

"I have a room just for you," Amy said softly, from where she stood in the corner. "You can have some dinner and a bath. You'll go to school tomorrow, so your teacher doesn't miss you too much."

"No," Lucy said, her voice rising with a fresh wave of hysteria. "I just want to go *home*."

I took another slow breath. "I'll bet there's a bathtub," I said. One of Lucy's many complaints about Beaumont House was that she had to take showers.

"Don't care."

"Maybe your brother would fill it up for you," Amy hinted.

I scooped Lucy up and stood. Carrying her was still no problem, weight wise. But she was getting so big, she dangled down to my knees. It seemed like just last week when she was just a little lump on my hip when I carried her.

Following Amy, I headed upstairs. We passed a bedroom, where a man was sitting across a desk from another child, a dark-skinned little girl. They seemed to be bent over a sheet of homework. The man looked up as I passed, and winked.

Okay. So the place wasn't exactly a scene out of *Oliver Twist*. But I still couldn't believe that I was supposed to *leave* Lucy here. Christ.

Lucy didn't let me leave the bathroom while she bathed. I think she worried that I'd slip out, even though I'd promised not to. So I rinsed her hair with a plastic cup, and tried to get her to stop looking so scared.

We figured out afterward that while I'd remembered her toothbrush, I'd forgotten to bring her socks.

"It's no problem," Amy said. "I've got some."

Of course she did. Because Amy's house was set up to accommodate other people's nightmares.

While I cajoled Lucy into eating exactly one chicken

nugget and two tater tots, Amy gave me a little of her own story. She was a daycare provider for years, but now she took in emergency foster kids, because it seemed like she could do more for them.

I wanted to hate her, but she made it impossible.

Her husband Rich came through to shake my hand. To his wife he said, "Sheena is in bed, and waiting for you to say goodnight to her."

"If you'll excuse me a minute," Amy said, leaving the room.

They were perfectly nice people. And so even though I knew Lucy would be safe here, it didn't warm me to the idea of letting the state do its thing. Because not all foster parents were Amy. And at eight years old, Lucy had a decade before she would be out of the state's clutches. Even if I liked Amy, there was no guarantee that she could stay here. If the wind blew a different direction, Lucy could end up in some godawful place, with people who took in too many foster kids as a paycheck. And there wouldn't be a thing I could do about it.

Eventually the dreaded moment arrived.

"It's bed time, Lucy," I said softly. "I'll come back tomorrow after school."

"Can you pick me up?" Slowly, I shook my head. I was pretty sure that Amy would have to do that. Social services had allowed me "supervised visits" with Lucy. And I wasn't about to fuck that up.

As I watched, Lucy's eyes filled again.

"No, little buddy," I whispered, hugging her. "It's going to be okay."

"I just want to go with you."

"I know," I said into her hair. "I'm working on it."

"Tell them I want to live with you."

"I'll tell them."

"Tell them I don't care where it is."

"I'll say it a hundred times if I have to."

"A thousand."

"Okay, I'll say it a thousand *times* a thousand. Which is a million. Or a hundred times ten thousand. Or…"

"Shut *up*, Bridge," she hiccuped.

Amy tried to insert herself, maybe hoping that Lucy would release me. "Is there a book you'd like to read with me now?"

"We're reading Harry Potter," I said, trying to be helpful.

"No." Lucy turned to Amy with a grimace. "*You* can't read me Harry Potter. Only Bridger. He does the voices."

I eased Lucy back, so she was standing on her own. "Amy probably has a lot of books," I suggested. "Why don't you pick one out?"

She didn't budge. And a single tear dripped down her cheek.

"I have to go now," I said, my voice cracking again. "You can wave to Scarlet. She's waiting for me in the car."

Lucy's eyes traveled toward the door. So I made my move, one foot in front of the other. She followed me, but I kept going until I'd reached the front of the house, my hand on the door.

"No!" Lucy yelped, and I had to take a big breath in through my nose.

"Tomorrow, Lulu. I'll be back." I dropped a kiss onto her head, and then pushed the door open. "Now wave at Scarlet. See?"

At that, I stepped onto the porch. I knew I should

shake hands with Amy or whatever, but I didn't think I could do it. So I kept moving, opening the door to Scarlet's Cayenne, sliding in. My girlfriend started the engine. She lowered the passenger window and leaned across me, waving at Lucy.

I raised a hand too, forcing myself to look up then. Waving, I met Lucy's red eyes one more time. Tears ran down her brave face as she waved.

"Just drive," I choked out. Mercifully, the Porsche pulled away from the curb. Seconds later, we were half way down the block. And I could give up the charade. I put my elbows on my knees and let my head fall into my hands. My throat pooled and my hands dampened.

I just stayed that way, trying not to totally lose it, as the car glided through the little streets, accelerating as smoothly as all that German engineering allowed. When the car finally came to a stop, I mostly had my shit together. I looked up and out the windshield. "Where are we?"

"Whole Foods in Milford," Scarlet said, her voice quiet. She reached over and squeezed my knee. "We missed dinner. And lunch. When's the last time you ate?"

"I don't know." *Yesterday.*

"Do you want to come in with me, or shall I go?"

I blew out a breath, not wanting to answer. I wasn't exactly fit for public consumption.

"I'll be right back," Scarlet said, reaching back between our seats for her pocketbook.

I slid my hands around her torso, pulling her towards me. "Thank you," I said into her shoulder, my voice rough.

She dropped her pocketbook and slipped her arms around me. "Anytime, Bridge."

"Sorry I left you out in the car so long."

"It's nothing," she whispered, holding me tightly. "It

was awful?"

"Worst hours of my life." And I said that knowing that it could still get worse. There was a very real possibility that I'd have to sit in front of Lucy sometime soon and tell her that I'd failed. That the judge ruled me unfit. That the bank took our house. That the school put me on probation for breaking their rules. The possibilities sat like a cartoon anvil on my chest.

Scarlet trailed her fingers into my hair and gave me a single kiss on the neck. "Don't go anywhere," she said, releasing me. "I'll be back in five. Or ten, if the lines are brutal."

"I'll be here," I said. Because that was the largest promise that I was capable of keeping today. Only that.

Sitting in her car, we ate a startling quantity of overpriced sushi out of little plastic containers. And I actually began to feel better.

"There are two more pieces of California roll," Scarlet said, offering me the tray.

"I'm out," I had to say, rubbing my stomach. "Honestly, that was great, though. I haven't had sushi in forever." It was out of my price range. Lucy and I ate a lot of sandwiches that I made on my desktop. What judge would consider that a meal?

"It was the first thing I saw," Scarlet admitted. "But I haven't had it in a long time, either. The Turner dining hall doesn't do sushi." Her eyes flickered into mine. "I just wish I could do more, Bridger. Seriously. Feeding you is all I could think of."

Well, shit. I had to reach out then, cupping her face in my hands and pulling her in. Her lips were so soft against mine. I dropped kisses onto her lips, her jaw, her neck. I stroked her lip with my thumb, then kissed her again, gently asking her to open for me. I'd missed her so much. And even with my whole life falling apart, showing a little love for her was something I needed to do.

But she ducked my deeper kisses. "What?" I asked.

"I probably have dolphin breath," she said, aiming her mouth over my shoulder.

"Dolphin breath?"

"You know... I smell like a tuna."

I began to chuckle. And maybe it was because we'd been fighting, or maybe it was because this was the most stressful day in my life. But I found that hysterical. I laughed so hard my gut hurt. I laughed until my eyes were wet again, and Scarlet was sweeping her hands across my cheekbones, chasing tears away.

For the tenth time that day, I fought for control. "I don't really care if you have dolphin breath," I said, my stomach still tightening with ripples of laughter.

She put the car in reverse and turned to look over her shoulder. "Noted," she said, maneuvering out of the parking spot. "Let's just get back. Then you can prove it to me."

— Scarlet

When we got back to Beaumont house, Bridger's room was dark and quiet. Lucy's mattress sat in the middle of the floor, broadcasting its emptiness. Wordlessly, I stepped into him, wrapping my hands around his waist. He put his chin on my shoulder and sighed. "Stay with me?" he whispered.

"Of course."

While Bridger returned a couple of calls, I went next door to fill Andy in on all the horrible things that had happened that day.

"You're shitting me," he said, his eyes widening behind his glasses.

"Nope."

"Why can't he just catch a *break?*"

I wished I knew.

"What can I do to help?" he wanted to know.

"I'm not sure," I answered. "This is only a few hours old."

"You have my number, right? I could... call funeral homes or whatever. Put me to work."

"Thanks, Andy. I'm sure there will be something." My heart swelled with appreciation for Bridger's friends. Whatever happened, I hoped Bridger didn't have to drop out of school. This place was just too precious to lose.

I borrowed Bridger's toothbrush, and changed into one of his tees. We lay down together in his bed, both exhausted from the day's events. Bridger curled his big body around mine, the way I'd always hoped he would. There had been so many nights these past weeks when I'd wished for this — to have a few hours alone with him.

But it wasn't supposed to be like this.

I slept awhile. But the bed was tiny. And so sometime in the night, I woke while trying unsuccessfully to roll over. When I opened my eyes, Bridger was lying on his back, staring up at the ceiling.

"Bridge," I whispered. "What are you thinking about?"

"Stuffed meatloaf," he said immediately.

"Um... what?"

"Stuffed meatloaf. With mashed potatoes inside. It was my mother's signature dish."

I propped myself on an elbow so I could see him better.

"Was it good?"

"Not really. I could never figure out why she went to the trouble. The potatoes would have been just as good on the side. And it took like an hour to assemble. Lucy asked me a couple of weeks ago if I'd make it for her. I had to tell her that you can't cook meatloaf in a microwave."

For a moment, we both listened to the dormitory's nighttime silence. Until I broke it. "I'm sorry about your mom, Bridge."

He made a face. "She did it to herself."

"Maybe it's not that simple. She made some mistakes, and then her body wouldn't let her out from under them."

"I never even saw her try."

I didn't argue, because it wasn't my place. Instead, I dropped my head to his shoulder and massaged his sternum with my hand.

"What do we owe them?" he asked.

"Who?"

"The parents who fuck up so badly. How much should we put up with as payment for being born?"

God, wasn't that the question of the hour? "I don't know. But I think about it all the time."

"I bet you do." Bridger's hand skimmed down the hair at the back of my head, and I snuggled in tighter.

"I feel guilty," I admitted.

"For what?"

"It depends on the day of the week. I was so oblivious, just living my own life, you know? So I feel bad for the victims. But other times, I worry that there's a zero-point-zero-zero-one percent chance that he didn't do it. And yet I've tried and convicted him ahead of schedule. Basically, I just feel guilty all the time. It's just that the focus shifts around."

"You're a good person, Scarlet Crowley."

Even though I'd heard it many times by now, the name sounded strange to my ears. "You're a good person, Bridger McCaulley."

"I'll try to believe it if you'll do the same."

"It's a deal," I told him.

Chapter Seventeen: *A Lot of Shifts at the Coffee Counter*

— Scarlet

"Wow," Bridger said. "That has to be him. He looks just like you."

I looked out of the coffee shop window to see my uncle striding toward the double glass doors. I hadn't spent enough time with Brian to bother checking for a resemblance. But it was true. My uncle and I had the same indecisive eye color, and the same wave to our hair. "You're right," I said. "That's him."

Bridger stood up. He'd dressed up in khakis and a button-down shirt today. But there was no hiding the exhaustion in his eyes.

Brian pushed through the doors, his gaze immediately scoping laser-like onto me. In a few long strides he'd reached me, pulling me against his chest in a powerful embrace. "My God, you're all grown up." He laughed, but the sound was sad. "So tall." He inhaled deeply and then stepped back, still holding my arms, and just staring at me.

"Thank you for coming," I said, feeling suddenly shy.

"Any time."

"This is Bridger," I said as Brian released me.

They shook hands, and Brian sat down.

But I didn't. "I'm going to get coffee for everyone. What do you drink?" I asked my uncle.

He put a hand on my arm, giving me a gentle squeeze. "Coffee black, one sugar packet. Thank you, Sweetie."

By the time I got back, they were deep in discussion. And

Bridger had begun to take notes on the pad in front of him.

"You have a real shot at guardianship," Uncle Brian said. "You're old enough, with great prospects and no criminal record. If her teacher will stand up in the courtroom and tell the judge that you've done a great job this year, that will help, too."

Bridger wrote 3rd grade teacher on his notebook. "Mrs. Rose is great, and she'll help us. But I just don't see why a judge would approve me," Bridger said.

"You're looking at it the wrong way," Brian insisted. "They *want* to keep families together. It's good common sense, and it saves the state money. It sounds like your biggest obstacle is housing."

"That's where the dean comes in," I put in. "He'll help you figure out your options."

Bridger was still frowning. "Even if they help me find somewhere legal to live, it will cost money. Which I don't have. A judge wants to see some income, no?"

"The money isn't as important as you think," Brian said. "Lucy has her own income, right? Her social security benefit will cover a lot of expenses."

Bridger's face was blank.

"Your father has passed, correct? And Lucy is under eighteen. She's entitled to his survivor's benefit. And now your mother's."

"But... my parents weren't retired when they died," Bridger said.

Uncle Brian shook his head. "Makes no difference. If any working adult dies leaving a minor child, the child earns a benefit until she turns eighteen. Did you ever see any mail coming into your house from the Social Security Administration?"

Bridger's eyes went wide. "Yeah I did."

"That was Lucy's check."

"*Fuck*. My mother probably spent it on..." Bridger let the sentence die, dropping his head into his hands.

Brian put a hand on his shoulder. "That's your ticket to providing for her. The judge will already know that."

"But how did *I* not know that?" Bridger asked the tabletop.

Because you don't ask anyone for help. Somehow I managed to keep that sentiment to myself. But it wasn't easy.

"How much money are we talking about?" Bridger asked.

"It depends on how many years your parents paid into Social Security. More than a thousand dollars a month, though."

My boyfriend's eyes opened wide. "*Damn*. That's a lot of shifts at the coffee counter."

"You'll have to contact the Social Security Administration," Brian said. "They need to know about your mother's death."

Bridger picked up his pen. "I'll add it to the list."

By the time Bridger's notes reached the bottom of the page, Brian had him feeling cautiously optimistic. "If the college helped me with housing, I might not have to drop out," he said.

"Dropping out should be your very last resort," Brian said, his voice gentle. "Now, if you'd consider completing your degree *before* you petitioned for guardianship..."

Bridger was shaking his head before Brian even got the words out. "I'm not waiting. I can't look Lucy in the eye and tell her that I feel like finishing school before she gets out of there."

Brian was silent for a moment, and I could see him choosing his words carefully. "I know she's important to you. But there's a big difference between the job you could get right now, and the job you can get eighteen months from now. It's not selfish to wait. Your sister would also benefit from a Harkness diploma on your wall."

Bridger rubbed his temples. "I get that. I do. But she benefits more by not being in the system for two years. I'm sure that there are good foster parents in the world. But you can't tell me that there aren't any creepers out there."

My uncle's eyes pinched shut for a second, and I saw him take a deep breath. "She's lucky to have you."

My uncle didn't press Bridger about his choices after that, and I loved him for it. I could tell just from a couple of hours in his presence that he was probably a kick-ass social worker. There was a calm way about him, and a lack of judgment.

Basically, he was the complete opposite of my father.

"How soon do you think I can get a hearing?" Bridger asked.

"I'm going to find that out for you while you meet with the dean," Brian said. "You'll need a lawyer, of course. The Harkness Law School probably has a pro bono program. I'll try to find a phone number for it."

"God, could this ever work?" Bridger asked, his eyes flashing with emotion.

Brian stood up. "I've stood in a lot of courtrooms with people who wanted custody of their kids, and I'd say you look like a better candidate than about ninety percent of them."

"But how many of them win?" Bridger grumbled.

"*Lots*," Brian answered. "Now I'm going to the courthouse to poke around and ask questions. You're meeting the dean. And Scarlet is going to study for her exams."

"I am?" I asked. Concentrating on schoolwork right now sounded impossible.

Bridger kissed me on the cheek. "We can't both flunk out. I'll call you as soon as I know more."

— Bridger

"Hey." Hartley was waiting for me outside Dean Darling's office, a somber expression on his face.

"Hey. Thanks for coming."

"Any time," he said, pushing off the wall. "You ready?"

"Let's do this," I said with more bravado than I felt. Hartley turned the old brass doorknob and ducked into the dean's ancient little office suite. I felt like I was walking to my doom. Since July I'd been pretending that I could pull it off, that I could take care of Lucy and be a full-time student like everybody else. I wasn't looking forward to being told to lower my expectations.

Dean Darling's secretary waved us inside, coming around her desk to take my hand. "Oh honey," she said, "I'm so sorry for your loss."

"Thank you, Shirley." This was all feeling way too familiar. When my father died, I walked around with a tight throat for a month as each neighbor and teacher in my life tried to comfort me.

It never worked.

The dean's office door opened, and the man himself beckoned to us. Hartley and I filed past him, taking seats in the spindly old wooden chairs opposite his desk. I'd never had to sit here before, thank God. Until this year, my academic career at Harkness had been smooth sailing.

Not anymore.

"I am very sorry to hear that you have lost your mother,"

the dean began. He had a fusty British accent.

"Thank you, sir."

"Please know that your final exams should be the last thing on your mind right now. You will take them whenever you are ready to do so. I've already reached out to your professors."

"Uh, thank you." I wondered how accommodating he was going to sound in a minute when I told him just how messy my life really was.

"I read in your file this morning that your father is already deceased. Do you have other relatives in the area? I ask because I'm worried for all the things you might be expected to take care of. A death is not only devastating but comes with a great load of bureaucratic hassle. There is a funeral to plan, and decisions to be made. Is there anyone who will help you with that?" The dean put his elbows on the desk and studied me.

"There, uh..." I started. *Shit.* "There are bigger problems than that. My sister has been placed with social services, and I have to get her back."

The Dean's face softened. "I was going to ask about Lucy next. Her name is also in your file."

"Yeah. This semester I've been..." I scratched the back of my neck.

"Just spit it out, Bro," Hartley whispered.

So I did. I told the Dean that I'd had Lucy with me in my room at Beaumont since July. And that getting her back was going to have to take precedence over everything, including, unfortunately, my next term at Harkness. And while I told my whole sordid tale, he watched me with a calm expression on his face. They probably teach that at Dean School — how to listen to fucked-up situations without scowling.

When I finished, it was quiet for a moment. He set down the gold pen he'd been fiddling with and said, "I wondered about the pink bicycle in the rack." Then he leaned back in his chair and folded his arms behind his head. "What you want is not an easy thing."

"I know," I grumbled. "The judge is going to laugh me out of there."

Dean Darling moved quickly, slapping his hands onto the desk blotter. "Dear boy, that is not true. And that is not what I meant. It's not an easy thing to be a student and take care of a child."

I just shrugged. "I'm already doing that. Taking care of an eight year old is a piece of cake. It's not like when she was little, and I had to follow her around all day making sure she didn't swallow pennies."

Dean Darling toyed with his tidy beard for a moment before speaking again. "You make a fine point, and it's obvious that you have more experience with childcare than I do. However, raising a girl into her teenage years would not be easy. And you'd be making every decision alone."

Bridger shrugged. "I'm going to be involved, no matter what. If the state says she has to live with someone else, that only makes it harder. It will limit the jobs I can take after graduation, if I have to stick close by. I'm not... This isn't a *whim*, for me, sir. It's my life."

The dean's voice was quiet when he spoke next. "A few times a year I have a student in my office, sitting in that chair, whose problems are vast. And usually there isn't a thing I can do about it. Often, the student's academic effort has lapsed so badly that it's too late. Occasionally, there have been mind-altering substances, paid for with his father's money. And he wants me to fix it all."

For a moment, the dean turned his head to look out the window into the courtyard. Then he turned to face me again. "Then we have you, Bridger McCaulley. You have a thick file with nothing in it but achievements, and no sign that anyone ever made that easier. Except for friends like Mr. Hartley here. Another of our hard-working achievers."

I glanced at Hartley, and found my friend watching the dean intently. Like me, he didn't have a clue where this was going.

"Shirley!" the dean called in a loud voice.

A moment later the door sprang open and her face appeared. "Yes?"

"I need you to find me a law school professor who hasn't left town for the holidays. Start with Blackwell or Potter. We are going to need some legal advice. And one of those gents will know whom to ask."

She closed the door and disappeared.

"Bridger," the dean began, and my name sounded more highbrow in his accent. "We are not going to throw up our hands and let you walk away from your Harkness degree. I have never solved this particular problem for a student before, but if it can be done, we will find a way." He took a binder off his bookshelf and flipped it open. "There is something called Married Student Housing. You may qualify for an apartment there if you have a minor child in your care." Dean Darling picked up his phone. "I'm going to ask the dean of graduate studies. One moment."

Hartley gave me a light smack on the arm with the back of his hand. "There you go," he said under his breath.

It's not a done deal yet, I cautioned myself. But a bubble of hope had already begun to swell inside my chest. While the dean made his call, I tried to tamp it back down.

Chapter Eighteen: *Approach the Bench*

— *Bridger*

The weekend was a blur of phone calls, meetings with lawyers, and visits to Lucy. While the rest of the student body hunkered down in the libraries, Scarlet and I survived on coffee, and practically lived out of her car.

But it was all worth it. On Monday morning, the lawyer that Dean Darling hooked me up with secured an emergency court date for the next afternoon. That left Scarlet and I pacing around my room, frantically phoning everyone involved.

"Brian is going to come to the hearing," Scarlet said after hanging up with him. She handed me my phone.

"Thank God it's in the late afternoon," I said. "So Lucy's teacher can be there. I left two messages for the dean already. I'm almost ready to storm his office if he doesn't call me back."

"He will," Scarlet said, kissing me on top of the head. "This is all going to work. Brian wanted to remind you to make sure you have something to wear that's appropriate for court."

"Oh, fuck." I looked down at myself. Old jeans? *Check.* Faded Harkness t-shirt? *Check.*

My girlfriend laughed. "Do you own a suit? Or are we driving to the mall right now?"

"I have a good sport coat and pants. But my ties are all stained."

"That's easy. We don't even have to leave town for a tie. How about a good shirt?"

"Define 'good,'" I said.

Scarlet tugged me out of my desk chair. "Come on. Time to go shopping."

"Right now?"

"Show me some hustle, McCaulley. There's not much time before the buzzer."

"You look great," Scarlet promised me the next afternoon while straightening my tie.

But I was too busy trying not to sweat through my shirt to agree with her. "Let's go," I said.

"Brian is waiting for you on Elm Street," she said, shrugging on her coat.

I held my room door open for Scarlet to pass. "Waiting for *us*, right?"

She paused on the landing, shaking her head. "I can't go with you."

"Why not?" She'd worked tirelessly with me these past few days. I couldn't imagine why she wouldn't want to see the outcome.

"Think about it," she whispered. "I'm not vain enough to imagine the judge will recognize me. But if there's even a tiny chance that some reporter hanging around at the courthouse knew who I was... you don't need that. You don't want the name Ellison associated with your custody case. Plus, my phone is going to show me sitting at the library while you're in court."

"Scarlet, can we please get rid of that crap on your phone now? Would you cut those assholes loose so I can stop worrying about you?"

"Soon," she promised, her eyes flicking away from me.

I wanted to argue. But I was out of time. So I kissed her instead, and went off to find her uncle.

"Always refer to a judge as 'your honor,'" Brian reminded me.

"Right." I'd probably watched enough cop shows to keep that straight. It's just that my head was buzzing with anxiety as we walked into the courtroom.

There were more people inside than I expected to see. *Jesus*. They were all there for me. Hartley and his mother sat together on a bench next to the men's hockey coach, of all people. Lucy's teacher nodded to me from the other side of the aisle, where she was seated with Dean Darling. Andy Baschnagel and *his parents* sat behind them. Holy fuck. At least I wouldn't have to tell anyone the bad news after I got shot down.

My young lawyer beckoned me over to take a seat in front. "I'll be speaking for you. But allow me to introduce you to the head of the litigation department at the law school, Judge Blackwell."

I offered him my hand. "It's good to meet you, sir..." I caught myself. "*Judge*."

Christ. One minute into the courtroom and I'd already fucked it up.

The older man just chuckled. "As long as the guy sitting up there..." he nodded toward the dais, "is 'your honor,' then it's all good."

"Thank you for coming," I said, although I wasn't entirely sure why he was here.

"Dean Darling and I play squash together at this hour of the week, usually," the older man said. "Since he had to cancel, I thought I'd come and watch one of my students at his first courtroom appearance."

"Thank you," I said again. God, I was nervous. Then I saw Lucy's foster parents appear in the doorway. I looked behind them, but my sister did not appear. "Where's Lucy?" I asked my lawyer.

"The child does not attend the hearing," he said quickly. "It's too traumatic when things don't work out."

I felt a stab right in the middle of my sternum. "That makes sense," I said quickly. I yanked at my collar, which suddenly seemed too tight. If the judge said no, I was going to have to make her cry. *Again.*

"Deep breaths," my lawyer said.

"All rise for the honorable Richard Cranmore!"

"It's show time," the retired judge muttered.

We turned our attention to the front of the room, where a gray-haired man climbed the dais and sat behind the bench.

"You may be seated," the clerk said.

The judge opened a file folder in front of him, and then looked out into the courtroom. "Good gracious," he said, fiddling with the reading glasses hanging around his neck. "I've got a dean and half the law school faculty in my courtroom today. Who is minding the college?"

A low chuckle traveled the room, but I was too busy sweating to find the comment funny.

Judge Cranmore scanned the paperwork in front of him. "Emergency petition for guardianship," he read. "Will Mr. Bridger McCaulley please approach the bench?"

I got up, and my two lawyers followed me.

The judge looked up from the file when I came to stand before him. "Petition for guardianship of Lucy J. McCaulley, made by Bridger McCaulley. Petitioner's relationship to the minor child is sibling. Is that a full sibling?"

"Yes, your honor," my lawyer said. "Their birth certificates are included in the file."

"Sorry, yes," the judge said, flipping pages. "Supporting documents include statements from the child's school teacher, foster parents, friends of the family... quite the file you've assembled here."

"They are all here today," the lawyer said. "The teacher would be happy to speak to you. Her statement describes Lucy's exemplary attendance and participation at school during the months she lived with her brother in his dorm room."

I tried not to flinch. But *seriously*. How did I not foresee that we would end up here?

The judge flipped through the statements in the file and then looked down at me. "You're a full-time student. Will you be able to continue your studies with custody of the child?"

The lawyer spoke up again. "Your honor, legal guardianship will actually make things easier for Mr. McCaulley, as he has been providing full support under strained circumstances. His custodial plan is in the file."

The judge waved a hand. "I've reviewed it. I just want to hear it from him."

I swallowed hard. "There are only two things I want to do. The first is to make a home for Lucy, and the second is finish my degree. I might have, uh, arranged things better. But I know I can do both. I've always taken care of her." From my back pocket, I pulled one of the photographs that I'd removed from our house in the fall. It showed Lucy in a baby carrier on my chest while I read a geometry textbook.

I'd been fourteen or fifteen when the picture was taken.

The judge looked at the picture for a long moment. Then

he beckoned a social worker toward the bench. "Does the state have any concerns about this potential arrangement?"

"Housing, your honor," the social worker assigned to the case said. "But I've been told that the College will provide suitable housing if guardianship is approved."

The judge lifted his eyes to the crowd in front of him. "Who would like to speak to that?"

Dean Darling stood up. "The McCaulley family will be afforded a small two-bedroom apartment in one of our graduate student buildings. Since Mr. McCaulley is part-way through a masters degree in cell biology, I did not even have to apply much force to the graduate dean's arm to get him to free up a unit. Mr. McCaulley's financial aid will cover about two thirds of the cost, and I'm told that the child's survivor's benefits will cover the balance. In addition, a hockey alumnus has generously stepped forward to supply both Mr. McCaulley and his ward with a dining hall meal plan for the second semester. Their new apartment has a kitchen, of course, but they will not need to use it until summertime, if they so wish."

"That is generous indeed," the judge said, and I had to agree. What's more, it was shocking. I didn't know any hockey alumni.

Dean Darling cleared his throat. "There are many people here who wish to see our student succeed. He has never asked for our help, but we want him to know that he is welcome to it."

"Well," the judge said with a nod. "Then we shall free up another place in our straining foster care system."

My gut stumbled when he said foster care, and so I didn't process the whole sentence. But then his next words sunk in. "Emergency motion for temporary guardianship approved." Just like on TV, he tapped a gavel against its base. "We'll revisit in three months to make sure that all conditions of the custody plan have been met."

I stood there a moment longer, replaying his words in my head, hoping that I'd just heard what I thought I heard.

Behind me, Theresa and Hartley let out a cheer.

— Scarlet

"Tomorrow?" I squealed into the phone at Bridger, who was breathless with relief. "Why can't you have her back tonight?"

"Paperwork," he scoffed. "But I got to give her the good news myself, over the phone. And Amy and Rich offered to take her to Chuck E. Cheese's to celebrate. And there's nothing like a little bribe to get you over the hump."

I laughed. "Where are you guys? I'm just walking back to Vanderberg." I'd been in the library, studying for my stats exam.

"It took me awhile to get out of there," he said. "I had to thank a whole lot of people who came to show their support, even though the judge didn't call on anyone except the dean. Now we're parking Brian's car about one minute away from you. Wait for us outside?"

"Sure." I hung up the phone and tried not to feel creeped out by the fact that Bridger's number would pop up on Azzan's spy report. Shoving the phone into my purse, I decided that it was time to let Luke take the spywear off. I'd left it on long enough that my father's handlers wouldn't assume that I'd noticed their spying. And it had occurred to me that if I traded up for a newer phone, the transition would look accidental.

I was so distracted by my own scheming that I didn't notice who was waiting for me outside of Vanderberg.

"Hi Scarlet."

I lifted my chin to find the district attorney Madeline Teeter standing outside my entryway door. "I told you I couldn't talk to you," I said immediately.

"I know you did," she said evenly. "But if you'll give me thirty seconds, I can explain why I came all the way down here to ask you a single question about the layout of your family home."

The layout of our house? That piqued my interest, although it didn't make much sense. The police had combed through the place with their search warrants several times after the arrest.

"Scarlet?" Bridger arrived, his arm coming around my shoulders. Brian joined us, too, flanking my other side. "Who is this?"

"The prosecutor," Brian supplied. "She interviewed me two months ago, after which J.P.'s security team followed me around Massachusetts for three days."

"I can't talk to you," I repeated. If I did, Azzan would find out, and then he'd threaten Bridger again. And I would do anything to spare him that heartache.

"Your father won't find out," Ms. Teeter said, reading my mind. "We're never putting you on our witness list."

"You can't promise me that," I protested. "Besides, I'm already on the list."

She shook her head. "That's just a front the defense is putting up. They'll never call you to the stand."

"Why not?" I asked.

The prosecutor rubbed her hands together. "I'd prefer to explain it to you in the office I'm borrowing downtown."

"Explain it to her here," my Uncle Brian said.

"Fine." She trained her serious blue eyes on me. "I'm not

putting you on the stand, because asking a daughter to testify against her father looks desperate. Unless the daughter has something crucial to say."

"Which I don't," I put in.

"I'm sure that's true," she said kindly. "If you did, your father's legal team wouldn't dare make you available. But they're not going to call you either, and I can prove it."

"Go ahead," Brian said.

The prosecutor pulled a file out of the elegant leather satchel she carried over her arm. Under the other arm was a paper tube, as if she were toting a poster around. "If your father puts you on the stand as a ploy to defend himself, I'm going to call a witness by the name of David Clancy."

That made no sense. "My hockey teammate's father? Why?"

"Because he — and several others, too — gave a deposition about your father's behavior toward you during hockey games. And it is not the kind of thing your father wants a jury to hear. Your father filled in as your team coach for a couple of games two years ago. Do you remember that?"

I nodded, steeling myself. Our regular coach had been out of town for a funeral. And with Dad in charge, I'd been a wreck. Those games did not go well for me, and now both my boyfriend and my uncle were going to hear the gory details.

"The witness said that you gave up two goals within three minutes, and your father was heard to shout…"

This next part was going to be even more humiliating than my hockey errors.

"…*You stupid little bitch. Only a whore could get herself fucked so hard as you just did.*"

Beside me, Bridger's body went absolutely solid, and Uncle Brian cursed under his breath.

"That sounds really bad out of context," I said, my face getting hot.

"Out of *context?*" Bridger's voice was tight. "There is no context in which that is an acceptable thing to say to your child."

"I was sixteen," I said, pointlessly. I don't know why I gave even a half-hearted defense of my father. Maybe because I felt like an idiot for living with a man who would say those things to me without realizing that he was capable of far worse.

Beside me, Uncle Brian bent down to put his hands on his knees, dropping his head.

"Are you okay?" Bridger asked, looking down at him.

"Give me a minute," he muttered.

"Please, Scarlet," the prosecutor said. "I will only ask you questions about the layout of your home. And your uncle can sit in on the interview. If you don't like the questions, you can just get up and leave. But I need this. And the boys who were victims need this."

My father had called me a whore in front of a few hundred people. But those boys got much worse.

"Okay," I heard myself say.

"The office is on South Street," she said.

"We just came from there," Bridger said.

Brian straightened up, his face red and strained. "I guess we're going back."

Ten minutes later, I found myself sitting in a little government conference room, which the prosecutor had borrowed from her colleagues in the Harkness County prosecutor's office. The tube she'd been carrying under her arm proved to be a detailed architectural floor plan of my New

Hampshire home. She and her assistant spread it out on the table.

"I need to ask you about your basement," Ms. Teeter said. "It doesn't seem very basement-like."

"Well, it's a walk-out," I supplied, pointing at the drawing. "These sliding glass doors open into the back yard. The house is on a slope, so only one side of the basement is really underground."

"And there aren't any walls or partitions down there?" she asked.

I shook my head. "The drawing is accurate."

She nodded. "Tell us about this utility space." She pointed at the little mechanical room under the stairs. "Is it roomy?"

"Not at all," I said. "You can barely get in there. My mother has always kept her Christmas wrapping paper in there, but I discovered it when I was in the second grade."

Brian let out a strangled chuckle and pinched the sides of his nose.

"Is it insulated?" the prosecutor pressed. "If someone was in there, could you hear it?"

"There's no way it's insulated," I said. "Why are you asking me this?"

She sighed. "There are some old stories about a basement. Or a dungeon. But there's nothing dungeon-like in your house. In fact, there isn't even a *door* on your basement."

That was true. It was all very airy and open.

"This has bothered me," the prosecutor confessed, "because I want rock-solid details in court. And — no matter what people say about lawyers — I want my complaint to be completely truthful. I don't have time for exaggeration. And this dungeon bit doesn't ring true to me. Has the basement *changed* at all in the last ten years? Did your parents have any work done down there?"

I shook my head. "The only renovations in the house that I can remember were the kitchens and bathrooms."

"The basement wasn't touched?"

"No. It was finished and modern when we moved into the place. That's why they chose to knock down the *other* house when they bought that second property. That one was really old..." I broke off that sentence. Something bothered me about that idea, and I couldn't figure out what.

"A second house?" the prosecutor asked, her voice hushed.

"Yes..." Again, my brain snagged on something. "My father wanted a big yard, so he could have an ice rink..." I pictured the rink and the yard. And the dark, shadowed corner of the property where I did not like to walk, ever since our yard had doubled in size.

"There are doors," I croaked, surprised at myself.

"What doors?" the prosecutor asked.

"There are..." I swallowed hard, and my throat was like sandpaper. "...Those doors in the ground. Like in *The Wizard of Oz*." I slapped my hand down at the edge of the floor plan. "Over there. Off the edge of your map. They were part of the old house."

The prosecutor locked eyes with her assistant. "Call the investigator. Check the search warrant to make sure that outbuildings are covered."

The assistant bolted out of the room, and a terrible shiver ripped down my spine. Those doors had always scared me. I never wanted to go near them. When I was eight or nine, I thought that monsters lived down there.

"Oh my God," I gasped, shoving my hands in front of my

mouth.

"Whoa," Brian asked, standing up from his chair so fast that it fell over. "This interview is over. We're done here."

The prosecutor held up two hands in a defensive position. "Okay. No more questions. And I'm going to step out. The room is yours. Scarlet, you've been very helpful."

I didn't answer her. Because there were tears stinging my eyes. I'd *heard* something in that abandoned old cellar. I was in grade school, and I was dawdling outside when I was supposed to be doing my homework. And I'd heard muffled shouting from that corner of my yard. "Oh my God," I said again. "Oh my God."

"Shh, shh," Brian said, righting his chair and pulling it close. He sat, wrapping his arms around me. "Shh. I'm so sorry."

"I think there was somebody *down there* once," I squeaked.

Brian swiped at my tears. "Sweetie, were *you* ever down there?"

Violently, I shook my head. "Never. I didn't really *know*. I didn't know. I didn't know. *I didn't know*."

He pulled my head into his shoulder. "You didn't know," he whispered, rocking me. "It's okay."

"It's not!"

"You didn't *hurt* anyone, Sweetie. You were a child. Just breathe for me. Deep breaths."

Slowly, I forced myself to calm down. "Can we leave, now? I really want to go." Maybe if I just got out of this room, the world would stop tilting.

"Whenever you're ready," Brian said. "Let's go and eat somewhere. We need to decompress."

"Decompress," I repeated, stupidly. When I looked up, I

saw Bridger standing very still across the table from us. His head was cocked to the side, as if trying to solve a puzzle. "Bridge?"

He stared for another long moment. "Sure, Scarlet," he said eventually. "Let's go."

Chapter Nineteen: *Take a Look at the News*

— Scarlet

Bridger took us to Capri's, which was a hole-in-the-wall pizza joint where the hockey team often hung out. But it was too early for the bar crowd, so we had a booth in the back corner all to ourselves. We ate a pie with sausage and olives. Bridger drank a beer while Brian and I had Cokes.

I snuggled against Bridger's shoulder, feeling worn out. I didn't know what to do with the suspicion that I'd heard something potentially terrible. And so long ago, too. I'd been Lucy's age when I'd started avoiding that corner of the yard.

"The dean said I'll have an apartment over on Osage Street before Christmas," Bridger said. "Apparently, things always turn over during the holidays, because some people depart over the semester break. Until then, Lucy will stay one more week in Beaumont, and maybe a week at Hartley's if we need it." He loosened his tie. "This week has been my worst nightmare. Thank you both for talking me through it."

"You are welcome," Brian said. "I'm happy for you." My uncle began to play with the straw in his drink, then. His face became somber. "But now we need to spend a little time talking about my worst nightmare."

"What do you mean?" I asked.

My uncle turned serious eyes on me. "There are some things you need to understand about your family."

"Okay?" I watched his eyebrows knit together.

"Did you know your father and I were adopted?"

"No. Really?"

"Really. Your grandparents aren't your blood relatives."

"He never said anything about it." But that wasn't surprising. My father wasn't a sharer. Not about anything.

"Your so-called grandfather..." Brian cleared his throat. "It was by design that he adopted two little *boys*."

Oh.

My insides clenched at the direction that I feared his story was taking.

Brian dropped his gaze to the tabletop. "He wasn't a good man. And it messed both of us up pretty bad. You already know some of what it did to me. I drank and I stole things. But J.P...." he sighed. "I thought J.P. had held it together. He was the one of us who seemed to rise above it. He was the big hockey star, with the great big career. That's what I thought, anyway. Until the news broke."

Oh.

"Shan..." he cut off the word. "Scarlet, I had no idea. And I just feel sick about this. I need to ask you something very important."

"Okay."

Brian looked up at Bridger and hesitated. "I'm sorry, man. But can she and I talk alone for a minute?"

Concern crossed Bridger's face. "If that's what Scarlet wants."

I reached across the table to put my hand on Brian's sleeve. "No. Whatever you have to say, he can hear." I was sick of hiding things from Bridger.

"Sweetie, I need to ask you a really personal question."

"*No*," I said. Brian opened his mouth to argue, but I stopped him. "I meant, no, my father never hurt me."

Brian's eyes welled up. "Sweetie, it's really important that you tell me the truth." His eyes flicked to Bridger again. "If he did hurt you, it would be really hard to talk about."

"I *would* tell you the truth. I *am* telling you the truth. Just like I told Bridger when he asked me the same thing. I'm not lying about this."

He still looked wary. "Sometimes people make themselves forget."

I shook my head. "Look, he wasn't a good dad. But... nothing like that ever happened. He yelled, Brian. About hockey, usually. But that's the worst thing I ever saw him do."

The tears spilled down Brian's face. "God, Scarlet. I hope that's so. Because that right there is *my* worst nightmare."

I felt Bridger squeeze my hand, and I squeezed back.

Brian blew out a long, shuddering breath. "I would never forgive myself..." he let the sentence die.

Bridger was still squeezing my hand. Actually, he squeezed it so hard it was beginning to hurt. "Ouch," I said gently. Bridger released my hand immediately. But he was staring hard at Brian.

"What's wrong, Bridge?" I asked.

My boyfriend chewed on his lip. "Dude, I have a question."

Brian looked up, wiping his eyes with his hands. "What?"

"Are you and J.P. blood relatives?"

At that, Brian grew very still. He didn't answer Bridger. His gaze fell to the tabletop again.

Bridger looked from Brian to me and back again. "Come on, it's a simple yes or no question. You and J.P. were both adopted. From the same parents, or not?"

"Why?" I asked, hating the sudden tension at the table. I didn't understand it.

Brian shook his head at Bridger.

"Well, shit," Bridger said. "Seriously? Are you going to…?"

"Hey, back off for a second."

"Why would I?" Bridger challenged.

"Back off *what?*" I cried.

"Take a good look at Brian, Scarlet. Your adopted *uncle*…"

Brian smacked a fist onto the table. "Give me a fucking minute, hothead." His face was red. "I'll get there, okay?"

"You are both scaring me," I said quietly.

Bridger forced himself to lean back against the wooden booth. Then he took both of my hands in his. "I'm sorry, Scarlet. Don't be scared."

But I was. Because as I studied Brian, and I had a sick feeling that I knew what he was about to say.

"Your mother," Brian said slowly, each word painful. "She and J.P. made me sign a document as thick as the phone book that I would never tell you this. And when I do, they will try to destroy me. I agreed to keep it a secret, because I was a stupid kid, and I thought it was the right thing to do."

The edges of my vision got a little fuzzy, because I feared hearing the next part.

Brian flexed his hands against the scarred wooden tabletop and dropped his voice. "I got your mother pregnant when we were nineteen."

Somehow, I managed not to gasp out loud.

"…And by the time she found out about it, I was in jail." He stared at me with wet eyes. "Sweetie…"

"So, J.P. isn't… He's not…?"

"J.P. is not your father. I am."

My throat constricted so suddenly that I had trouble

asking the next question. "I'm not even *related* to him?" Never before today had it ever occurred to me that my father was not really my father. At the edges of my shock, I could feel an oncoming wave of relief. I was having the reverse of a Star Wars moment. Darth Vader had no claim on me.

Brian shook his head. "That's the only silver lining here."

But the emotions were rolling over me, and it seemed they'd never stop. "But... you *left* me with him?"

"I know, honey. But your mother..." he closed his eyes, looking utterly exhausted. "I'm not excusing it. But it was her idea. She wanted his money, and the lifestyle. And he wanted... I never quite knew what he wanted from this deal. He wanted a family. He said he couldn't have children. And maybe it's even true. Now I think he just wanted to be a part of a normal-looking family. He was hiding behind you and your mother. I didn't ask myself why he wanted this weird bargain. But for years, I thought they knew best. You were doing so well."

"How do *you* know? You weren't even *there!*"

"I tried," he whispered. "But they didn't trust me. One hockey game a year. That's what they gave me." Tears ran down his face. "I didn't know he was going to *hurt kids.*"

"I could fucking kill you right now," Bridger said, his voice like gravel.

"*I* could fucking kill me right now," Brian spat. "This year has been... I couldn't find her. I even came to campus here and walked around, looking for you, Sweetie. There was no Shannon Ellison in the directory." He threw his hands in the air. "I'm so sorry. I went to your house last year, they threw me out. Their thugs threw me out. Their legal team came down on me hard. That asshole Azzan had me tailed on and off, just to be intimidating."

"Okay," I breathed. I could feel the stress coming off Brian in waves. I reached across the table and grabbed both his hands. "Okay. It's okay. Some day the trial will be over." I was telling myself just as much him.

"I'm so sorry," he said again. "I was so young, and they convinced me that a rich athlete was a better deal for you than a broke felon." His voice broke. "They told me I was a shit person, and I believed them."

Reeling, I wished the world would slow down for a minute so I could catch up. "I don't know what to say."

"You don't have to say anything. When I came here to see you on Friday, I didn't know if I was going to tell you this or not. Then I thought I'd wait until Bridger's case was settled, and talk to you about the trial. But we haven't had even a moment's peace."

That was certainly true.

"...But I haven't *ever* stopped thinking about you. Not one single day. Your mother told me that if I made myself scarce, they would give you everything. She told this to me during prison visiting hours, honey. I sat there in my shitty orange uniform and believed her."

It still wouldn't quite sink in. Except that I could practically hear my mother's voice in that story. She'd rather eat nails than have a baby out of wedlock with a criminal. My whole life, she'd made decisions based upon appearances. And she'd paid the price.

God, how depressing.

"What now?" I asked.

Brian opened his hands. "No matter what those assholes in New Hampshire try to do to me, my door is open to you. I'm finished being afraid of them."

"I need to think," I said, rubbing my temples with two

hands. My eyes felt sandy with exhaustion. It had been the most emotional day of my life, and I didn't even know what to say to him. "I think we should see each other again over my Christmas break," I suggested.

His face softened. "Can we? I just hate dropping this bomb on you and then driving away. But I have to be in Massachusetts tomorrow morning. An ex-con can't ever blow off his job. There might not be another one."

I nodded. "I know you took time off from work to help Bridger."

"I wanted to." His voice was rough again. "I'm going to head home now, then. Be safe, Sweetie." He stood up. So I did too. He stepped close to me, hugging me again just as hard as when I'd seen him in the coffee shop a few days ago. That fierce hug made even more sense now than it had then. "I'm sorry," he whispered. "I truly am."

"I know it," I said.

Bridger held out a hand. "Thank you for everything. And I'm sorry I got a little crazy there a minute ago."

Brian shook my boyfriend's hand. "Bridger, you are a man who protects the people he loves. There's nothing wrong with that. Goodnight to you both. We'll talk soon."

After Brian left, Bridger and I sat there a minute. "*Jesus.* Are you okay?" he asked me.

"I will be." My reality had been transformed in the past few hours. It was all going to take some time to understand. But when I stood up from that booth, Bridger stood up, too. And he took my hand. Together we walked out of Capri's, and through the streets of our college town. As we waited for a traffic light, the warm heel of his hand rested on my lower back, and I felt calm.

When I'd driven away from my childhood home on

Labor Day, I'd been so alone. But I wasn't anymore. In silence, we walked back to Beaumont. I followed Bridger up to his room, and he kissed me on the forehead at the top of the stairs.

"Sleep will help," Bridger said, fishing his keys out of his pocket.

The moment he said it, I yawned on command.

"I'm going to tuck you into my bed," he said. "And we're going to watch a pointless movie on my computer."

"God, don't pick a drama," I teased. "We've had enough of that."

He grinned. "We are going strictly comedy for awhile. You can even choose a chick flick. As long as the couple gets naked before the credits roll, I'll hang with it."

We went inside his room, and I closed the door. "If you want naked people, we don't need the movie," I pointed out.

Bridger turned to look at me, a smile playing on his lips. "You are a smart girl, aren't you?" He removed his sport coat, hanging it on the back of the desk chair. And then he crossed the room to me, pushing the hair back off my shoulders. He pressed his lips to my cheekbone. "Are you sure you're okay?" He dropped tiny kisses along the side of my face. "I mean, it's not every day that you find out that you're your own cousin."

I giggled into his neck. "I will be okay," I told him, reaching up to loosen the knot in his tie. "As soon as I get your hands on me." He yanked the tie off, and then I went to work on the buttons of his dress shirt.

We'd been alone in his room for four sad nights. We held each other, but nothing more. Now that Lucy would soon be back, I could think of no better way to use up the last few hours of privacy. I needed to stop thinking about the traumatic revelations of the day. And I wanted his skin against mine, his touch taking me out of my own head.

The gleam in Bridger's eye as I undressed him was a thing of beauty. It made me feel powerful. He leaned in to kiss me as I pushed the shirt off his shoulders. "Patience!" I demanded, ducking out of the way. I did it just because I could. Stepping back, I eased my own shirt over my head, teasing him. And when I could see him again, that interested gleam in his eyes had ignited into full-blown desire.

He was watching me. So I skimmed my hands down my belly and drew the zipper of my jeans down slowly. "You're killing me right now," he said.

"Good." I began to ease the fabric down off my hips. But before I got very far, Bridger was there, sinking to his knees in front of me, kissing the deep V of skin I'd revealed below my belly button. *Holy hell*, that felt good. Then he yanked down my jeans and began nuzzling me, his lips ghosting over my silk panties.

A shocked whimper escaped me. I could feel the heat of his breath on all my most sensitive places. Then he opened his mouth, and the friction of warm, wet satin against my body was almost too much. I felt my knees begin to buckle.

Strong hands clamped around my hips, and I heard a muffled chuckle. "Lie down, baby." He set me onto the bed and then with one big tug removed my jeans and socks. "You said you wanted my hands on you," he said. "How about my mouth?" Without waiting for an answer, he began dropping wet, open-mouthed kisses down my belly and onto my hip. I trembled with anticipation.

This wasn't something I'd ever done before, and I wondered if maybe I'd be too self-conscious to enjoy it. But Bridger's gentle kisses circled and teased. And when he finally landed at his intended destination, it seemed that the day's revelations weren't over yet. My body lit up like the Christmas tree in the center of Fresh Court, and I pushed all the day's worries right out of my conscious mind.

An hour later, we lay collapsed together in a sweaty heap. I traced my fingers along Bridger's ribs, feeling limp and blissed-out. I could feel his heart thumping under my ear. From next door, I could hear the muffled sounds of Andy's TV. "I hope that fire door is thick."

Bridger chuckled. "Will you freak out if I tell you that you're kind of a screamer?"

My heart stuttered at the very idea. I still thought of myself as a good girl. A *very* good girl. In spite of a pile of evidence to the contrary. "I won't freak out," I said, while freaking out a little. "But I will be embarrassed, and try to reign it in."

"That's a shame," Bridger said. "Because it's really hot."

"Do you promise?"

He rolled so that we could lie eye-to-eye. "Best. Thing. Ever," he whispered. "You make me feel like a sexy beast."

"You *are* a sexy beast."

His eyes flared. "What would you say if I told you that the beast wanted some celebratory ice cream."

I considered the idea. "I'd say it's cold outside. And we're not wearing any clothes."

"We can get dressed and go out for dessert. When we come back, I'm going to undress you again." He let his fingers drift down my naked back, grazing my bottom. It felt so good that I shifted suggestively against him. I couldn't help myself. "Mmm..." Bridger said, kissing my ear. "Ice cream first. Because you're going to need the calories. I plan to make this an all-nighter."

I slid off of him and began hunting for my clothes. It was hard to argue with that logic, even if the only kind of all-nighter I'd ever before had was the kind where you cram for a test. Though getting naked with Bridger was certainly *instructive*. I felt insecure about that, too. He had so much more experience than I did. It probably showed.

"What's that frown for?" he asked, pulling open a dresser drawer. "We can stay in if you want."

"It's not that," I said with a shake of my head. "I like your idea of fun."

Bridger grinned, and I noticed that he was fixing to go commando in his jeans. "Then what's the matter?"

"Absolutely nothing. It's just that I hope I... please you."

He looked up quickly, the grin still in place. "Like you can't *tell?*"

"Well..." I couldn't really. I knew his body reacted to mine. That was obvious. But I also knew that I was still only beginning to learn all the ways there were to touch him. "I hope that if there's some way I could improve, you'd tell me."

He dropped a shirt back into the drawer and closed the distance between us. "Every time is better than the last," he said, cupping my face in one of his big hands. "Don't you *ever* think you're inadequate, Scarlet. Experience isn't important."

"I don't have a complex about it, Bridge. But sometimes I wonder if you used to have more fun..."

He shook his head. "That's not how it works, although I didn't understand that until I met you."

"Understand what?"

He came so close to me that all I could see were those luminous green eyes. "You're the best I ever had, Scarlet. Because I love you. When other people touched me, it felt good. But when you touch me, it feels good and it also means something. And that's *potent*."

He ducked his head to kiss the sensitive spot underneath my ear. "Mmm," I said in appreciation.

I skimmed my hands over his bare chest, and he groaned. "Honestly," he said. "You make me feel like a teenager again. We don't get that many chances to be together, so I have to fantasize about you all the time."

The idea made my skin heat. "Not tonight."

"You're right," he swatted me gently on the backside. "Now put a shirt on, because I need me some Ben & Jerry's."

After we both dressed, and I'd brushed out my I-just-had-sex hair, Bridger tapped on Andy's door. "You want anything from Scoops?" he called.

The door opened a few seconds later, and I made myself busy flipping through Bridger's copy of our Music Theory textbook. As if Andy was really going to believe I'd been sitting here reading tonight.

"Are we celebrating your victory?"

"Yeah. Lucy comes back tomorrow." Andy grinned, holding up a hand for a high five. "So. You want ice cream?"

"Sure. Can I tag along? I need to get away from this chemistry book for a few minutes."

"Get a coat."

With Bridger holding my hand, we went out into the chilly night. The courtyards and pathways were still. Harkness was a quiet place during exams, except for a few end-of-year festivities. "Hey, Andy? Isn't your date with Katie tomorrow night?"

"Yeah," he said. "Unless she's changed her mind."

"She wouldn't do that." I protested. "Katie is great. You have to look beyond the Barbie hair and the shiny lip gloss.

There's a really generous person under there."

"Cool," he said. "And speaking of generous, Hartley was looking for you earlier, Bridge."

"Yeah?"

"He's got the hockey team all organized. Some of them are going to help you plan a funeral, and other guys are going to help you clean out your mom's house."

Bridger flinched. "I don't know if I want anyone's help with that."

I squeezed his hand. "Tomorrow, right? We deal tomorrow."

"Good plan." He squeezed back.

We were finishing our cones when my phone rang. It was my mother calling. I refused the call, but she tried again a minute later.

"Tomorrow," Bridger murmured.

That sounded fine to me. The problem was that I'd upset the applecart by talking to the prosecutor. And if Azzan and friends didn't like it, they might get in the car and drive here to express their displeasure in person. "I've got to take this. But I think I know how to get rid of them. Wish me luck."

First, I pulled up that phone call recording app that Luke had told me about. After activating it, I answered my mother's call.

"What have you DONE?" she screeched.

"Don't you dare scream at me," I said.

There was a brief silence, perhaps because my demand surprised her. "Azzan needs to speak to you. The police were back today, and he thinks you might be involved."

"Why would he think that?" I asked, wondering what she'd say.

"I don't know. But you will answer his questions."

"Only if you answer mine. Mom, did you authorize Azzan to follow me and read all of my texts and emails?"

There was a pause. "Of course not."

"Did Dad, then?"

Another pause. "No."

"Thank you. Because having me *tailed* isn't what I thought you meant when you said that family was supposed to help family."

She ignored that. "When are you coming home for the holidays?"

"I'm not, Mom."

Her sigh was like a fire-breathing dragon's. "You are. And you'll pack appropriate clothing for appearing in a courtroom."

"None of that is going to happen..." I heard her winding up to yell, so I spoke quickly. "...And you're going to shut up a minute and let me tell you why." I took a deep breath. "I'm done. All I want from you is my tuition. You pay the bursar bills and leave me alone. And if you try to involve me in the case, I'm giving an interview to the *New York Times*."

"You wouldn't."

"I would. And the first thing I'd tell them was that you lied to me for my entire life."

On the other end of the line, my mother gasped. "I'll kill him."

"You can't. Because I figured it out for myself. I read the newspaper too, Mom." I was ad libbing this part. But I could tell that she was freaking out well enough to believe me. "One of the longer articles talked about Brian. It mentioned adoption. There was a picture, too. And my boyfriend said 'you look just like your uncle.'"

I glanced up at Bridger. He was watching me, admiration on his face.

"I put it together myself," I lied. Even though I was still upset with Brian for his part in the deception, I didn't need to throw him under the bus to make my point. "I'm sure the newspaper would be very interested in those facts. It really speaks to Dad's credibility, you know?"

"Don't do this," she said, her voice broken.

"Okay," I said, my own voice rock steady. "Just let me be a student, and don't expect to hear from me. Now give the phone to Azzan."

For a minute I didn't hear anything at all. A couple of hundred miles away, my mother was having either a breakdown or a strategy session. Just when I was about ready to hang up, the Asshole of the Year came on the line.

"Shannon," he said, his voice gruff.

"Brrr!" I said, giving him the buzzer. "Try again. You want to talk to me, use my name."

"You little *bitch*."

"That's not it either." By now I must have completely lost my mind. Because talking back was starting to be fun. "Azzan, it's illegal to track somebody's phone messages without their consent. And it's illegal to threaten my boyfriend to keep me under your thumb."

"Now you're just whining," he said. "Tell me what happened today. Why were you inside an office building on South Street?"

"If you want to know, I need you to apologize."

In the silence that followed, I could practically feel the waves of aggression coming at me through the ether. "I do my job," he spat.

That wasn't good enough for my purposes. I needed to

get him to cop to some of the crap he'd been pulling on me. "You do it *illegally*," I tried.

"I was never going to plant drugs in your boyfriend's dormitory room, you little bitch. And good luck proving that I said it."

Yes! I shot out of my chair, grinning like a maniac. Across from me, Bridger raised an eyebrow. But I could probably get him to say even more. "There's no way for you to know where I was this afternoon."

"Your parents pay for your phone. If they installed some tracking software on it, there's nothing wrong with that."

"Interesting," I said. Because my mother had blown that theory, and I had it on tape. "Well, it's been fun talking to you tonight. But I'm afraid we're not going to keep having these chats. Ask my mother — she'll tell you why."

I disconnected the call and then stared at the recording app. I'd tested it ten days ago, but only once.

"What's going on?" Bridger asked.

"Hang on. I can probably show you." A few seconds later, the app chimed. *Recording Saved*, the screen read. I tapped the "share" button, and shared the call with Bridger. "Can you check your email? I need to know if this worked."

He took out his phone and tapped it. "What do I do? Follow this link?"

"Yeah."

He waited, and thirty seconds later I heard something. Bridger tapped "speaker" and then my mother's voice came from the phone, denying that she'd authorized my electronic tail.

Bridger and Andy listened to the whole thing, wincing whenever Azzan called me a bitch. But when it was over, Bridger grinned. "You are sneaky."

I paced the ice cream place, too amped up to sit down. "Don't cross me this week, guys. Because I'm kicking ass and taking names." Then I "shared" the conversation I'd recorded with Azzan, and also with my techie friend Luke. Then I put on my coat and practically skipped back to Beaumont beside Bridger and Andy.

That night, I had the familiar dream again. But this time, it played out a little differently. The puck disappeared into a dark place. And when I skated over to retrieve it, the hole had transformed. This time, there were two rectangular doors in the ice. In the dream, I knew it was urgent that I get them open. But there were no handles on the doors.

And I was afraid of the sounds coming from within.

"Shh," Bridger said into my ear.

My eyes flew open. It was dark, and I was naked in his bed. "Sorry," I gasped.

"It's okay," he said quietly. "You were dreaming."

I gave my heart rate a minute to descend back into the normal range. "Bridge? I think I might need to tell the prosecution what I think I heard," I said. "That means I might end up in that damned courtroom after all."

"Shh," my boyfriend said, curling his warm body around mine. "Sleep now, worry later."

"Okay," I whispered. He kissed my shoulder, and I pushed the scary thoughts out of my mind. I focused instead on his soft breathing, and the feel of his skin against my back.

I must have fallen asleep again. Because the next thing I knew, sunlight poured through Bridger's windows, and someone was knocking on the fire door.

"Hey guys?" came Andy's voice. "I think you need to take a look at the news. I have the TV on."

"Argf," Bridger said.

But Andy had my attention. So I rolled off Bridger's bed and pulled on my clothes. "Can I come in?" I asked, tapping on Andy's door.

"Sure."

I stepped into his room. A news channel played on mute on the screen. But a ticker strip at the bottom of the screen read: *Shocking new physical evidence discovered underground. J.P. Ellison Takes Guilty Plea Bargain. Gets 25 Years.*

"Oh my God," I said, staring at the screen.

"Wow." Bridger came up behind me, his hands landing on my shoulders. "What does that mean?"

"No criminal trial," I said. "And he'll lose the civil suits. I need to get a job. And I have to do the summer term at Harkness."

"Why?"

"I need to get as many credits as I can before he loses everything."

"Welcome to my world," Bridger said, kissing the back of my head.

"There's always financial aid," Andy said.

"I know," I said. "Somehow, it will work out. I've thought about this a lot. Mostly I'm glad that he earned all that money in the NHL. It isn't *exactly* blood money."

"The settlement would protect your tuition money, wouldn't it?" Andy asked.

"I have no clue. And I can't count on anyone giving me a straight answer."

"Come on," Bridger said, tugging on my hand. "Breakfast now. Worry later."

"Last night you said that worrying was back on in the

morning."

He pinched my backside. "The day starts after breakfast. And I get to eat it in the dining hall like a real student, because Lucy is on her way to school right now with Amy. The dining hall makes omelets to order, and I want one."

"Do you get to pick Lucy up today?" I asked, following him back into his room.

"Yes ma'am. After my meeting with the graduate housing office."

"Can I drive you both out to the foster parents' home later to pick up her things?"

"That would be awesome. Now let's go have ourselves an omelet."

Chapter Twenty: *Meatballs and Furniture*

— Scarlet

After breakfast, I made myself spend an hour in the library. Then I gave my computer geek friend Luke a call. "Did you listen to the call I shared with you?" I asked him.

"You are starring in a cop show, aren't you?" he said. "Just admit it."

"I wish," I laughed. "I'm ready to ditch the creeps now. Can you clean that off my phone?"

"But of course! I'm working from eleven o'clock until six. Bring it in anytime."

I was still smiling by the time I got home to Vanderberg. I hadn't spent much time there these past few days, only dropping by to shower and change clothes. When I pushed open the door to our suite, both Katies looked up from their books.

"Hi, guys!" Since exams were beginning in less than seventy-two hours, I didn't find it strange that they were both home studying.

But I did find it strange that their eyes tracked me silently across the room.

"What?" I asked, shedding my coat.

"We watched the news this morning in the nail salon," Blond Katie said.

Oh crap. "The news?" I asked. As if playing dumb would help.

"There was a picture of you," she went on. "*Shannon.*"

With a mighty sigh, I sat down on the rug opposite Blond Katie. "Yeah. Okay. I changed my name."

"You *lied* to us," Blond Katie said. "Why would you do that?"

247

"Because my father..." I got stuck on that word. The idea that he was not my father would take some time to seem real. "I'm not him. And a lot of people don't understand that."

They just stared at me.

"He, um, pled guilty this morning." That was another attitude adjustment that I needed to absorb. I could stop beating myself up now, wondering what had happened. If he told the world that he did it, I didn't have to go ten rounds in my head every day, trying to discover the truth.

"You're not from Miami beach," Ponytail Katie said. "I knew you weren't tan enough!"

I shook my head.

"You weren't home-schooled!" Blond Katie yelped.

Again, I shook my head. "But I might as well have been. I was a pariah. And I didn't want be one in college, too. I'm sorry I didn't tell you. I just didn't know how else to get out from under it."

Ponytail Katie slammed her book closed and stood up. "That's not cool. You can't live with someone and lie all the time." She stomped into her single. When her door slammed, I felt the reverberation in my chest. *Here we go again.* Miserable, I looked toward Blond Katie, waiting for her to do the same.

But she cocked her head, studying me. "Must have been pretty bad. To make you change your name."

"It was hard on me to be the town punching bag. But a boy killed himself. It was worse for him."

"Did you know him?"

I shook my head.

"Weird."

"Yeah."

She chewed her lip for a second, and then she stood up.

"I'd change my name, too," she said. Then she went over to shrug on her coat. "I'm going to the gym."

"Okay," I said, wondering where we stood now.

She paused with her hand on the knob. "Are you going to stay a Scarlet? Now that it's over?"

I opened my mouth to tell her that it was never going to be over. But that would only sound like whining. And for the first time in a year, I finally felt as if my life were headed in the right direction.

"Yeah," I said finally. "I'm going to stay a Scarlet."

"I like it," Katie announced, opening the door. "It suits you."

"Thanks!" I called after her.

— Bridger

"Bridge!"

At two-thirty, Lucy came tearing out of that elementary school and right into my arms. Today it didn't matter that she was a big girl with a reputation to uphold. She *threw* herself at me. I picked her all the way up, and she did her best impression of a spider monkey. "Hey now," I said. "I told you I'd be here." I'd called her before she went to school this morning, telling her to look for me in my usual spot by the bike racks.

She opened her mouth and broke my heart. "But things go wrong."

"They do, sometimes," I admitted. "We had some trouble, didn't we?"

"Yeah."

"It's going to get better now," I promised. "There are more people around to help us than I thought."

"Not Mom," she said simply.

Fuck. My eyes began to sting. "Not Mom," I agreed. "We're going to feel bad about that for awhile. We haven't really said goodbye to her yet."

"You mean, like a funeral?"

"Yeah. Like that. We'll do that next week."

Hartley and Theresa had talked me into having a memorial service for her this weekend, and the dean had offered up the use of one of the college chapels.

But I drew the line at a casket. "Too macabre," I'd told them. Lucy had already endured her mother's slow withdrawal and disappearance from her life. Putting a box of remains in the same room with her would just be too much for her to process. So I'd chosen cremation. And when Lucy was older, I planned to let her scatter the ashes.

I'd explained this carefully to Hartley and his mother, at which point Theresa's eyes had welled. "You're really good at this," she said. "You're already one of the better parents I know."

The praise had made me feel unworthy. "I just make it up as I go along," I'd stammered.

She squeezed my shoulder. "That's how it *works*, honey. That's all any of us do."

I hoped she was right, or else I was in way over my head.

Setting Lucy down on the sidewalk, I took her hand and led her down the concrete pathway. Being her legal guardian — being her parent — was absolutely what I wanted. There was no part of me that regretted it. But that didn't mean I knew what to do with Lucy's grief.

A couple of hours later, I found myself hugging Amy goodbye, while Lucy hopped from foot to foot, eager to leave.

"Call us any time," Amy said to me. "If you have a

babysitting emergency, or just need to vent."

I didn't see myself taking her up on it, but it was an awfully nice offer. "Thank you."

"You have a lot of people to support you," Amy said, reading my mind. "But it's always good to have one more."

"You've been great," I said, meaning it.

Rich offered me his hand to shake. "Even so, you hope you don't see us again, right?"

"Take care," I chuckled.

"You too," Amy said. "All of you."

Lucy ran out of the house, her winter coat under her arm.

"Put that coat on," I called after her.

"Good luck with that," Rich smirked.

By the time I got into the car, Lucy had already buckled herself in behind Scarlet. "Are you sure it's okay with the college that I'm in your room?" she asked, biting a fingernail.

"They know about you now," I explained. "And it's just for a few nights. Soon we'll have our own place."

"What does it look like?" she asked. "Tell me again." She seemed nervous, which didn't make that much sense to me. I'd hoped that tonight she'd finally be able to relax. But the last week had really shaken her. I was just going to have to ride it out.

"Well, I only saw the apartment for a minute," I told her. There had been a harried young mother at home when the housing office had sent me over for a peek. She'd had a fussy baby in a sling around her neck, and a toddler tugging on her skirt, too. So I'd spent only two minutes checking the place out, trying to figure out what I'd need to furnish it. "Let's see. The kitchen is at the end of the living room. There's no wall between them, but there's a counter that divides it."

"Tell me about my room."

"Um, the walls are white..." It was small, and the graduate students who'd been living there had somehow wedged two cribs into the room. Space was probably the reason they were leaving. "There's a window over the bed," I said, grasping for details. "We'll find you a little desk for homework."

"Will it look the same as my old room?" Lucy wanted to know.

I didn't know quite how to answer that. *Smaller, actually, but without the meth lab in the dining room.*

Scarlet bailed me out. "It's going to look cooler," she said. "A big girl's room. I think we should put your name up on the wall. Or maybe on a sign on the door."

When I turned to look at Lucy, she was chewing her lip. "I like that. Mandy's door has a sign that says 'no muggles beyond this point.'"

"Good one," Scarlet agreed.

"We should get some dinner," I said, looking at my watch. "The dining halls are about to close."

"I've got a better idea," Scarlet said.

"What's that?"

"How do women recover from stress, Bridge?"

So she'd noticed how twitchy Lucy was, too. "I dunno. Spa treatments?"

"Close," she said. "Shopping."

"Where?" I asked.

"Ikea, of course."

First, we ate meatballs. And then we turned Lucy loose in the kids' department. "I like that pink lamp," she said. "And, look!" She pointed to a kind of filmy fabric thing that hung from the ceiling, draping around the head of a bed. "That's like

252

the bed curtains in Harry Potter!"

"We're not get anything yet," I cautioned. Lucy was going to want everything in the store.

"Oh, I am *so* buying that," Scarlet murmured. "It's cool, and it's thirty bucks."

"Christmas," I hissed.

"Deal," she whispered, tucking a lock of hair behind her ear and smiling at me. She drew a little notepad out of her purse and began writing.

"What's that for?"

"It's a list of things you need. So far I've added a desk for Lucy. A couple of lamps for reading. We'll get to the kitchen stuff in the next room."

"This is going to give my credit card a workout."

"Nope." Scarlet smiled. "Your Coach's wife asked Hartley for a list. And Hartley asked me to make it."

"Because that's not a job for anyone who has a dick?"

She rolled her eyes at me. "Hartley put it more delicately than that."

"Scarlet, I can't let the hockey team furnish my apartment."

"Why? Because you'll end up with a TV, a video game console, and nothing else?"

"No. Because I don't want them paying for things."

She stuck the notebook in her back pocket. "I'm thinking you don't really have a choice. But look on the bright side. Stores will be visited, but not by you."

I grabbed her waist and kissed her. "Thank you."

"For what?"

"Everything." I kissed her again. I ought to feel wrecked right now. Everything I'd dreaded about this year had actually happened. And we were going to be okay. Even though I had a boatload of problems to manage, debris to clean up and a gale force of uncertainty in my life. Scarlet. Hartley. Theresa. Amy and Rich. The dean. The coach. Andy. The number of people who had my back was astonishing. Leaning on them made me feel weirdly strong, when I'd always assumed that the opposite would hold true.

"Ew. No kissing," Lucy complained. "That's gross."

Scarlet giggled. "Let's look at tableware instead. That's almost as fun."

* * *

We got back to Beaumont after Lucy's bedtime. But Hartley and Corey were waiting with champagne and ginger ale to welcome Lucy back.

"Thanks," Lucy said, accepting a glass from Corey.

"You're welcome. But I have something else, too. The dean asked me to give it to you." She took a Harkness ID out of her purse, on a pink lanyard. When she turned it over we could all see that it read LUCY MCCAULLEY on the front, with her school picture.

"It's just like Bridger's!" Lucy yelped, putting it over her head.

"That's what you use to check in to the dining hall."

"Can we eat there tomorrow?" Lucy asked.

"Hell yes," I said. "We'll have to be ready for school a little early. But they have five kinds of cereal, and there's always bacon." Christ, I missed the dining hall. It made life effortless.

Hartley popped the cork on a bottle of bubbly and began pouring into my collection of stolen dining hall glasses. "Maybe Andy wants one?" Hartley asked.

"He's out on a date tonight," Scarlet said.

Corey looked toward the fire door. "I'm positive I just heard him over there."

Scarlet frowned, probably hoping that the set-up with Katie hadn't been a disaster.

Corey raised a hand to knock on the fire door, but something held her back. She turned, with an amused expression on her face. "You know, I don't think he's going to want one."

From the other side of the fire door came the distinct sound of a moan.

"Is he okay?" Lucy asked.

"He's fine," Corey said quickly. "He's, uh…"

"He's watching the basketball game," I said, just as another moan could be heard. "And his team isn't doing that well." (Big lie there! It sounded as if his team was doing *very* well.)

"Dance party!" Scarlet announced, leaping over to my computer. She tapped the touch pad, and a second later Macklemore began to rap. Scarlet cranked up the volume and began to boogie. "Come on, Lucy! Shake it."

My girlfriend was brilliant.

But my sister just stood there for a second, looking confused. So Corey got into the swing of things, circling her hips. She swatted Hartley on the arm, too. Watching the three of them, Lucy began to move, shaking her skinny body and bouncing her arms.

Then we were *all* dancing, drinks in hand, on a Wednesday night in December. Macklemore segued into Skrillex and then into Avicii. I watched Scarlet shake out her silky hair. She caught me oogling her and winked. Hartley took his girlfriend's hand while they danced, to help her balance. Lucy climbed up on the window seat to better see the action. It was silly and glorious. The last few months had made me feel old and defeated. But just then, I felt young again.

Young, and surprisingly happy.

THREE MONTHS LATER

"She had not known the weight until she felt the freedom."
— *The Scarlet Letter by Nathaniel Hawthorne*

Chapter Twenty One: *Division is Hard*

— *Scarlet*

"I forgot nine times seven!" Lucy yelled from her bedroom.

Bridger's hands were currently coated with ground meat, so he did not go into Lucy's bedroom to help her. "What's the rule of nines?" he called instead.

"Oh yeah..." came from the bedroom.

"Do you want me to help her?" I asked.

"She'll get it," he said. "I need you to paint some ketchup right here on top. I think I'm done with the gross part." He held up the wooden spoon he'd been using to shove mashed potatoes into the center of the baking dish and began to laugh. "I feel like I just *violated* two and a half pounds of ground meat."

His laughter was infectious, and my giggles made it difficult to smooth on the ketchup. "Remind me why anyone thought stuffing a meatloaf was a good idea?"

With a grin, he just shook his head, reaching for a paper towel. "I hope she appreciates it."

"Do you mean Lucy, or your mom?" I asked quietly.

His green eyes looked sad. "Lucy, of course."

"She will," I promised.

"I know." He kissed my cheek on the way to the sink, and I hefted the dish into the preheated oven.

Most nights, Bridger and Lucy ate in the Beaumont dining hall. And when I wasn't eating with The Katies, or having rehearsal for the folk music group I'd joined, I often met them for dinner. But Lucy had been asking him to make their mother's stuffed meatloaf, and tonight — a Sunday — he'd finally given in.

Unfortunately, we didn't have their mother's recipe. Bridger and Hartley had cleaned out the house before the bank sold it. He didn't let me or Lucy help. "Not much to save," he'd said of that sad task. He'd taken his father's bureau, and a dresser for Lucy, which I'd painted pink one Saturday during Christmas break.

His mother's meatloaf recipe would therefore remain lost. So I'd chosen one off the Internet. I'd doubled the garlic, though, just as my own mother would have done. It gave me a guilty stab to think about my mom all alone now in our house. She and I didn't speak. But the more distance I'd put between last year and my new life, the more possible it seemed that I could eventually get past a few of our differences.

Eventually.

I'd spent Christmas break here, with Bridger and Lucy. And I'd also spent a few days visiting Brian in Boston. "You don't have to come, if you're not ready," he'd said when he invited me. "But you'll always have a standing invitation."

I went. It wasn't an easy few days for us, but I was glad

to have done it. My next visit would probably be easier. We spoke on the phone once a week, and had plans to see a classical guitar concert in Boston next month.

From the kitchen counter, Bridger's phone chimed. "Someone's messaging you," I said.

"Tell me who it is?" he asked, his hands in the dishwater.

I picked it up. "Hartley. He wants to know where you're eating because he needs to ask you something."

After drying his hands, Bridger took the phone and rung Hartley. "I cooked tonight," he said when his friend answered.

"*Who* cooked?" I prompted.

"Listen, lady," he lifted his handsome chin in my direction. "It was me who was just up to my ears in raw hamburger."

"Fair point."

He went back to his call. "So if you want to see me, come over." There was a pause. "Nothing. Just bring your pretty face. No rush. It won't be ready for an hour." He hung up.

"Did you see any of last night's game?" I asked, stealing a crumb of Parmesan cheese off the cutting board where I'd grated it.

"I watched the whole thing this morning, as soon as the video was loaded," Bridger confessed. He still had the team password, which gave him access to the game tapes. "It was awesome."

I'd gone to the game in person with The Katies, watching the Harkness men's team clinch their quarterfinal series against Cornell. Now they were off to the conference semifinals. "When Hartley made that goal through the five-hole, the place went nuts."

"It's just wild to see the team in first place." Bridger took a head of broccoli out of the fridge and unwrapped it. "That's never happened before."

"Actually, it last happened in 1982."

"Stickler," he grinned. Then he rinsed the broccoli under the sink.

And it killed me. Bridger was rinsing a head of broccoli, while his hockey team was preparing to sweep the conference. He didn't even appear frustrated. I didn't know how he could stand it. Watching last night, I'd been bitten by the bug again. Every time Hartley's team took possession of the puck, I'd wanted to run out and get my skates sharpened.

"Let me cut that up," I said, nudging him away from the cutting board. "You open the wine."

"Now we're talking."

Hartley came through the door forty-five minutes later, carrying a bag from the cupcake bakery on Bank Street.

"Whoa!" Lucy said, swooping in to relieve him of the bag. "Ooh!" she squealed. "The mini ones!"

"Hold up," Bridger said, lifting it over her head. "Dinner first."

"I just want to peek!"

He didn't budge for a second. "Is your math done?"

She nodded, jumping for the bag.

"Even the division?"

"There wasn't any today," she said. "I hate division. It's hard."

Bridger chuckled. "Is it?" He lowered the cupcakes. "If we divided those evenly, how many do you get?"

Lucy slid the plastic clamshell out of the bag and eyed it for a second. "Three."

"Good girl. Now what do you say to Hartley?"

"Thank you thank you thank you!" she said, skittering off

to admire the tiny cupcakes in peace.

"Wine?" Bridger asked Hartley.

"Of course."

Bridger poured it, and then went to check on the meat. "This looks great," he said, reaching for the hot pads.

"Smells good," Hartley agreed. "What did you make?"

Bridger chuckled. "You tell me."

The kitchen area was tiny, so I traded places with Hartley. "You made a stuffed meatloaf? Seriously?" He laughed. "That reminds me so much of middle school. Dinner at your house, after a bantam game."

"I know, right? Let's eat it."

We sat around the coffee table, because the tiny cafe table where Lucy and Bridger usually ate together wasn't big enough for four. With our knees tucked underneath the table, everybody tried a bite.

"Wow," Hartley said. "This is so much better than..." Bridger gave him a warning look. "...I remembered," he finished.

"No," Lucy argued, chewing. "It's just the same. Bridger made it *just* the same."

"That's what I meant," Hartley said, forking up another chunk. "It's exactly the same. The garlic is a nice touch."

Bridger winked at me, and I smiled. In a weird way, Bridger's mom and my mom had collaborated on this dish. The two women who'd caused the most trouble in our lives were here at the table, too. I filed that thought away to examine later.

Hartley helped himself to the broccoli, and then pointed his fork at Bridger. "I have an important question for you. But I guess it's also a question for Scarlet."

I met Bridger's eyes, but he gave a little shrug, letting me know that he had no idea what this was about.

"Did you hear about Mike Graham's concussion?"

Bridger winced. "That looked bad on the tape. But when Orsen came into the coffee shop, he told me Graham was going to be okay."

"He will be," Hartley said. "But he's out for the rest of the season."

"That sucks. He was your second best enforcer."

"I'm shorthanded, Bridge. I want you to come to practice tomorrow."

Bridger's fork halted halfway to his mouth.

"I know you have obligations. But there are just two conference finals. And then four NCAA championship games. Six games in five weeks. And that's only if we made it all the way."

"Which you *will*," I piped up. "Bridger, tell him yes!" I shouldn't have spoken up like the pushy girlfriend that I was. But *God*. How many times in your life do you get a chance like that?

"Not sure how that would work," Bridger dodged. "We'll talk about this later." He ate his bite of food and looked away.

I knew he was right — we couldn't get into the nitty gritty details of Bridger's family obligations with Lucy sitting right there. But I could see his wheels turning across the table from me.

Do it, I begged silently.

"I haven't been on skates for a year, dude," he said while Hartley washed the dishes.

"It's like riding a bike," Hartley insisted, handing him a rinsed plate.

"Okay. But I haven't been to the varsity weight room more than five times this season. And that's *not* like riding a bike."

"I don't care," Hartley argued. "We're going to end up dressing a couple of walk-ons. I'd rather have you."

"Mike is a defenseman."

Hartley just shrugged. "You might have to play D. Or someone else might have to. Coach will figure it out."

Bridger shook his head. "There are so many problems with this scenario."

"No there aren't!" I hissed, checking over my shoulder to see if Lucy was listening. But she was flipping channels on the TV. "I'll cover you, Bridge. Lucy's been asking me to teach her to play the guitar."

"Practice can go pretty late," Bridger argued. "That's a lot of guitar."

"Six games, tops," Hartley said. "Three is more likely. My mom can help out if it goes into the end of the month. She's got spring break."

"I'll think about it," Bridger said.

"Think quick. Practice is at four o'clock tomorrow."

"I will." He glanced at the clock on the microwave. "Right now I have to chase Lucy into bed. Are those teeth brushed, buddy?"

Hartley and I finished up in the kitchen while Bridger tucked Lucy in. "Do you think he'll do it?" He asked me.

"If he doesn't, I'll be devastated," I admitted. "If one of your goalies gets injured, you have my number, right?"

Hartley grinned. "I'll keep you in mind." His face became serious then. "There's something I've been meaning to mention to you."

"What's that?" I put the last forks into the drawer and

closed it.

"I got my first pair of new hockey skates when I was ten. Up until then I only had yard sale equipment. One pair was orange, and the other kids used to mock me."

That seemed unlikely. "Until you skated circles around them."

"Well, sure," he smiled. "But they never fit right, you know? Not until Steel Wings came along and gave me the real thing."

"Oh."

Oh. That shut me up, and fast. In one of the newspaper articles, I'd read that my father's charity had given out two million dollars' worth of equipment. Until now, I'd never met anyone who'd received any of it.

Hartley's big brown eyes held mine. "They cost eighty bucks, Scarlet. They were the nicest things I'd ever owned. And I kept them on my desk so I could look at them between games."

"That's..." I didn't know what to do with that. "Aren't you glad you never met the founder, though?"

He leaned back against the counter and crossed his arms. "Of course I am. I'm not trying to excuse what he did. But the help he gave me was straightforward. And it was real."

"Okay," I said softly. "Thank you for telling me."

Hartley pulled me into a quick hug. "No problem. I've got to run and try to do some homework before next week drags me under."

"Thanks for the cupcakes," I said.

He winked, reaching for his jacket. "There's a dozen more in it for you and Lucy if you can get his ass to practice tomorrow."

"I'll do my best."

— Bridger

After I brushed my teeth, I turned the lights out in the living room. Then I locked the front door. As the bolt slid into place, I felt a powerful contentment. The people I loved best were both on the same side of this door, home with me right now.

While Hartley's offer thrilled me, I already had what I needed. It was right here in this modest apartment.

I tiptoed into my bedroom and clicked the doorknob lock into place. Lucy never wandered into my room in the night, but it was more fun getting naked with Scarlet if I knew that she couldn't accidentally get an eyeful.

My girlfriend laid in the middle of the bed, hogging both pillows, her hands behind her head. There was a gleam in her eye, and I felt it in all the right places. With one hand, I stripped the t-shirt over my head. And I swear that gleam burned brighter. "Get over here," she said.

The demand wasn't Scarlet's style, but I loved it. And so did the most ambitious part of my body. I stripped off my jeans, followed by my rapidly tightening underwear. Then I climbed onto the end of the bed, watching her track me with that heated gaze.

Crawling up her body, I trapped her under the sheet. "Did you want something from me?"

"I did. I *do*," she corrected.

I dropped down, supporting myself on my forearms. My pelvis molded into hers, and the only barrier between us was the sheet. Holy shit, she was naked under there. "What is it that you wanted?" I asked. "I like you bossy, by the way."

"Good thing," she said, arching up to me. "Because I'm going to boss you around tonight."

I swear, the *whoosh* of a flame that her words lit inside

me was practically audible. I was on fire already, and she hadn't even touched me yet. "Boss me," I challenged. "Let's hear you."

Scarlet put her hands on my bare ass and said, "go to practice tomorrow."

I laughed. "That's not where I thought this was going."

"Oh, there are *lots* of places this could take us," she whispered, stroking me with soft hands. "Just promise me you'll go."

With one hand, I peeled back the sheet between us as far as I could without climbing off her. "What do I get if I go?"

Scarlet's brow quirked. "You get to skate in the semis, dumbass."

"*Jesus*, I love you," I said, dipping my head to kiss the creamy breast that I'd exposed. "Sexy and tough in one pretty package."

Her face softened then. And as I continued to tease her nipple with my lips, she melted beneath me. I wiggled my way under the sheet, kissing every bit of skin I uncovered along the way.

Maybe she'd already said her piece. Or maybe I'm just that good a lover. But I didn't hear any more attempts at negotiation. There were only soft sighs, and the feel of her velvet skin against mine. She was loving every minute of it. In no time at all I was reaching into the nightstand for necessary equipment. And then lowering my body onto hers, teasing her with myself, and then moving away again.

"Hey!" she said, and I laughed.

"Got a plane to catch, Scarlet?"

"You're not a nice person."

"Oh, but I am." I dropped my lips to her belly and began kissing her there. Meanwhile, my hand slid to a place that made her gasp. I looked up at her. "Scarlet," I said, removing my hand. "How good a hockey player are you, anyway?"

"Umm," she gasped. "Who cares, Bridge…"

I chuckled into her belly button. "How good, Scarlet?"

"All state MVP," she mumbled.

I lifted my head. "Could you take me one-on-one?"

Her eyes popped open. "I'm trying to. Right now."

I hitched myself up on her body, grinning. "I'm serious. Who would win?"

She dropped her head onto the pillow in frustration. "You could out shoot me," she told the ceiling. "But I might be more maneuverable. And you couldn't deke me very easily. Too many hours spent watching for defensive gaps."

I looked down at her. "Do you have any *idea* how sexy that is? I want to play you. I think I can win, as long as you're wearing clothes. Will you play me sometime?" she didn't say anything, so I slid my hand back where it was before. "Please?" I begged.

"Sure," she smiled. "I'd love to."

"Yesss…" I said, finally pressing forward, sliding home. Scarlet's eyelids fluttered closed, and I caught her moan in my mouth.

Life was very, very good.

— *Scarlet*

The student section was crammed full of fans. It was standing room only. But Lucy and I made our way to the adjacent section, where the VIP seats were. Every guy on the team received two tickets to give out. We found ours next to Corey and Theresa, and right in front of the women's hockey team.

"Lucy!" Theresa said. "I hear you're coming for a

sleepover at my house if the team goes to Philadelphia."

"I hope they do," Lucy said. "That would be fun."

After we got settled, Coach Samantha Smith — the very woman I'd had to quit to in September — touched Corey and I on the shoulders. "How have you been, ladies?"

"Great!" Corey enthused. "I promised Hartley that if they made it to the Frozen Four, I'd paint his number on my face."

Coach laughed. "The way the team looks, you might have to go through with it."

"It would be worth a little humiliation to see them do that well," Corey said.

Coach turned to me. "And how are you doing..." she stopped. "I'm sorry, I forgot your name."

"Scarlet," I supplied.

"*Scarlet*," she said with an apologetic look. But I wasn't offended. She'd recruited me for an entire year as Shannon.

"She's famous, Coach," the girl sitting beside her said.

Crap. My smile melted away as I examined the girl, who wore a *Harkness Women's Hockey* jacket. I didn't think I knew her.

Coach's eyebrows lifted, as if she wasn't sure what to say either.

"...She's famous for catching Bridger McCaulley," the girl said with grin. "Nobody's ever done that before."

"That's my brother you're talking about," Lulu chirped. "He isn't very easy to catch, because he's fast."

The player's cheeks turned pink. "That's... exactly what I meant," she said, while the other girls around her laughed.

Coach winked at me, and the subject was dropped.

"Good evening!" boomed the announcer over the sound system. "And welcome to the Eastern College Hockey Conference semifinal game between Harkness College and

Quinnipiac!"

The crowd gave a loud cheer, and U2's familiar guitar intro to *Where The Streets Have No Name* began to swell under the announcer's words. "Allow me to introduce your team. From Etna, Connecticut, your captain Adam Hartley!"

Now, you'd think that our bench would cheer the loudest, but it sounded to me as if every female at Harkness College gave a fan girl scream. One by one, the players skated to their blue line as they were introduced. "From Harkness, Connecticut, left wing Bridger McCaulley!" Lucy popped up to shriek along with a couple thousand other fans, and even from the tenth row I could see that Bridger's smile was enormous.

"All rise," boomed the announcer over the sound system. "...For the National Anthem, sung for you tonight by Harkness's own Something Special."

"This is it!" Lucy said, standing up, putting a hand over her heart.

The lights dimmed, and the crowd grew quiet. On the upper deck, the girls' singing group leaned in to their microphones and sang the national anthem. I must be turning into a giant sap, because I actually teared up. There was no place in the world I'd rather be tonight than here.

From the face-off on, I was glued to the action. Both teams wanted this game *bad*. It was fast, intense, and glorious. The only bad moment was when Bridger was cross-checked into the boards. He went down hard, and Lucy panicked a little.

"He's *fine*," I insisted, pulling her into my lap. "Just give him a second."

Coach Smith tapped Lucy on the shoulder, offering her a Skittle. And by the time the little girl turned back toward the ice, Bridger was skating again.

I looked over my shoulder. "Thank you," I mouthed.

Then Coach leaned in. "Will you have coffee with me next week? I'd like to stay in touch."

I wasn't expecting that. The idea that Coach wanted to chat about next season sent butterflies into my stomach. I took a deep breath of the icy rink air and let myself consider it. The sounds echoing around me — of steel scraping ice, and the puck smacking the boards — were as familiar to me as breathing.

"You know, I'd like that," I told her.

"Awesome," she said.

I turned back then, to catch Bridger hopping over the wall for his shift. Lucy wiggled in my lap, and the puck skidded across my line of vision. I checked the clock. There were only two minutes left in the period.

It was the goalie's job to see the whole ice at once. I'd spent the past few months feeling that I'd failed at the job. But tonight I understood that if you kept your heart in the game, there would always be one more period to play. And excellent people to play it with.

Game on.

Thank you!

Thanks for reading *The Year We Hid Away*. I hope you enjoyed it!

Reviews help other readers find books. I appreciate all reviews, whether positive or negative.

Ready for More?

Would you like to know when the next *Ivy Years* book is available? You can sign up for the new release e-mail list at <u>www.sarinabowen.com/theivyyears</u>

The Ivy Years Series:

Book 1: *The Year We Fell Down*
Book 2: *The Year We Hid Away*
Novella: *Blond Date*
Book 3: *The Understatement of the Year*
Book 4: *The Shameless Hour*

The Gravity Series:

Book 1: *Coming in From the Cold*
Book 2: *Falling From the Sky*
Book 3: *Shooting For the Stars*

About the Author

Sarina Bowen is a Vermonter whose ancestors cut timber and farmed the north country since the 1760s. Sarina is grateful for the invention of indoor plumbing, espresso products and wi-fi during the intervening 250 years. On a few wooded acres, she lives with her husband, two kids, and an ungodly amount of ski and hockey gear.

CPSIA information can be obtained at www.ICGtesting.com
Printed in the USA
BVOW06s2147220916

463059BV00014B/56/P